●●●●●●●

She cried out in shock and reflexively wrapped her legs around his waist. Marcel backed her against the counter and set her on top of it. Now they were the same height. He looked into her eyes and smiled when he saw Donna's expression of shock and wonderment. Her legs were spread wide to accommodate him. With the counter supporting her, he was able to release her ass and undo the buttons on his shirt. Donna watched, still somewhat in a daze. She barely felt him lift her off the tiles. And she wasn't a small woman. She knew he was strong, but...

Marcel got his shirt off, and everything became crystal clear. Of course he didn't have any trouble lifting her. Under the bright lights in the kitchen, Donna saw that every muscle he'd been hiding under his tee-shirts was as beautifully sculpted as she imagined. His massive pectorals were the most impressive, but his arms and shoulders were equally enticing. Every bulge fought for her attention. Donna wasn't aware that her mouth hung open. Marcel stepped closer, and she held both hands up – not to stop him, but to feel the goose bumps that were scattered across his chest.

She sucked air between her teeth the moment her hands came in contact with his dark flesh. He was so hot. And hard! She felt his powerful muscles ripple beneath her fingertips. She felt his heart thumping strong against his sternum. Her bottom lip slipped into her own mouth as she fondled him at will. His nipples were big and dark. She couldn't resist tasting them. Marcel's hand moved to the back of her neck as she ducked down and suckled his nipple unexpectedly. He looked up to the ceiling and took a deep, slow breath.

Donna licked one nipple, and then the other. She sucked them both and nibbled them softly. She stopped when the heaving of his chest became more pronounced. She looked up at him, her lips wet, her face flushed with heat.

"I want you," he said. "I need you. Now."

His eyes were low and drunk with passion.

The yearning between Donna's legs was white hot.

She nodded and grabbed hold of his shoulders, so he could help her off the counter.

●●●●●●●

1

LIFE AFTER

LIFE AFTER

KEITH THOMAS WALKER

For Melissa Carter,
Sorry I don't have an
autographed picture to send you,
but this autographed book is just
as nice. Plus I have my picture on the
back. ☺ thanks for being such a
supportive reader! Much love
and God bless!
2/3/15

KEITHWALKERBOOKS, INC
This is a UMS production

LIFE AFTER

KEITHWALKERBOOKS

Publishing Company
KeithWalkerBooks, Inc.
P.O. Box 331585
Fort Worth, TX 76163

For information write
KeithWalkerBooks, Inc.
P.O. Box 331585
Fort Worth, TX 76163

All characters in this book have no existence outside the
imagination of the author and have no relation whatsoever to
anyone bearing the same name or names. They are not even
distantly inspired by any individual known or unknown to the
author and all incidents are pure invention.

ISBN-13 DIGIT: 978-0-9882180-4-8
ISBN-10 DIGIT: 0988218046
Library of Congress Control Number: 2014901184
Manufactured in the United States of America

First Edition

Visit us at www.keithwalkerbooks.com

KEITH THOMAS WALKER

This book is for Fern Reynolds-Gordon

MORE BOOKS BY
KEITH THOMAS WALKER

Fixin' Tyrone
How to Kill Your Husband
A Good Dude
Riding the Corporate Ladder
The Finley Sisters' Oath of Romance
Blow by Blow
Jewell and the Dapper Dan
Harlot
Plan C (And More KWB Shorts)
Dripping Chocolate
The Realest Ever
Jackson Memorial
Sleeping With the Strangler

NOVELLAS

Might be Bi (Part One)
Harder

POETRY COLLECTION

Poor Righteous Poet

Visit keithwalkerbooks.com for information about
these and upcoming titles from
KeithWalkerBooks

ACKNOWLEGMENTS

Of course I would like to thank God, first and foremost, for giving me the creativity and drive to pursue my dreams and the understanding that I am nothing without Him. I would like to thank my wife for being my first and most important critic, and I would like to thank my mother for always pushing me to be the best I can be. I would like to thank Janae Hampton for being the best advisor, supporter and little sister a brother could ever have. I would also like to thank (in no particular order) Brandy Rees, Denise Bolds, Sabrina Scott, Dianne Guinn, Kierra Pease, Sharon Blount, BRAB Book Club, Beulah Neveu and Uncle Steven Thomas, one love. I'd like to thank everyone who purchased and enjoyed one of my books. Everything I do has always been to please you. I know there are folks who mean the world to me that I'm failing to mention. I apologize ahead of time. Rest assured I'm grateful for everything you've done for me!

LIFE AFTER

CHAPTER ONE
RISING STAR

"I hear your concerns, and I agree that the problems we're having with the Transportation Authority are unacceptable," the chairman of the city council said. "There's no good reason why we couldn't get this worked out before it turned into this, this *debacle*," he stated. His eyes were filled with fire and compassion. The many bus drivers who attended tonight's meeting nodded and voiced their agreement.

"I saw bus drivers on the picket line this morning on my way to the office," the councilman said. "I saw the resentment and the frustration in their eyes. I stopped and talked to them. I understand why they're saying the city isn't doing enough to keep them safe. We're not doing enough to fix the roads they have to travel on."

"Yeah, that's right!" someone near the back of the room shouted. "No one's doing anything to help us! No one cares!"

Nolan Hodge scanned the crowd, hoping to make eye contact with the man who interrupted him, but it was no use. The city council meetings were usually dull affairs, just a bunch of elected officials trying to balance a constantly insufficient budget. But tonight was different. Tonight the room was packed with everyday Joes. The working class. Most of them worked for the transit system, and they were mad as hell.

One of the city's biggest unions threatened to shut Overbrook Meadows down, if their demands weren't met. The mayor called their bluff, and today not one of the 78 city busses left the lot this morning. The shuttles that ushered passengers to nearby Arlington and Dallas were unmanned as well. Bus drivers

and mechanics lined nearly every downtown street with picket
signs and chants of unity and fair wages.

The mayor was brokering a deal to get the busses running
at that very moment, but that didn't stop Nolan from jumping on
the opportunity to elevate his standing in the community. Two
weeks ago he announced his plans to run against Mayor Victoria
Monroe in the next election. It was clear that he was already on
the campaign trail.

"I argued for the union long before it came down to this,"
he informed the crowd. "Every quarter I argued for more money
to fix our streets. I told the mayor we needed better security at the
transit centers downtown.

"I was one of the loudest opponents of the mayor's Cedar
Lake development plan," Nolan reminded the crowd. "But that
went through without a hitch. We spent *fifty million dollars* on
that project, and for what? The people in Cedar Lake don't ride
the city bus to work!"

The crowd erupted in cheers.

"What about the people on the north side? What about the
people on the south side? They never get to play on that
multimillion dollar golf course."

The crowd got even more boisterous.

"Even if they wanted to play golf, they couldn't get there,
because the damned buses aren't running!"

The people were on their feet now. Nolan tried to get them
under control, though it was clear he enjoyed basking in their
affection.

Nearly lost in the sea of people was Donna Hodge. Her
heart warmed as Nolan embarked on another one of his tirades. A
slight smirk appeared in the corner of her mouth. Her husband
was the whole package. Not only was Nolan brilliant and an
excellent speaker, but he was also a handsome devil – definitely
the best-looking elected official the city had ever known.

Nolan Hodge had fair skin, a hard, square jawline and
naturally wavy hair that he wore short on the sides and a little
longer on top. He was clean-shaven, with a thin nose and dimples
that appeared in his cheeks when he flashed his megawatt smile.
Tonight he wasn't smiling, but it was still very easy to become
enraptured. Nolan wore a black suit with a white shirt and no tie.

He was powerfully built, though not much of him was visible behind his desk.

Donna was the only woman Mr. Hodge had eyes for, and his current demeanor was a huge turn-on. She loved it when her husband went off on people while standing up for the common man. The fact that he was attacking the city's mayor – *publicly* – was even more delicious. Donna felt her kitty shudder at the thought of what she wanted to do to him when they got home. A moment later she felt her ears burning when he mentioned her name.

"My wife, Donna, is a middle school teacher," Nolan said. He looked around and locked eyes with her and smiled. It was such a loving smile. There were over two hundred people in the room, but Nolan had the power and the state of mind to make Donna feel like she was the most important person in his life.

God, she couldn't wait until she got him home! Many people appreciated this city councilman, but none of them could express their appreciation like she could. That fact made her extremely giddy.

"She tells me about the problems in the school district," Nolan went on. "I talk to the superintendent. I talk to parents. They tell me about promises the mayor made. But where's the commitment? We have fifty million dollars for Cedar Lake, but we can't spend five hundred thousand to get most of our potholes fixed?"

The crowd erupted in cheers again.

Most members of the city council smiled and nodded their approval, but one woman sighed silently. The muscles in her cheeks clenched as she faintly rolled her eyes. Donna caught all of this, and she kept track of everyone who slighted her husband, no matter how minor.

"Yes, I'm back on the Cedar Lake development," Nolan said, "because I was against that project from day one! I gave the mayor a detailed analysis of where that money could be better spent. I told her we needed to beef up the police department's Special Crimes Unit long before we had a serial killer in our midst. We lost five lives to the Sleeping Strangler. Many in the police department believe those murders could've been solved sooner if the investigators were allowed to work overtime on the case. But there was no money for that.

11

"Now, I'm not giving a campaign speech right now," Nolan said.

That brought knowing grins and chuckles from some. The same councilwoman who rolled her eyes earlier frowned as she looked down at her watch. Donna's nostrils flared as she watched her. She decided that she didn't like Mrs. Heather Preston at all.

"I'm just speaking for the people," Nolan went on, "as I've always done. Thank you for your time. I pray that everyone has a safe trip home. Thank you. God bless."

Nolan's rant (which was surely not a campaign speech) garnished him a standing ovation. No one was more proud of him than Donna. Tonight he blew her away. She knew that he was going to win big on Election Day. It wasn't so much about his looks or his charisma or the way he electrified a crowd. Nolan would win because on top of all of that, he was *right*, and the current mayor was constantly *wrong*.

Sometimes things could be as simple as that.

●●●●●●●

An hour and a half later, Donna and Nolan sat at a large table at *Mille Fleurs*, which was the classiest French restaurant in the city. On Donna's right was Nolan's political advisor, the great Oscar Lane, and next to Nolan sat Frederick Mueller, a police lieutenant for the 8th district, and his lovely wife Carla.

Their plates were taken away by then, and everyone was on their second or third glass of wine. The atmosphere at the table was festive. Nolan had simply delivered a powerful speech tonight, but Donna felt as if he'd won the mayoral race already.

"The transportation strike couldn't have come at a better time," Oscar commented. He was a dark-skinned gentleman with wire-rimmed glasses and a big belly that threatened to burst at least one of the buttons on his shirt. He didn't look like much, but Oscar was a brilliant strategist. So far he had groomed Nolan into the perfect candidate.

"Did you really talk to some of those people on the way to work this morning?"

"Hell no," Nolan said. "But I did see them. The streets were packed downtown. Even if I wanted to stop, I couldn't find anywhere to park."

"It's great that you included that in your speech," Oscar said. "Made it real personal."

"I'm glad you didn't bring up my name," Lieutenant Mueller said. Frederick, or Freddie, as he preferred to be called, had been a family friend for over a decade. Nolan knew him from his days as an assistant D.A. Freddie continued to be Nolan's lifeline for information about the police department.

"I was holding my breath when you brought up the strangler," he said with a chuckle. "You know the mayor's gonna wanna know who told you about the overtime, or lack thereof."

"That was genius!" Oscar nearly shouted. He downed three drinks during dinner and was more jovial than Donna had ever seen him. His chubby face glistened under the soft lamp lights. "Preying on people's fears is *excellent*. But the strike, I couldn't have prayed for better. I love the way you kept going after the Cedar Lake development. You had the perfect crowd for it."

"It is pretty over there," Freddie mused.

"I know," Nolan said. "I try to make it out there at least once a week. I love Cedar Lake. I think I'll move my family out there one of these days."

Donna couldn't help but laugh at that.

"But those goddamned bus drivers are out of their minds," Nolan continued. "How the hell do they expect to get twenty dollars an hour with no college degree?"

Everyone laughed, but Freddie raised an eyebrow. "Well, you'd better not break any of the promises you're making to the police," he warned Nolan. "I could give a damn about a bus driver myself, but if any of your budget cuts ever hurt the department—"

"Y'all ain't gonna do shit but complain to the next councilman," Nolan said, and they all laughed again. "No, but seriously," he said, wiping a joyful tear from his eye, "you now I got your back, Freddie. The police and schools, those are two things I sincerely care about."

He reached into Donna's lap and squeezed her hand. His touch was warm against her lower belly. He smiled at her, and she pleaded with her eyes, *Can we please get out of here, so I can fuck your brains out?* Nolan raised an eyebrow, as if he understood her completely.

"Hey, guys, it's getting late," he told his friends. He checked his watch and saw that it was after eleven. "I'm tired, and Donna had a long day at work."

Donna didn't yawn on purpose, but she welcomed the visual effect. She covered her mouth daintily. "Oh, excuse me."

Freddie leaned forward, with his elbows on the table. "So, you think you're gonna pull it off?" he asked Nolan. "Think you might actually win this thing?"

"He's gonna win," Oscar answered for him. "The last poll had Monroe only three points ahead. After tonight, Nolan will be four points ahead of her. And if need be, we still have our ace in the hole."

"What's that?" Freddie asked, eager for more dirt on the despised mayor.

"I really don't want to talk about that," Nolan said seriously.

"Come on," Freddie urged. "I told you about our overtime problems with the strangler case. I thought we were friends."

"We are," Nolan said. "I just don't think it's appropriate for this setting. We got women here."

Now Freddie was really intrigued. "Damn. What'd she do, sell one of her daughters into prostitution?"

"Even better," Oscar said. "Six months ago she sent her youngest daughter to Mexico for an *abortion*."

Freddie's eyes widened. "No shit?"

"No shit," Oscar said, his eyes twinkling.

Freddie sat back and folded his arms over his stomach. "Not Mayor Victoria Monroe; one of the staunchest anti-abortion republicans in the state."

"Yep. She did," Oscar said.

"How old is her daughter?" Freddie asked.

"Fifteen. Fourteen at the time of the procedure."

Freddie shook his head, still smiling.

"And she was late term, too," Oscar said. "She waited until she was almost showing before she told her mom, and they waited another month trying to figure out what the hell they were going to do about it. The doctor said the baby was five months when he got it out. Probably could've survived in ICU."

Donna brought a hand to her mouth. Freddie's wife looked equally disturbed.

14

"You talked to the doctor?" Freddie asked.

"No, I don't speak Spanish," Oscar said. "My secretary talked to him. He sold us pictures and everything."

"Pictures of what?" Donna dared to ask.

"Pictures of the mayor's daughter, and pictures of the dead baby," Oscar said casually. "I got 'em on my phone. Wanna see?"

Donna was shocked to see him actually reach for his cellular. "Oh, that's disgusting," she said, her eyebrows knitted.

"Yeah," Nolan said. "Nobody wants to see that shit, Oscar. What the hell's wrong with you?"

"I'm just saying," Oscar said, expressing no shame. "I got 'em."

"Nolan, you're not going to let him drag an aborted baby into this, are you?" Carla asked.

"I don't know," Nolan said. "Maybe. If we have to."

Even his wife was surprised by that. "Really?" Donna said.

Nolan gave her a look and then fixed somber eyes on everyone at the table. "I think you all need to calm down and take your emotions out of this. The mayor is a lying, hypocritical bitch, and she needs to be exposed as such. Because of her and Governor Powell and all of the other Bible-thumpers, women in Texas have to travel damned near to Oklahoma for an abortion.

"If that's truly the mayor's stance, then she needs to abide by those laws as well. She should've bit the bullet and told us, '*Hey, my daughter's a slut. My bad. Here's my grandbaby.*' But no, she sends that little girl out of the country to get rid of it. So yeah, if it comes down to it, and there's even a fraction of a chance that I might not win, then that story's getting leaked, with my blessing."

"We can get a billboard," Oscar suggested. "*Does Mayor Monroe have a grandchild?*" he read the imaginary placard aloud. "*Yep, here it is!* And we'll put the picture up there, big as day."

Donna's eyes widened.

Nolan shook his head in disdain. "You know, you really are a sadistic bastard. But I'm glad you work for me," he said with a smile. "I'm running for governor in a couple of years," he announced for the first time. "I cannot let someone like Victoria Monroe stand in my way. I will not."

The bad taste in Donna's mouth was quickly replaced with excitement and admiration for her husband.

"You wanna run for governor?" she asked him.

He nodded. "Yeah. But I gotta win this race first."

"And you're gonna win!" Oscar said. He was very enthused. Donna was too.

"You think you can turn Texas blue?" Freddie asked doubtfully. "We haven't had a democratic governor since..."

"Ann Richards," Nolan said. "1991."

"But you think you can do it?"

Donna had butterflies in her stomach as she watched the men talk. *Governor?* Really? She knew her husband was ambitious, but she never imagined he dreamed this big.

"I think the people in this state are tired," Nolan said. "They're tired of the lies, tired of all the arguing in the senate, tired of getting their rights and government assistance taken away. Everybody's tired, and they're turning against the republicans. A change has come. You'll see."

"I think you're right," Freddie decided.

"Good," Nolan said and rose to his feet. "Now I gotta get home. Who's taking care of this check?"

Both of the other men at the table looked away sheepishly.

"You cheap bastards," Nolan said with a grin as he reached for his wallet. "When I'm mayor, I'm not paying for anything in this town. You hear me? Not a goddamned thing!"

CHAPTER TWO
MR. AND MRS. HODGE

"How was your day, baby?"

Nolan drove a brand new Infinity Q50. It was four doors and sleek black with dark tint and an immaculately clean interior. He had it for a few months, but it still had a new car smell. Donna's SUV was new as well, but hers was the "family car," and it was not nearly as clean. Their son Colton played every sport imaginable, and she spent a good deal of time ushering him and his buddies from one event to another.

Nolan still seemed to glow as he sat behind the steering wheel of his luxury vehicle, finally piloting them towards home. Donna couldn't take her eyes off of him. She found it endearing that after all that took place tonight, her husband still had the courtesy to ask about her uneventful day.

Donna worked as a Math teacher at Wedgewood Middle School on the west side. She loved her job, but she was very happy it was Friday. A lot of her students were considered "at risk," and it was a struggle to keep them focused on most days. Donna desperately needed the weekend to recharge and remind herself that her job was truly meaningful.

She smiled at her husband and shook her head slightly.

"My day was fine, pretty boring compared to yours. Why didn't you tell me you were thinking about running for governor?"

Nolan looked over at her and grinned.

Donna grinned back at him.

"You're beautiful, you know that?" he said. "Did you wear that to work, or you had time to change?"

Donna wore a coffee bean colored pant suit with a beige camisole. She was tall and not as thin as she'd like to be, but there was no denying her curves were sexy. She kept her tummy flat, for the most part, and Nolan was a breast man. He watched with wonderment when her chest swelled during her pregnancy. That was fourteen years ago. Thankfully Donna's cup size never receded after their son's birth.

Nolan stole glances at his wife as he drove west on the sparsely populated freeway. The interior of his car was dark, but the street lamps illuminated Donna's face every quarter mile. Her hair was long and frizzy by nature, but today it was straightened and layered, with reddish highlights that accentuated her dark skin tone. She had bright eyes with long lashes. Her lips were full, glistening with a thin coat of gloss.

"Thank you," she said and found herself blushing slightly. She found it odd and delightful that Nolan could still make her feel that way after so many years together. "But tonight is not about me, and you know it. Why didn't you tell me you were eyeing the governor's office?"

Nolan's grin spread from ear to ear.

"I didn't really think about it until tonight," he replied. "After my speech."

"That was an awesome speech!"

"Thanks. I was nervous at first, but then everything started coming together."

"You were nervous? Whatever!"

"I was," Nolan said with a chuckle. "I knew I had to pounce on the strike, but I didn't know if I wanted to go that hard or not. We're not supposed to use council meetings as our personal platform. I didn't want anyone to think I was taking advantage of my position."

"I'm sure what's her face thought that," Donna informed him.

"Who's that?"

"That duck-face lady," she said. "Preston."

"Oh, Heather? Why do you say that?"

"I caught her rolling her eyes a couple of times," Donna said. "And then she checked her watch when everyone was applauding."

Nolan smiled at that. "I hear she and the mayor have been friends since college. Heather's been doing a lot of dry-snitching lately. I can't say anything in our meetings without it getting back to the mayor."

"Well, your speech tonight is *definitely* gonna get back to her. But governor? Baby, that's huge! The people love you!"

"I still have to win the mayor's seat first."

"Baby, you got that in the bag. There's no way Monroe can dig herself out of this hole."

"Overbrook Meadows is still 60 percent white," Nolan cautioned. "And Monroe has served three terms. It won't be easy to dethrone her."

"Well, you certainly won't have Cedar Lake's support," Donna joked. "Everybody there is gonna hate you."

"Those votes are already committed to Monroe," Nolan said. "I didn't risk anything by going after them. Oscar did the numbers."

"Oh my God." Donna brought a hand to her face and rubbed her forehead. "Baby, you gotta fire him. That man is out of control."

Nolan laughed. "I can't fire Oscar. He's doing an excellent job."

"I think he's more concerned with running a smear campaign than he is about the actual issues. And you know that doesn't work. They tried it with Obama. *Two times.*"

"This is different. Obama had the facts on his side. But there's nothing Monroe can do to explain her daughter's abortion. That's a gold mine. She might even drop out of the race if she finds out we're going to use it against her."

"Just try to keep your hands clean," Donna urged him.

"Oscar knows what he's doing," Nolan assured her. "And I do too."

"Yes you do, Mr. Hodge. Or should I say, *Mr. Mayor?*"

Nolan locked eyes with her for a moment. He liked the way his wife was looking at him. "That sounds good. Say it again."

"What? Mr. Mayor?"

"Yeah. I love the way that sounds. I can get used to that."

"I think *Governor Hodge* sounds better."

Nolan grinned. "I like the sound of that, too."

"You know what would be even better?" She placed a hand on his thigh and moved it slowly towards his zipper.

"What's that?"

Donna brushed his manhood and then squeezed it through his slacks. "How about *Mr. President*?"

Nolan began to grow steadily beneath her palm. "Getting a little ahead of ourselves, aren't we?"

"I don't think so," Donna said. "But I do like the idea of getting *a-head*. You were so awesome tonight, I think you deserve something special..."

Nolan cleared his throat. "That would be nice."

Donna tried to unzip his pants with her left hand, but she couldn't manage it. She unbuckled her seatbelt so she could turn and use both hands. Nolan exited the freeway and kept both eyes on the road. Donna dug in his boxers until she managed to free his meat. It popped up hard and ready. Donna wrapped a hand around it, loving the heat it emitted.

"What would my loving mayor like from his dutiful wife?" she asked.

"Damn," Nolan muttered. "I'm actually at a loss for words. This is sexy as hell."

Donna stroked him slowly, up and down. She used her thumb to titillate the sensitive head. "Surely there's something my mayor desires from me tonight."

Nolan stopped at a light and turned to watch her. His chest rose and fell visibly.

"I, I don't..."

Donna licked her lips and then sucked the bottom one into her mouth. When she let it go, it glistened with spittle. Nolan looked around anxiously. They weren't the only vehicles at the intersection, but there was no one on their right or left. Nolan didn't think anyone in the opposite lane could see inside their car, but he wasn't the voyeuristic type.

"Are you too proper to ask me to suck your dick, Mr. Mayor?"

He raised an eyebrow, and Donna felt him jump in her hand.

"That's all I could think about tonight," she said. "During your speech, I wondered what it would be like if you left your desk and walked up to me and pulled your dick out."

Nolan laughed nervously.

"And at the restaurant," Donna continued, "I wondered what your friends would think of me if I crawled under the table and did it there."

His mouth fell open.

Donna giggled teasingly. "I'm just kidding, baby."

"Kidding about then or now?" he managed.

"I know Mr. Straight-Laced Hodge isn't going to let me give him a blowjob in the middle of the street," Donna said.

"I'll probably wreck," Nolan stated. "But I think it might be worth it."

"Probably."

"But you're not wearing your seatbelt. If I kill you, while you're doing that, I don't think I could live with myself. And what would I tell people?"

Donna saw that he was smiling. But he was also serious. Nolan was one of the most cautious people she knew, almost to a fault.

"We'll – I'd hate for you to run into a phone pole," she teased as she withdrew her hand.

The light turned green, and Nolan got moving again.

"We'll be home in eight minutes," he said. "I hope you don't change your mind by then."

Donna shrugged. "I don't know. I guess we'll see."

"What do I have to do to get some assurance?"

"Hurry up."

"You want me to speed?"

Donna feigned a yawn. "I'm getting sleepy. We're not there yet?"

Nolan put the pedal to the metal, and the Infinity's motor roared like a lion.

●●●●●●●

They pulled into their garage five minutes later. Nolan unbuckled his seatbelt and turned to watch his wife as the garage door rattled closed behind them.

"Baby, do you *really* think I can win?"

Donna was surprised by the question. "I thought you were already working your way towards the governor's mansion. Why are you having doubts?"

"Because people are stupid, and some of them are racist."

"Monroe's daughter had a late-term abortion in *Mexico*," Donna stated. "If that's not enough to get her out the office, this Godforsaken city deserves her. You're the best, baby. Don't ever forget that."

Nolan grinned. "Thank you. And did I mention how nice you look tonight?"

"Yes, but I don't mind hearing it again."

He leaned towards her. Donna closed her eyes as their lips met over the center console. Nolan's lips were full and warm. The electricity between them made her heart flutter. She felt the temperature rising as well, mostly between her legs.

Nolan reached and fondled her left breast. The nipple quickly hardened beneath his fingers. He slipped his tongue inside her mouth and she moaned pleasantly. He sucked her bottom lip into his mouth and did the same to the top one. Donna's breaths quickened. She felt her panties becoming moist.

She reached into his lap, pleased that he didn't zip up after the fondling at the stop light. Nolan was already rock hard. Donna looked down and saw his essence glistening at the tip. The sight of it made her mouth water.

She licked Nolan's lips and said, "Mr. Mayor, you still haven't asked me to suck your dick."

Nolan loved it when she talked dirty to him, but he was generally too reserved to reciprocate. Tonight was no exception. He remained mute, but his hand made its way to the back of her neck. Donna allowed him to pull her head down between his legs. His dick jumped in her mouth the moment she sucked him in. She took him in deeply, all the way on the first gulp. She loved that Nolan wasn't particularly long or wide. His seven inches was perfect for her mouth and hands and all other warm, wet places. She backed out, sucking hard and slow. The taste of his pre-cum was salty and exotic, like caviar.

Nolan's legs stiffened, and he inhaled audibly. He kept a grip on the back of his wife's head as it moved up and down on his pole. He loved the brightness of the garage. He loved how Donna's eyes were closed, her lips wet, her cheeks concave. He loved the sounds she made as she sucked. His toes twisted in his shoes, like they were throwing gang signs. Not many women could pull off a sideways blowjob so effectively. Donna's beauty and professionalism made the experience much more enjoyable for Nolan.

Early in their marriage, she promised to be the best wife he could ever hope for. She promised to be the best mistress as well, so that he'd never have to seek love elsewhere. Donna kept her promises many times over. Nolan's dick knew where home was, and it was always very happy to be there.

It took less than three minutes before he told her, "Damn, baby. I'm finna cum."

Donna stopped sucking long enough to tell him, "Don't worry. I won't spill any in your car."

●●●●●●●

The couple met at Jackson Memorial Hospital fifteen years ago. Donna was twenty-two at the time. Nolan was young and fit at twenty-five. Donna went to the emergency room to see a friend who had come in by ambulance after a multiple vehicle collision. She knew her friend wasn't seriously injured because Tricia called her after the accident and told her which hospital she was going to. The woman at the information desk said Tricia went to X-ray and couldn't have any visitors until she returned.

Donna took a seat in the waiting area and was soon approached by a handsome fellow who quickly struck up a conversation.

"Hi," he said. "My name is Nolan Hodge."

"Hi," Donna said. She frowned at him, rather than reveal her identity.

"I'm a lawyer," Nolan said. He offered her a card.

Donna didn't take it. "I don't need a lawyer."

Nolan wore a white golf shirt tucked into neat khaki slacks. He was clean-shaven, his hair thick and curly. He was thin and muscular with dreamy hazelnut eyes. Donna was quite a looker as well; a natural beauty with big brown eyes and a slim, yet curvy figure.

Nolan asked, "Can I take a seat for a moment?"

Donna looked over at the empty seat next to her. She had her purse in it. Before she could respond, Nolan picked up her purse and handed it to her as he sat down. Donna's eyes widened.

"Excuse me."

"I'm sorry," Nolan said. "I don't mean to be rude."

Up close, Donna thought he smelled wonderful, but she kept her frown intact.

"I was wondering if you're here with someone who was involved in that accident on 820," Nolan said. "There was a huge pile up, caused by an 18-wheeler. I know that several injured people were brought here."

Donna couldn't believe he said that with a straight face. "Are you serious?"

"Yes. I'd like to offer my services to anyone seeking representation."

Donna laughed at that. Nolan smiled, too.

"Are you serious?" she asked again.

"What?" Nolan said, still grinning. "I don't get it."

"I didn't know ambulance-chasing, blood-sucking lawyers like you really existed."

"Whoa. There's no need to be offensive."

"I mean, I heard about it," Donna said. "But I never met one in real life before. You're literally *chasing ambulances*. Like, for real."

"Okay, I'll cop to that," Nolan said. "But I'm not a bloodsucker."

"You make money off people's misery."

"No, I want to help people *profit* from their misery. There's a difference. The people I work for are already miserable. I help them get their life back on track. So, are you here with someone who was involved with that accident?"

"Maybe..." Donna said. She was aware that she was flirting. She could've told him *No* and ended the conversation, but the more Nolan talked, the more interested she was in him. Smart men were always a weakness for her. A smart, *hustling* man was an all-new level of awesomeness.

"Could you tell me your friend's name?"

"No. Absolutely not."

"Well, could you give him or her my card at least? I'll make it worth your while."

Donna frowned again, thinking he was some kind of pervert.

Nolan laughed. His teeth were nice. His smile was infectious. "I don't mean anything *illicit*," he said. "What I meant was, I can offer you a finder's fee, if I take your friend's case."

"How much?" *Ugh*! Donna didn't mean to ask that. Now the lawyer knew she *did* have a friend who was involved in the accident.

"Depends on the case," Nolan said. "Usually around two or three hundred dollars."

Hmmmm. Donna could use that money. It must have showed on her face.

"What do you do for a living?" Nolan asked.

"I'm a teacher." Donna didn't know why she divulged. She realized Nolan could be very disarming.

"A pretty, young thing like you?" he said. "This must be your first year."

Donna rolled her eyes at the flattery.

"Well, I know teachers aren't paid enough," Nolan said. "You deserve a lot more money for what you're doing for the community. I'm sure a few hundred dollars could help. All you have to do is give your friend my card and maybe encourage her – or him – to call me."

"I'll give her the card," Donna said, and she finally took it from his hand. "But I won't encourage her to call you. She can call whoever she wants."

"Fair enough," Nolan said. "Will you tell me your name now, so I'll remember, in case I need to pay you for the referral?"

"I'm Donna."

"That's a beautiful name."

He smiled at her, and Donna felt her face flush with heat.

"Hey, uh, on a personal note, do you think you might like to have dinner with me sometime?" Nolan asked.

She shook her head.

"Why not?"

Because you look like the kind of guy who takes waaay too many women to your den of desire. You probably have notches on your bedpost and everything!

"Because you're too cocky," she told him.

"Most people think I'm confident."

"Only cocky people run around telling people how confident they are."

"I'm gonna be somebody important," Nolan told her. "One day, I'm gonna be the big man in this city."

"Well, if that ain't cocky, I don't know what is."

He laughed again, and Donna felt her heart swell. She didn't know why his laugher affected her like that, but it did. After only a few minutes of knowing him, Donna decided she wanted to be the one to keep a smile on his face.

"Here," Nolan said. He produced another business card, seemingly from thin air. "You keep this one. If you change your mind about going out with me, my cell number's on there."

Donna didn't say anything, but she accepted the card.

Nolan rose to his feet and told her, "Hope to see you again, Donna," before making his way to the next potential customer.

Donna had to admit that she was not happy to see him go. She began to feel jealous when he parked his perfect keister next to another woman, so she looked away and tried to put him out of her mind altogether.

●●●●●●●

Contrary to her icy reception, Donna was very supportive of Nolan when she gave the card to her friend. Tricia wasn't badly injured, only a broken clavicle, but Nolan took her case. He promised to get her car fixed, get her free therapy and get her $5,000 for her "pain and suffering" when the 18-wheeler's insurance company finally settled the case.

That could take three to six months, but Donna didn't have to wait that long to get her referral fee. Nolan called her a few days after Tricia signed with him and said he had a $300 check with her name on it. He offered to mail it to her, but Donna said she'd come to his office to pick it up. When she got there, Nolan asked her out a second time, and she said yes.

Their courtship lasted eight months. They were married on a beautiful autumn afternoon. Donna was six weeks pregnant at the time, but no one could tell. Nolan never wanted another child after their son was born, so Donna put her dreams of three or more children on the shelf. Thankfully that was the only major concession she had to make as Nolan Hodge's wife.

Over the next decade and a half, she groomed Nolan into the man he is today. But the ambition had always been there. Nolan worked as an independent attorney for three years before taking a job as Overbrook Meadows' Assistant D.A. He stayed in that position for eight years before joining a prestigious firm to work as a defense attorney.

Donna wasn't surprised when he announced one day that he was running for city council, and she was not surprised when he got elected. For as long as she'd known him, every goal Nolan set his sights on was eventually obtained. Now he had his sights set on the mayor's office as well as the governor's mansion.

Donna didn't know where the next decade and a half would take them, but success was almost guaranteed. She looked forward to growing old with Nolan and celebrating his many accomplishments. Her career as a school teacher paled in comparison to her husband's endeavors, but Donna was happy with her job, and, as Nolan told her the first day they met, she was also doing something important for the community.

•••••••

Nolan's dick pulsated in her mouth as it pumped semen down the back of her throat. Donna continued to suck hard and slow. She wrapped a hand around the shaft and used her saliva as a lubricant as she milked him dry. Nolan threw his head back against the seat's headrest and moaned, panting slightly. His grip on the back of her head tightened. The slurping sounds his wife made as she consumed his essence made Nolan's heart shoot up his esophagus and rattle in the back of his throat.

"*God damn,*" he breathed. "*Baby, that feels so good.*"

Donna kept her promise not to spill a drop in his beautiful car.

"Mr. Mayor, you were all full," she said when she finally removed her lips from his throbbing pole.

"Co, Colton's with my brother?" Nolan managed.

Donna nodded. Nolan's brother Brandon took his role as godfather very seriously. He picked Colton up from school at least once a week so he could spend time with him. This weekend, Colton planned to be with his uncle until Sunday.

"Gimme a minute," Nolan said. He was red about the face, still enjoying the tremors of an awesome orgasm. "How long will it take you to get out of that suit?"

"Not long," she replied.

"Hurry up."

The seriousness of his request made everything below Donna's waist shudder in anticipation.

•••••••

She made it inside first, but the light on the answering machine was blinking, and she thought she had time to check it. She knew it couldn't be anyone important, or they would've called her cellphone. But her son was away, and the voicemail would've been on her mind for the rest of the night, if she didn't listen to it now.

She pressed play and was still standing next to the coffee table when Nolan appeared in the hallway. He looked like he was upset that she didn't follow his instructions.

"Oh, baby, I'm sorry," Donna explained. "Just checking these messages."

Nolan peeled off his sports coat and let it fall to the floor behind him. He kicked off his shoes and left them there as well. He approached his wife. The look in his eyes was dark and hungry.

Donna deleted the last of the messages and gave him her full attention.

Nolan kept his eyes glued on hers as he unbuttoned his shirt. "You have a hard time following instructions, Mrs. Hodge?"

Her eyes widened. Her pulse quickened to the point that she actually felt the blood rushing through her veins. She shook her head.

"I think you do," Nolan said. He took off his shirt and pulled his tee shirt over his head. "Here I am butt-naked, and you're still fully dressed."

Nolan was not naked when he started that sentence, but he managed to slip his pants and boxers off before he finished it. Donna felt a coat of lubrication moisten her nookie at the sight of his nude physique. Nolan played basketball all the way through college. He still practiced with their son a few days each week, and he never allowed Donna's good cooking to give him a potbelly. Donna thought he was as fine as he was the day they met, especially with his hard dick pointing right at her.

"Let me go—"

"No." He approached her with the speed of a black panther and took hold of her arm before she could leave the room. "You had your chance, Mrs. Hodge. Now we're doing it *my* way."

Donna knew what Nolan's way was like, and she was both thrilled and anxious about the prospect. Nolan was a stickler for the rules in most cases. He never sped, ran red lights or even cut in line. But when they were home alone, sex was one facet of his life where he was free to show another side of himself.

He pushed her onto the couch roughly and grabbed both of her ankles before she could react. He pulled her shoes off and tossed them over his shoulder. Donna heard one of them hit the coffee table and knock something off before it fell to the floor.

"Baby, hold on."

Nolan ignored her. "Lay back." He hovered over her and pushed her shoulders back when she didn't comply. He took hold of her legs again and pulled them until her spine was completely flat on the seat of the sofa. He reached between her legs and hastily unbuttoned and unzipped her pants. He lifted her hips and pulled the pants off her legs with the panties still entangled.

Goosebumps sprouted on her thighs the moment they were exposed. Her legs snapped closed reflexively. Nolan pried them apart just as quickly. He dropped to his knees, and without so much as a *How do you do?* he buried his face in her hot snatch.

"*Oh, baby!*"

Donna cried out, mostly in surprise, until she felt her husband's warm tongue on her most sensitive region, and everything was suddenly very nice, and she had no idea why she would fight something so wonderful. Her back arched as tendrils of pleasure stretched in all directions.

Contrary to his caveman tactics, Nolan was surprisingly patient when it came to cunnilingus. He licked her slowly, until her clitoris hardened and throbbed, and then he zeroed in on the bulb, sucking with his lips and massaging it with his taste buds. The pleasure was immediate, and it was explosive. Nolan claimed her treasure like he found it at the bottom of a rainbow, and

Donna saw all of the rainbow's dazzling colors as her kitty began to quiver and yearn for more.

She was slightly uncomfortable because she still had her suit jacket on, but she heard the garment rip when she reached for Nolan's head, and suddenly she had a lot more range of motion. In the back of her mind she wondered how badly her jacket had torn, but in the here and now she didn't give a damn about the suit.

Nolan brought her to the verge of climax twice, but both times he altered his tongue action and didn't focus on her clitoris again until the trembling in her legs subsided. The third time it happened, he withdrew his tongue completely. Before Donna could protest, Nolan rose and penetrated her fully, shoving his dick balls deep in her wet center on the first stroke.

"*Aaah!*"

The sudden thrust caused Donna's walls to contract and squeeze his hard rod. Nolan grunted and smiled down at her disheveled state.

"*Damn, baby,*" he moaned. "*You're so tight.*"

He was on his knees, pumping his hips slowly yet forcefully.

Donna couldn't move, let alone respond to him. A levee in her love box opened, glazing his dick with another coat of lubrication. The contractions of her walls continued to squeeze him pleasingly. Donna felt like her clitoris was about to explode with joy. She managed to relax her legs, hoping to prolong the pleasure he gave her.

Her orgasm started as a trickle in her belly. It was a tsunami by the time it rolled down to her womb. Her body clutched him even tighter, and her clitoris pulsated rhythmically, enjoying every bit of friction his dick provided. Donna saw heaven behind her closed eyelids. She gripped the couch cushions so hard her hands left sweat stains that were there for half an hour. Her legs shook uncontrollably. Nolan propped them on his shoulders and plunged deeper still. Donna felt him all the way in her chest.

When the thunderous pounding of her heart finally slowed from a stampede of wild stallions to a somewhat normal pace, she told him, "*Ooh, you getting it, Governor.*"

Nolan began to pound her box harder, as if upset by the comment. But he told her, "*Suh, say it again.*"

Donna looked up at him with a wistful smile parting her lips. *"Ooh, Governor Hodge. Get it, boy."*

Nolan could only last a few strokes longer before he shuddered and pumped another load of his essence deep inside her. Donna rolled seamlessly into a second orgasm. She rode this one slowly, like a tiny raft lost at sea. It felt so good, she thought she might lose consciousness.

Nolan told her, *"I love you, baby."*

"I love you," she said, barely above a whisper.

Donna didn't know it, but that was the last time she'd ever utter those three little words to the man of her dreams.

CHAPTER THREE
IN THE BLINK OF AN EYE

The next morning Nolan woke up at eight and was out of the house by 9:30. Donna didn't bother with breakfast because Nolan didn't eat anything heavy before lunchtime. That started years ago as a diet, but it was now a way of life for him. He took a banana, a granola bar and a bottle of orange juice and slung his golf bag over his shoulder. Donna followed him to the door and kissed him on the cheek.

"Don't forget we have that dinner party tomorrow," Nolan said.

Donna actually enjoyed having guests over, but she still gave him a little attitude.

"So you get to go play, and I have to clean up the house?"

"You don't have to do it by yourself," Nolan said. "Call my brother, and tell him to bring Colton to help you."

"Yeah right. I'm sure Colton would love to cut his weekend short to help Mama clean."

"I'll help you when I get back."

"*Yeah right!*" Donna said, and this time she had to laugh. "You're not gonna help me clean, and you know it. You haven't seen a mop in so long, you probably forgot how to work one!"

He wrapped his free arm around her waist and pulled her close. Donna wore a baby blue robe that felt like clouds from heaven. Nolan wore khaki slacks with his golf shirt tucked in neatly. The dress code at Cedar Lake was strictly enforced, even for mayoral candidates.

"Why don't you go to the mall when you're done, and get yourself a new pair of shoes?" he offered.

Done and done!

"Okay," Donna said and kissed him on the lips. "Have a nice day."

Nolan gave her booty a squeeze before they separated. "You too, baby. Don't work too hard."

● ● ● ● ● ● ●

Donna didn't need her son's help with the chores, but she hadn't seen him since she took him to school yesterday, and she missed him. She knew he'd sleep late at his uncle's house, so she waited until eleven before she called his cellphone.

He answered after a few rings. "Hey, Mama."

Colton was in the eighth grade at Wedgewood Middle, which happened to be the same school where Donna was employed. She made sure not to have him as a student any of the three years he'd been there, but it was nice working in the same building with him. Because of their proximity, Colton was an excellent student. Or maybe he'd still be a good kid at a different school. That remained to be seen. Donna did not look forward to when he got promoted to high school next year and left her behind.

Colton was the spitting image of his father, right down to his wavy hair and golden-brown eyes. He was tall and thin and naturally athletic. As an only child, he was certainly spoiled, but Colton remained grounded. He was popular at school, and so far he didn't get loopy in the head over the many little girls vying for his attention.

"How are things going?" Donna asked him. "Having fun with Uncle Brandon?"

"Yeah I am," Colton said. His voice was laced with excitement. "We went to the Mavericks' game last night! Uncle Bran got me a signed basketball! I'm never going to use it. He said it's a collectible."

"Wow. That's awesome!" Donna said.

"The Maverick's lost, but we still had fun. That stadium is huge, Mama. It's all brand new."

"I know. I want to get out there one of these days."

"You should," Colton said. "Today we're going to Sycamore for my basketball tournament. I think we're going to the movies tonight. I don't know yet."

"You still have your allowance?" Donna asked him. "I don't want Brandon spending all kinds of money on you."

"I have it," Colton said. "But he won't let me spend my money. I tried to buy some stuff at the game last night, but he kept telling me, 'Man, put your wallet up.'"

Donna laughed. That sounded like Brandon.

"Where's Dad?" Colton asked. "Playing golf?"

"You already know."

"What are you doing?"

"About to start cleaning up. We're having a get-together tomorrow. Wanna come help me clean?"

"Sorry, Mama, I got my game today."

"Everybody's got an excuse. Have fun, boy. I love you."

"Love you too, Mama. Bye."

●●●●●●●

Donna called her friend Tricia next. Tricia was certainly not interested in cleaning her friend's house, but she was all for shoe shopping afterwards. She showed up at noon with lunch from McDonalds. Donna knew the chicken nuggets weren't healthy (and didn't contain much chicken meat), so she only indulged once every few weeks.

Donna met Tricia during their college days at Texas Lutheran. Tricia went on to make a killing in the medical field, while Donna molded young minds each year for far less pay. Donna usually met with Tricia and their other friend Kendra for happy hour on Friday nights. She had to cancel on them yesterday because of Nolan's meeting.

Ten minutes later, the ladies sat at the kitchen table chowing down on the fatty foods. Donna had a tee shirt and shorts on by then. Tricia was dressed for the mall in jeans and a tank top. Donna had bigger boobs and hips, but she envied her friend's tall, slender build. Tricia's skin was dark and beautiful. Her hair was plaited to her head in thick cornrows.

"How'd the meeting go?" she asked around a quarter-pounder with cheese.

34

"Oh my God," Donna said. Her face lit up. "You should've been there! Nolan was on fire. He *owned* the mayor!"

"She was there?"

"No. She was probably somewhere hiding her face in shame," Donna said with a laugh. "That bus strike did her in, and Nolan definitely let her have it."

"Yeah, I saw him on the news this morning," Tricia said. "They showed some of his speech."

Donna knew there were reporters at the meeting, but she didn't know her husband made the news. She hated that she missed it.

"But the buses are running again today," Tricia said. "They said the mayor fixed everything with the union reps."

"Bullshit. She only fixes stuff when her back's against the wall. She had no choice but to give them what they wanted last night."

"But they still made it sound like she solved the problem," Tricia reported. "They said she got everything back to normal."

"Ugh, they make me sick," Donna said with a frown. She was referring to the mayor's people as well as the news outlets that went out of their way to show Monroe in a positive light. "Nolan's the one who made that happen."

"Do you think he'll win the election?" Tricia asked.

"He's definitely gonna win," Donna said. "Last night I found out we got an ace in the hole."

"What's that?"

"I can tell you, but you'd better not tell anyone. Seriously. If the story gets out before we expose it, the mayor will come up with some way to explain it. Or people will forget about it in the next two months before the election."

"I won't tell anyone, Donna. You know me."

"Well," Donna said, eager to share the gossip, "it seems that Monroe's youngest daughter got herself pregnant last year."

Tricia's eyes widened, and then she frowned. "Wait, that girl's not pregnant. The mayor had her whole family at one of her speeches last month."

"She's not pregnant *anymore*," Donna corrected. "The mayor took her to Mexico for a *late-term abortion*. The doctor over there said the baby was five months at the time. He took pictures of the mayor's daughter and the dead baby."

Tricia's eyes grew even wider. "Oh snap!"

"I know!" Donna said. She was on the edge of her seat.

"Y'all gonna expose her?"

"Nolan said he won't unless he has to. But, yeah, it's looking like he will."

"*Daaaamn*," Tricia said. "That'll win him the race for sure."

"I know!" Donna was ecstatic.

"You're gonna be the mayor's wife!" Tricia announced.

"Nolan said he's running for governor after this."

"Are you kidding me?"

"No, I'm serious!" Donna was exhilarated to the point of trembling.

"Oh, my God, Donna! Your life is gonna be totally different! Texas never had a black governor. You think he can win?"

"Girl, I'm just focusing on this mayoral race right now. I can't even see that far ahead. But Nolan thinks he can win. He never set his sights on anything that he didn't get."

"I know," Tricia said. "I still remember when he set his sights on *you*. Do you remember when he took my case, after that wreck?"

"I was just thinking about that yesterday!"

"I almost didn't sign with him, because I thought he wasn't professional," Tricia confided. "The first time I met with him, he spent just as much time asking about me as he did about you."

Donna grinned at that.

"But if I didn't sign with him, you never would've got your referral fee," she went on. "And if you didn't get your referral fee, you two never would've gone out..."

"I don't know about that," Donna said. "Nolan later told me that he never gave anyone a referral fee – except me. He just said that so he'd have a reason to contact me again."

"Awww, ain't that cute."

Donna nodded. "It is."

"And that's some big-time tricking, too," Tricia teased. "That man paid $300 just for a *chance* to ask you out. And that was after he already saw *me*. I wonder why he didn't ask me out."

"Obviously I'm much more desirable."

"I guess so," Tricia said with a smile. "I'm so happy for you, Donna. All of your dreams are about to come true."

"They already have. I don't need to be the mayor's wife to be happy."

The doorbell rang.

Donna went to answer it with her smile still in place. She didn't think anything was amiss when she saw Freddie standing on her porch with another police officer. Freddie wore his full uniform, which looked amazing under the afternoon sun. He had colorful stripes and pins on one lapel and his shiny gold badge on the other.

Donna's smile didn't falter when Freddie removed his hat and held it in both hands. His mood seemed very somber and official. His eyes were glazed. He took a deep breath and sniffled, and that's when Donna's whole body went numb. The smile slipped off her face slowly, like a guy finally realizing his winning lottery ticket is actually a prank.

Freddie told her, "I'm sorry, Donna. There's been an accident."

And that's when the ground fell from beneath her.

She stared at him for a long time. She blinked. She felt her heart beating, which was strange because she felt completely calm. She also noticed that Freddie had a small tear on his jacket. It was less than a quarter inch long, mostly concealed by his shiny, gold badge.

"You, No, Nolan's not here," she told him. "He wen, he went to play golf this morning."

How could Freddie not know that already? Nolan played golf every Saturday morning. Last night he told Freddie that he was going to Cedar Lake, as a matter of fact. What the hell was wrong with the lieutenant? He and Nolan were good friends, but surely Freddie could go twenty-four hours without checking up on him. Jeez. What was this, some kind of man crush?

Freddie shook his head. "I'm sorry, Donna. Nolan's been in an accident. He didn't make it. I'm sorry."

Donna's expression was stuck somewhere between confusion and *Get the fuck away from my house, you lying bastard*! She looked from Freddie to the policeman he brought with him. That man had his hat off, too. He held it down by his

37

waist in the same manner as Freddie. What the hell was this? Did these assholes go to a hat-holding class or something?

The only time cops and military personnel held their hats like that was while standing on some woman's porch when that unlucky woman was a brand new widow. But Donna wasn't a fucking widow! Her husband was playing golf! He played golf every Saturday morning. No one had accidents on a golf course! The most that could happen was he got beaned in the head with a stray ball. Nolan could've called her himself to tell her that.

"Put, put your hat on," Donna told Freddie. "What are you doing? What are you doing, man?"

Tears blurred her vision. She stumbled to the left. Freddie was quick to catch her. His grip on her arm was strong. Donna shoved his hand away.

"Don't touch me," she bawled. "Get away from here. I gotta call Nolan."

Tears rolled down Freddie's cheeks. He sniffled and wiped his nose with the back of his hand. "Donna, he's, he's gone. Nolan's gone."

"Shut up!" She punched him in the chest. Hard. "Stop it, man. What are you doing? Where's Nolan? What happened?" Tears streamed down her face. Her heart sank deep into the pit of her stomach and shriveled up like a raisin. She felt like everything inside her was dying. It was dead already. She suddenly had to vomit.

Tricia appeared in the doorway behind her. Her eyes widened as she surveyed the scene. "What, what's going on?" she asked Freddie.

"Nolan's been in an accident," he said. "It was a bad accident, and he didn't make it. He passed away about an hour ago."

Donna emitted a fierce wail as she fell to her knees. Her cry was drenched with shock and hopelessness and fear and dread and sorrow. Her howl sliced through the quietness of the spring afternoon and broke the heart of all who heard it. Even the birds in the trees above stopped chirping out of reverence for this poor soul whose life was forever changed, irreparably damaged by a terrible twist of fate.

Tricia sat on the porch with her and held her and cried with her for as long as Donna wanted to cry. Freddie stood stoically, unable to control his emotions as well. Donna didn't hear his apologies or assurances that they would get through this. She couldn't hear anything past her own sorrow and the huge ripping sound of her soul being torn in two. Her life, her soul mate was gone. Despite the bright sun rays warming her skin, there was only darkness now. Donna knew that she would never see the sunlight again.

●●●●●●●

Thirty minutes later the four of them were in Lieutenant Freddie's unmarked town car on their way to the coroner's office. Donna's face was puffy, stained with fresh and old tears. Her eyes were red and swollen. She grabbed a pair of flip flops and her purse before leaving the house. She didn't remember if she locked the front door or not. Tricia was still with her, holding her hand as they huddled in the backseat. Tricia didn't bother telling her it would be alright, because that was a lie. Things would never be the same. Nolan's death turned the whole world upside down.

Freddie knew a lot about the accident. He said Nolan was travelling north on Grantland Circle when he was struck by an SUV travelling east on Brentwood Drive. He said the driver of the SUV was a fourteen year old boy who stole the car from his step-father and decided to lead police on a high-speed chase when they tried to pull him over. Freddie said the boy ran a light at the intersection and T-boned Nolan's Infinity. He said the damage was massive, and Nolan was killed instantly.

"Wha, what are you, that's not right," Donna cried from the backseat. "Nolan was going to play golf. He wasn't on the east side."

"I, I don't know why he was in that area," Freddie said. He tried to make eye contact with Donna in the rearview mirror.

"It can't be," she said. "It can't be him." Her heart was actually filled with a glimmer of hope. This was all a big mistake. Nolan was playing golf at Cedar Lake, which was all the way on the west side of town. This was a huge misunderstanding. They could still have the dinner party tomorrow.

"I identified him myself," Freddie said. His features were wrought with pain and empathy.

"It can't be," Donna moaned. But a part of her brain tried to inject logic: Nolan and Freddie had been friends for over a decade. And Freddie was a seasoned police officer. There was no way he could screw up an identification this badly. Plus Nolan had his ID and credit cards in his wallet. Freddie wouldn't have come to her home with this somber news unless he was one thousand percent sure.

Donna forced the truth away as the pain hit her all over again. She emitted a fierce scream that reverberated through the small confines of the car and permanently damaged the psyche of everyone who was forced to hear it.

"It can't be him!" she cried. "It can't be, Freddie. He, he just went to play golf. You just ate dinner with us last night! He can't be dead! He's gonna be the mayor, Freddie! He's gonna be gov-"

Her throat caught, and it was difficult to squeeze another breath down her windpipe. In a way, she hoped she would choke to death on her own tears. Surely that would be easier than the future that lay ahead of her. Donna thought of Colton. She realized she had to continue living for him. But that thought was a double-edged sword. Donna knew that if her husband was really dead, she'd have to tell their son, and the torment would start all over again.

She shook her head fiercely. "No. He's not dead. He can't be. Let me see him, Freddie. Take me to him!"

Donna was so distraught, she didn't realize that they had already pulled to a stop in front of the morgue. Freddie took a deep breath before he got out of the vehicle and went around to help the new widow.

●●●●●●●

Nolan was dead.

That was a fact.

Donna stared at her lifeless husband for a long time as she drifted between life and death, real or make-believe, like a heroin addict. No one rushed her. The chaplain entered the room and started talking. Donna was detached by then. She didn't hear much of what the man said. She heard "Jesus" a few times and "God's plan," and some other stuff that didn't make one bit of difference because her husband wasn't Lazarus, and no one was going to resurrect him.

Nolan was dead.

The medical examiner said they were going to do an autopsy to determine the exact cause of death. They said it was mandatory for trauma victims. Donna didn't think she needed an exact cause of death. *Banged-up* was sufficient.

She didn't want to leave her husband at the morgue, but Donna had to notify her son. Colton was playing in a basketball tournament. Donna didn't know if his team participated in the first round yet, or if they advanced to the second round. She debated whether she should pull him from the game or let him finish before she gave him the grim news.

She decided that it would be wrong not to tell him right away. There might be some resentment later if Colton found out how long she knew before she came and got him. Plus Colton was the closest thing Donna had to a living, breathing Nolan. She needed to see him and hold him, so she could convince herself that not every bit of her husband was gone. Nolan would still live on through their child.

•••••••

Freddie took her to Sycamore Park, where the basketball tournament was in full swing in the community center. Donna found Nolan's brother Brandon in the stands. His face immediately filled with dread when he saw Donna's distressed condition. She was flanked by the police lieutenant and her friend Tricia. Brandon handled the news better than expected. He didn't scream or break down in the crowded gym. His eyes welled with tears, and he sobbed quietly.

Brandon told them Colton was the star of the team today. They wouldn't have won the first game of the tournament if not for his two three-pointers in the fourth quarter. Colton's team was currently at halftime of their second game. They were in the locker room, most likely being drilled by their coach because of a lackluster first half. Again Donna wondered if she should let her son finish before she broke the news.

The question became moot when Colton's team suddenly rushed in from one of the side doors. They looked determined and energetic as they took over one half of the court for their lay-up drills. Colton looked for his uncle in the stands, and he was surprised to see his mother there with the Lieutenant Freddie and his play-aunt Tricia. Everyone looked like they were crying. Colton didn't ask for his coach's permission before running to them.

●●●●●●●

The rest of the day was like a never-ending nightmare parading as reality. Every minute, every hour brought more grief. Colton was a lot stronger than his mother envisioned. Brandon and Tricia stayed with them until well after nightfall.

They started Nolan's autopsy, which kicked off another phase of death that Donna honestly didn't think she could handle. She had to choose which funeral home would prepare her husband the best. She wondered what suit he should wear at his funeral and how to get the life insurance money to pay for everything. She was thirty-seven years old. On her last birthday, she felt like she was getting old. Today she felt much too young to have to figure these things out. She was too young to plan her husband's final farewell. Too young to wear the title *widow*.

She was physically exhausted and emotionally drained when she crawled into bed that night. Sleep did not pay her a visit. Her bedroom was cold and lonely. Nothing anyone said today helped to comfort her broken heart and tormented soul. Everything around her was a stark reminder of her husband and the fact that he was never coming home.

And the small part of her that looked at things rationally would not let go of the fact that Nolan died on the *east side* of town when he was supposed to be playing golf on the *west side*. Donna didn't think she could ever fully accept this tragedy until she got an explanation for that.

Unfortunately the only person who could give her an explanation was Nolan.

And Nolan was dead.

CHAPTER FOUR
SIX FEET

The next five days passed slowly and painfully, like a gallstone making its way through a sore kidney. Donna found that she did have the strength to get through the most traumatic experience of her young life. The strength came from a well of courage that was added to her DNA over many generations.

Thankfully she didn't have to do it alone. Many people called and visited in the days following Nolan's death. His brother Brandon was always there. He brought groceries and took the trash out and spent a lot of time with Colton. The boy didn't want to come out of his room on most days, but Brandon had a way with him. He made sure Colton got some sunshine and didn't try to keep his feelings bottled up, as men tended to do.

Tricia and Donna's other good friend Kendra were always there as well. They were excellent lifelines. Donna could not drown at sea with the two of them constantly in her room, helping her get presentable for the other guests. On that first Sunday, it seemed as if the doorbell rang nonstop.

Donna's parents came, as did Nolan's parents. Everyone was in shock. Everyone felt as Donna did; that this couldn't be. Nolan was young and vibrant. He was a wonderful husband and lawyer and politician. He was going to do great things with his life. It wasn't his time. This wasn't fair. Sometimes God's plan didn't make any sense at all.

Nolan's colleagues at the law firm brought flowers and hams. Members of the city council did the same. No one would leave the house until they spoke with Donna personally, even though the front room got so packed at times, people started milling around in the kitchen and den and even the back yard. Tricia and Kendra and Brandon took the role as greeters and hosts. They piled hams on the kitchen counter and then piled them in the fridge and in the deep freezer when they kept coming.

Some people cried openly. Some tried to keep it together, telling light-hearted jokes about Nolan. People hugged and smiled awkwardly. Some paced in the front yard, avoiding eye contact with everyone. A few never made it out of their car. They just sat there and watched the house and cried. They banged on the steering wheel and then drove away, knowing they could not look Nolan's widow in the eyes without making things worse.

Even the mayor came. She was a tall, middle-aged woman, more handsome than pretty. She told Donna, "I'm terribly sorry for your loss. Overbrook Meadows has lost one of its biggest champions. It's very rare to meet someone like Nolan, let alone to know him personally. He truly cared about the city, about the people."

"Thank you," Donna said. She almost apologized for Nolan's scathing attack on her on the eve of his death, but Mayor Monroe took the high road.

"Even as a political opponent, I admired Nolan and his honesty and even his fiery speeches." She smiled half-heartedly. "I hope to accomplish many of the objectives Nolan fought for at the city council meetings. A scholarship fund for inner city schools is already being set up in his name. Nolan will have a legacy in Overbrook Meadows. He won't be forgotten."

Of all the visitors, Donna spent the most time with Lieutenant Freddie Mueller. Knowing more details about the accident wouldn't change the fact that Nolan was gone, but Donna was insatiable for details, and Freddie was an endless source of information.

The driver who struck Nolan was fourteen year old Jeremiah Walton. He was white. Donna was surprised by that, though she wasn't sure why.

"Jeremiah doesn't come from the best home environment," Freddie told her. "His mother works at Walmart and struggles to keep food on the table most days. Jeremiah has two brothers and a sister, all younger than him. The father took off when he was in grade school, and Jeremiah doesn't get along with his step-father.

"He doesn't have much of a juvenile record, but his mom says he's not a good student. His recent interest in marijuana and pill-popping has made things much worse. Jeremiah was forbidden to leave the house minutes before he took his step-father's Explorer for a joyride. His mother called the police immediately. A high-speed chase ensued before Jeremiah had a chance to figure out what his goal was exactly."

Donna listened quietly, wondering why God put her husband in the middle of a perfect storm.

"The kid was travelling 55 miles per hour in a residential area when he struck Nolan at the intersection," Freddie said. He watched Donna's eyes, wondering how much she truly needed to know. She waited expectantly, hanging on every word. "Nolan had the right of way," Freddie said. "The light had just turned green. He was only going eleven miles per hour. Jeremiah never had time to stomp the brakes. Nolan never saw him coming."

Donna hoped that last part was true, but of course there was no way to know for sure.

Freddie said the accident was captured on video by a traffic light camera, but Donna didn't think she would ever want to see that. The pictures Freddie showed her of Nolan's totaled car were bad enough. It looked like the impact was so powerful, the driver's door got pushed all the way to the passenger side. Freddie watched her expression as she studied the photos, and he put them away hastily. Donna never wanted to see the battered Infinity in person.

Jeremiah's step-father did have auto insurance, but Jeremiah was already excluded from the policy, so it wasn't likely Allstate would foot the bill for any of this. Some of Nolan's colleagues at the firm were already vowing to fight the case with every attorney in the building. They promised to leave Jeremiah's mother and step-father completely destitute when it was all said and done. But Donna wasn't interested in tormenting an already struggling family. She didn't believe Nolan would want that either.

The only question left unanswered was why Nolan was on the east side to begin with. Records showed that he never played a round of golf at Cedar Lake that morning. They didn't have any family in the area, and none of Nolan's friends or political contacts came forward to say that he was meeting with them that day. If it was something unexpected, Donna was sure that Nolan would've called and told her where he was going beforehand. If not her, then Oscar or Brandon should have some insight, but they were perplexed as well.

Donna was almost afraid of what she would discover if she fully investigated the matter, but she knew it must be done, starting with Nolan's cellphone. But she didn't have to do it now. Today she had to focus on burying her husband and keeping her and Colton from going crazy in the process. If Nolan had secrets that tainted his good name, she knew she couldn't take it, on top of everything else.

●●●●●●●

Nolan Hodge's funeral was beautiful. Nearly a thousand people attended. It was Friday, March 21st, at one o'clock in the afternoon. The sun was bright and pretty in the sky. The trees were full and green.

The pastor didn't speak long. He left room for the people. A lot of them wanted to speak about what Nolan meant to them and how sorely he would be missed. None of their speeches were long-winded, but all of them were tear-jerkers.

Donna was the perfect widow. Colton, the perfect son. He held his mother's hand as they sat together on the first pew at Ebenezer Baptist Church. She held his hand at the end of the service, when they approached the casket.

Donna was grateful that Nolan's face was not damaged in the wreck. Even in death, he was a handsome devil. She hugged as many people as she could. Someone from Nolan's firm told her there was a fund set up, and there was no need for her to worry about finances.

The procession to the gravesite was massive. People lined the street in some areas and watched them go by. Donna thought she would break down, as they lowered his casket. But she didn't. Colton was there for her. He was always there.

Nolan Hodge's funeral was beautiful. Donna was the perfect widow.

●●●●●●●

Later that night, when the last of the well-wishers were gone, Donna told Freddie and Brandon and Tricia and Kendra that they too needed to head home to their loved ones. She went to talk to her son. She found Colton lounging in the den, watching TV. He used the remote to turn it off when his mother sat next to him.

"What are you watching?"

He shrugged. "Nothing."

"Why'd you turn it off?"

He shook his head slightly and shrugged again. Donna scooted closer. She reached and rubbed his head, brushing his hair slightly with her palm. Colton's hair was short on the sides and a little longer on top, like his dad. He had his father's croissant complexion as well.

Donna thought it might be difficult to look him in the eyes in the days to come. Her heart would yearn to see Nolan again. Sometimes she'd think she saw him, but after a few blinks, she'd realize it was Colton.

"What are we gonna do?" the boy asked. His voice sounded very small. His eyes welled with tears, and he looked away from her.

Donna pulled him close and held his head against her chest. Tears blurred her vision as well. She looked to the ceiling and tried to keep them in.

"Baby, what do you mean? We're going to get through this," she assured him. "It'll be hard, but... But it won't be hard forever."

"Everything already sucks without Dad here," Colton said. His voice was wrought with grief.

His small body felt warm and sick. Donna gave up the battle against her own tears. She continued to rub Colton's hair, and she began to rock slightly. The room was quiet, except for their breaths and their sniffles and the slight squeak of the sofa as she rocked.

"It's only been a week," Donna said. "I miss him, too. But it will get better. I promise."

"Is Dad in trouble?" Colton asked.

The question stunned Donna. She frowned. "No, baby. Why do you say that?"

"Because people are talking about him being on the east side," Colton said. "They talk about it like it's a secret, but I heard some of them. Is that where he had his accident?"

Donna wiped the tears from her eyes, putting her grief on hold, so she could concentrate on the conversation.

"Yes. That is where he had his accident. But he's not in any trouble."

"Then why do people talk about it? They wanna know why he was over there."

Donna blinked quickly. She didn't talk about any of that when Colton was present. She couldn't believe someone else was reckless enough to do so. Or maybe they were discreet, and Colton eavesdropped on them. However it happened, he now knew about the mystery, and that was bad. Donna realized it was equally bad if so many other people were discussing it. She had to put out all of those little fires, starting with the one in her home.

"He was visiting Oscar," she said. "He was going to Cedar Lake, but Oscar called, and he headed there first. The other car hit him before he made it."

Donna realized she was drawing a line in the sand with the lie. She did so effortlessly. Nolan was a mountain among men in his son's eyes, and that image would remain.

"Then why are people asking about it?"

"Because he wasn't where I thought he was, at first," Donna said. "But I found out where he was going, and that's it. I wish he hadn't gone over there, because maybe this wouldn't have happened if he went straight to the golf course. But no one knows the future, baby. The world can seem cruel at times. That's why we have to make the most of every moment we have. We have to make sure to tell the people we love how much we care about them. We should tell them every day."

"I love you, Mama."

Donna's heart melted. Tears squirted from her closed eyes. "I love you too, baby." She kissed the top of his head.

But she thought about what she told him.

I wish he hadn't gone over there, because maybe this wouldn't have happened...

She still didn't know where Nolan had gone or was going that day. A part of her wondered if she should take the same advice she forced upon her son and let it go. Maybe it was best not to know.

CHAPTER FIVE
THE WILL
AND THE INTERLOPER

The next few days felt like months, but time did move on. Donna knew that she would eventually reach the acceptance phase of the grieving process. And all in all, she didn't think she was doing too badly. She missed Nolan with every beat of her heart, but she was past the point of thinking this was some ongoing nightmare that might be over if she stayed in bed long enough.

In fact, getting out of bed was the one thing that helped her the most. Donna found that even a mundane task, like taking her car to the carwash and scrubbing it by hand, was a healthy and welcomed distraction from the ugliness of her empty bed, the mini-heartbreaks she endured every time she saw Nolan's evening loafers waiting for him next to the nightstand or his cologne bottles going unused on the bedroom dresser.

On Tuesday Donna gathered nine hams and other pre-packaged food items the mourners brought to her home in the days following Nolan's accident. She took the rations to the Salvation Army on Lancaster, for the homeless people who frequented the area. She got Colton to help her. He didn't want to, but Donna knew that he needed to get his mind on something different as well.

On Wednesday Donna did some of the laundry that had been piling up. She suffered another mini-heartbreak when she sorted through the clothes. Each one of Nolan's garments was special to her. She purchased the majority of his outfits, and she remembered when and where she got most of it. She thought of how good Nolan looked in a particular shirt, and how he always made sure his dress socks matched whatever pants he wore them with.

It wasn't enough for Nolan to wear dark socks with dark slacks. He had to make sure blue went with blue and black with black. Donna remembered how he would come to her sometimes with a sock in each hand, asking which was which. She laughed and told him that if he couldn't tell, no one else would notice. Nolan thought that was foolish talk. He chided Donna for trying to keep him down.

"You don't want me to look good."

"There's nothing I can do to take away from your glory," she'd say, and he'd smile smugly.

Memories like that weren't bad, but they weren't all light-hearted, especially at nighttime. That's when Donna's king-size bed seemed to grow three times its normal size, and she hugged Nolan's pillow, hoping his lingering scent would offer some sort of comfort in the late hour.

She didn't think it was working, because sleep was fleeting. When she did manage to catch a few winks, Donna awakened with tears in her eyes, the remnants of a dreary dream already fading from her mind. She feared that the pillow might be hindering rather than helping the recovery process, but she couldn't bring herself to wash it – just as she couldn't bring herself to move Nolan's house slippers from their spot on his side of the bed.

She slipped her dainty feet into them once and her heart swelled in her chest, even though she was reminded of the huge void in her family unit and the big shoes she now had to fill.

● ● ● ● ● ● ●

On Thursday, Donna awakened bright and early and went to the kitchen to make coffee. She thought she was the only one up, but she heard the television in Colton's room. She assumed he left it on all night and was surprised to see him up and focused on a video game.

He told her, "Hey, Mama," when she appeared in the doorway.

"Morning," Donna said. She went to get her coffee and took a seat at Colton's desk when she returned. He didn't look away from the television screen.

"Can you turn that off?" she asked him.

"I'm playing online."

"I don't see what that has to do with it."

"I can't turn it off in the middle of a match," Colton explained. "I'll have to quit, and it'll count as a loss."

"That's a good explanation," Donna said. "Turn it off."

Colton complied with minimal griping. Donna watched him closely. At thirteen, it was hard to tell when his behavior was due to depression or when it was typical adolescent foolishness. On one hand, she was glad that he was enjoying his electronics, rather than balled-up in a fetal position sobbing. But staring at a television screen didn't seem like a productive way to deal with his father's death.

"How long you been up?" she asked him.

He shrugged. "I don't know."

Colton wore a tee-shirt with gym shorts. His shirt was clean, but it had a slept-in look to it.

Donna already knew the answer, but she asked anyway; "Did you take a bath this morning?"

He frowned and shook his head.

"How about last night?"

He shook his head again.

"I don't want you wearing the same thing every day," she said.

"I just got up," he complained.

"I don't want you rolling out of bed and turning on your video game, either. If you have enough energy for that, then you have enough energy to clean your room and take a bath."

Colton scratched his head. He looked irritated, which was actually a welcomed sight compared to the tears.

"How you feeling?" she asked him.

"I don't know," he said. "Okay, I guess."

"Brandon said you didn't want to go to the Mavericks' game tomorrow night."

The boy stared at her but didn't respond.

"Why not?" Donna asked.

He shook his head. "I don't know, Mama. I don't, I don't think that's right."

"Why not?" Donna asked, eager for him to vocalize his feelings.

He frowned. "It won't be fun. How am I supposed to have fun with Dad dead?"

Donna nodded. "I understand, and I feel the same way. It seems like nothing is fun anymore. Even some of my favorite shows aren't funny. I can't watch them."

Colton listened but didn't respond.

"But I'm sure you know that your father doesn't want you to be sitting around doing nothing. He wants you to get out and have fun, at some point."

The boy inhaled slowly and blew it out quietly. "Are you saying I have to go?"

Nolan's funeral was only six days ago, so she didn't push it.

"No, I'm not saying that. I'm only saying we have to get our lives back on track, or at least try to. Eventually we have to start doing things that make us happy."

Colton seemed to accept that.

"On that note," Donna said, "I think Monday's a good day for you to get back to school. Me too. I'm going back to work on Monday."

The boy was not pleased to hear that. "I thought you said we have to start doing things we *like* to do."

Donna smiled, glad to hear that his humor was still alive and kicking.

"You do like school, smarty-pants."

"Speak for yourself."

Donna laughed softly. To her recollection, that was the first time she did that since hearing about Nolan's accident.

"You're not going to your game this Saturday, either?" she asked.

Colton's smile faded, and he shook his head.

Donna expected that response as well, but she looked forward to him playing ball again. Sports was his biggest past-time, and it was also the one that would remind him the most of his father. Nolan taught Colton everything he knew about basketball and football. Donna couldn't imagine her son shooting around on the goal in the backyard without Nolan there to catch his rebounds. But she knew that must happen. It was vitally important to Colton's well-being.

However, one week probably wasn't enough time. It was enough time to be off school, though. And it was enough time to avoid some of the chores, but life must go on.

"Today I need you to help me cut the grass," Donna said.

Colton frowned at that. "I don't know how to work the mower."

"You mowed the lawn before. I know you have."

"I just push it, once Dad gets everything set up. I can't start it by myself. I don't know how to check the gas and stuff."

"I'll help you."

"You don't know how to work it, either."

"It's not rocket science," Donna said. "It's a basic lawnmower. Didn't your friend Myron do that all summer; go around offering to mow people's yards?"

"Yeah, but he's been doing it by hisself for a long time."

"Do you want me to go pick him up, so he can show us how?" Donna offered.

Colton shook his head.

"Then we have to figure it out on our own."

She wondered if he really didn't know how to work the mower, or if he was unwilling to take on one of *Dad's chores* without Dad in the picture. This was one of many humps they had to get over. Luckily they could do it together.

"Go ahead and take a shower and get dressed, and I'll make you some breakfast," she said. "What do you wanna eat? Cereal?"

"Just a banana and a granola bar," Colton said. "And some juice."

That was Nolan's typical breakfast, and it was the first time Colton ever requested it for himself.

Donna told him, "Okay," and left the room quickly, lest he notice the fresh tears in her eyes.

●●●●●●●

Contrary to Donna's suggestion that they try to move on with regularly scheduled business, she was not interested in meeting with Nolan's lawyer on Friday morning. Mr. Atwell wanted to go over Nolan's will, which totally screwed up any plans to not fret over his death that day. Donna called Mr. Atwell at nine a.m. to cancel their eleven o'clock appointment. To her surprise, Mr. Atwell would not let her back out.

"Mrs. Hodge, I don't mean to cause you any additional stress, but an issue has come up, and we need to discuss it. Better sooner than later."

Donna sighed. If it wasn't one thing, it was another. Losing a loved one was bad enough, without having to deal with the legalities. "What sort of issue?"

"It's, um, it's something I would much rather discuss in person," the lawyer said. "If you don't want to come to the firm, we can meet at my office on Camp Bowie."

Donna felt like he was reading her mind. Going to Nolan's old law firm was one of the reasons she wanted to cancel their appointment in the first place. Nearly everyone in the building knew Nolan and was aware of his death. Donna was not eager to take part in the pity-party that would ensue the moment she entered the building.

"What's the address on Camp Bowie?"

He gave it to her, and Donna agreed to meet at the original appointment time.

Two hours later she walked into Mr. Atwell's office and took a seat. She only met the lawyer a couple of times over the years, but she remembered that Nolan spoke highly of him.

Mr. Atwell was a short, unattractive man with a bad comb-over and thick glasses that seemed to slide down his long nose far too often. Watching him push them back towards his eyes every few minutes was a mild distraction. His office was neat, and his desk was tidy. The only thing on it was Nolan's will and other financial documents regarding his estate.

Donna was surprised that she was the only one at the meeting. From what she saw on television, everyone mentioned in the will would gather together for an official reading. But Mr. Atwell told her there were not a lot of people mentioned outside of her and Colton, and he planned to meet with them sometime next week.

The full balance of Nolan's estate was $190,000. That included his retirement fund from the law firm and the District Attorney's office, as well as two life insurance policies. His peers at the firm had also raised $32,000 (and counting) in another fund that was solely for Donna. And then there was $20,000 Donna was due for a third life insurance policy she had with her school's insurance.

The sudden influx of resources was not comforting. Donna would trade all of that in a heartbeat, if there was a chance she could have her husband back.

Mr. Atwell said Nolan's will was fairly basic. He obviously didn't envision dying at such an early age and hadn't updated it since he was 35. He wanted the home, boat and all other vehicles to go to Donna and Colton. Likewise, he wanted 70% of his money to go to his wife and son. Of the remaining 30%, Nolan chose to donate 10% to a few of his favorite charities and divide the rest between other relatives.

That all seemed very reasonable, which was how Nolan lived his life. Donna wondered why Mr. Atwell felt the need to meet with her in person, but then he closed his main file and opened a much smaller one. He cleared his throat and looked extremely nervous when he began to speak again.

"There's an, um, problem," he said.

Donna's nostrils flared, but otherwise she kept her inner turmoil to a minimum.

"There's a woman," Mr. Atwell said.

Donna's nostrils flared again. This time she sucked her next breath audibly and couldn't stop from pursing her lips. *There was a woman. That sonofabitch.* A part of her knew what the lawyer was about to tell her, but she played dumb. She stared at him like she had no idea what this woman had to do with Nolan or his money or why he was traveling north on Grantland Circle, when he was supposed to be playing golf on the morning he died. No, this *woman* certainly had nothing to do with that.

Donna's eyes twitched and began to well with tears.

"She's been making calls," Mr. Atwell continued. "Well, first it was her personally, and now it's her lawyer. So far we've managed to keep this quiet, but she went through several people before she got my number. She didn't tell them much. I'm sure no one knows anything yet. But this has the potential to get very messy, and we need to discuss what we're going to do about it."

"Do, do about what?" Donna managed, still playing the fool. He hadn't dropped the bomb yet, but the lawyer told her enough to ensure that the remainder of the day would be filled with a new kind of hurt.

Mr. Atwell sighed, but he was man enough to maintain eye contact as he broke the young widow's heart all over again.

"She and her lawyer, they want to talk about Nolan's estate. According to the woman, she'd been having an affair with your husband, and she says she's pregnant with his child. She believes she should be included in the discussions regarding his will. Her lawyer has threatened to sue Nolan's estate, if she doesn't receive some sort of compensation."

The clock on the wall read 11:22 a.m. Donna glanced at it, thinking she would always remember this as the *second* moment her life was completely ruined. The first time was when Lieutenant Freddie came to her door with his hat in hand. She hated that even in death Nolan could continue to break her heart. She knew it was wrong to think like that, but the news of a pregnant mistress quickly replaced her sympathy for him with raw hate.

How could he?! Why would he?! She was everything for him. She prided herself on being the best wife and mistress he could ever want. How could he be so selfish? With no proof whatsoever, Donna had already accepted the horrible story as fact.

She asked, "How much does she want?" because her brain was racing, and that was the only thing she could think of that didn't involve screaming or cursing or threatening to dig up her dead husband and kick his ass.

Mr. Atwell took her reaction to mean she was aware of the affair.

"So, you don't want to dispute her allegations?" he asked.

Donna sniffled. Tears rolled down her cheeks and blurred her vision. That was good. She felt like if she couldn't see Nolan's lawyer, then he couldn't see her, either. Her heart thumped sickly in her chest. She honestly didn't believe she could survive this torment. Surely there was only so much heartache a human body could endure.

"I, I don't know," she managed. "Does, does she have proof?"

"No, I mean, not really. She has a few pictures and some of his personal belongings. But the most definitive proof will come when her baby is born. We can do a paternity test, to see if it is

57

indeed Nolan's child, but... Mrs. Hodge, I know this is terrible news. I'm very sorry to be the one to inform you. I can't imagine what you must be going through right now."

That was not true. Not only had Mr. Atwell been dreading this moment for the past few days, but he saw the devastation with his own eyes. Donna was already hurting when she walked into his office. She now looked like she had nothing left at all. He hated Nolan for putting him in such an awkward situation.

Donna hated her dead husband, too. She felt like Nolan was lower than dirt. How could he do this to their family? And the bastard never even had to face his sins while he was living. Nolan was lucky to be dead. If Donna could get a hold of him right now, she would undoubtedly kill him.

"Nolan, he died on the east side, when he was supposed to be playing golf at Cedar Lake," Donna said through shuddering breaths. "I, I kept wondering what he was doing over there. Everybody did. Does, does she live on the east side?"

"I..." The lawyer looked through his notes. "I don't have that information right now. But I can find out for you. So, you suspected Nolan was having an affair?"

Donna shook her head. "No. But we didn't know where he was going that day. Ever since he died, I've been wondering..."

She was a sniveling wreck. Mr. Atwell pushed a box of Kleenex across his desk. Donna grabbed it and pulled it into her lap. She yanked four tissues at a time and blew her nose noisily. Mr. Atwell cringed at the anguish he was forced to take part in.

Nolan had to be a fool to cheat on this woman. Mr. Atwell didn't know much about Donna's personal life, but he always thought she was a perfect wife. She was beautiful and kind, and she adored her husband. Creeps like Nolan made him sick to his stomach. Prior to his death, he was a shoe-in for mayor, maybe even governor one day. It seemed that men who had it all were always the greediest. They always wanted more, regardless of how their selfishness affected the people closest to them.

"Even if she does live on the east side of town," the lawyer said, "that doesn't mean Nolan had an affair with her, and it doesn't mean she's carrying his child, either."

Donna wished that was true, but she didn't want to get her hopes up. What kind of woman would seek out a dead man's lawyer, unless she had proof of their relationship? If she hired an attorney, that gave further credence to her story. Donna didn't think any lawyer would take the mistress' case, unless he was confident she was carrying Nolan's child.

"How, what does she want?" she asked. "How much?"

"They asked for a million dollars."

Donna's jaw dropped, but the counselor was still talking.

"That's just a preliminary number," he said. "They have no idea how much Nolan's estate is worth, so they're starting with this unreasonable amount. If everything they say is true, I'll tell them how much money we actually have and argue them down to a portion of it, which will be around $45,000. But that's only if you want to settle. We could tell them to go to hell – but that may lead to a huge scandal. They'll file a lawsuit, and then the whole city will know about it. Ultimately, it's up to you, Mrs. Hodge. My personal opinion is we should make them prove everything first."

Donna felt completely dead inside. It was hard to believe that three weeks ago she was contemplating how awesome it would be when the man of her dreams got elected mayor. Now all she had was a dead, selfish asshole who most likely lost his pathetic life while going to visit his pregnant whore. Yet, even through the anger, she still loved and missed Nolan dearly. The conflicting emotions were driving her crazy.

"What's her name?"

The lawyer frowned, but he told her. "Bettye Sanders."

"Do you know where she lives?"

"No, Donna. I really don't. I can find out for you."

"Do you have her phone number?"

"Yes, but you do realize it would be a bad idea for you to contact her, don't you?"

"I don't want to call her. I'm just going to check through Nolan's phone, to see how often he talked to her."

"That's a good idea," the attorney said. "But don't call her."

"I won't." Donna sniffled and folded her arms over her chest. She stared at him until he wrote the number on a sticky note and handed it to her.

Nolan's phone had been turned-off since the day of his accident. It was ringing off the hook when Freddie gave it to her. He had already put it on silent. Most of the calls were from people who heard about the accident and wanted to see if he was okay.

Some of them had already been told that Nolan was dead, and they were praying he'd answer, and they'd see that it wasn't true.

Donna knew that Bettye Sanders was in the phone somewhere. She'd avoided looking, mainly because she knew it would hurt when she found out and also because she told Colton that his father's whereabouts that morning didn't matter. Nolan was dead, and he was perfect, and that's how they would remember him. But now... Now she knew better.

"She says she has some of his belongings," Mr. Atwell said, reading from his file. "I'm going to get her to take pictures of them. I should have something by tomorrow."

Donna nodded.

"So, what are you thinking?" he asked. "Are you willing to pay to get these people out of your hair, or do you want to fight it? I'd say—"

"If the baby is his, then we have to pay," Donna said. Her face was deadpan, puffy and shiny from crying.

"My thoughts exactly. But Bettye says she's only six months pregnant. So we won't know if that's Nolan's child any time soon."

Donna's eyes flashed open. She nearly screamed at him. The baby was *three months away? Three months?* How was she expected to live a normal life for that long, while waiting to learn if Nolan fathered that woman's child?

"*We have to wait until the baby is born?*" she shrieked, suddenly breaking free of her near comatose state.

"There are non-invasive prenatal paternity tests available," the lawyer said. "But as of now, the results don't stand up in court. The problem is fetal DNA can remain in the mother's bloodstream for up to twenty years. And this isn't Bettye's first or second child. An amniocentesis *would* stand up in court, but the risks for that procedure are too high. If we make her do that, and she loses the baby, well, that would be a worst case scenario – especially if it turns out to be Nolan's."

Donna just shook her head. Her husband's death brought the kind of pain that kept on giving.

"We need something of Nolan's," Mr. Atwell said. "A toothbrush would be nice. I need it pretty soon, because if there's DNA on it, it might deteriorate in the next few months. When do you think you can get it to me?"

Donna chuckled, but her features didn't register any amusement. So there it was. They weren't just talking about it anymore. This was really happening. A paternity test for Nolan's bastard child. Donna didn't know what to feel anymore. But she knew she had to stop crying. Nolan was no longer worth her tears.

"Mrs. Hodge, are you alright? I mean, I know you aren't. But is there something I can do for you?"

Donna continued to shake her head, suddenly feeling self-conscious. She knew how bad she looked right now. Mr. Atwell didn't deserve this. He was just the means by which Hurricane Nolan spread its destruction.

She returned the Kleenex box to his desk and rose to her feet. "Thank you," she said on her way out of the office. "I'll get you a toothbrush. Please, try to enjoy the rest of your day."

"If there's anything you need, let me know." The attorney waited until she was gone before he buried his face in his hands. "Fuck me," he muttered. "And fuck you too, Nolan!"

CHAPTER SIX
HAPPY HOUR

Donna woke Colton bright and early on Monday morning and made him get ready for school. His protest was minor. It was hard to tell if this was the usual *I hate school* griping, or if it was lingering depression from losing his father. It didn't matter either way, because Donna already told him he had to return to school that morning. He should've been ready for it. She felt a lot worse than he did, and she was returning to her regularly-scheduled life as well.

When they got in the car and had a few minutes to talk, Colton commented on her sour mood.

"What's wrong?"

"Nothing."

"It is something," he said. "Whenever you won't look at me when I ask you that, it means there is something wrong."

Donna gave him a quick smirk. "Or it could mean I'm driving, and I'd like to pay attention to the road, rather than look at your goofy tail."

"You been mad all weekend," the boy said. "Did something happen?"

You mean something like me finding out your father was cheating on me? Something like his mistress contacting our lawyer and demanding some of Nolan's insurance money because she's pregnant with his child, and she's upset that he won't be around to help raise the little bastard? Something like that?

"Something like what?" she said.

"I don't know. It just seems like, I don't know. You used to be really sad. But now you seem really mad."

Donna frowned. Keeping secrets from her son was not the easiest thing to do. She and Colton had always been close. Nolan's death brought them even closer. She thought she hid her feelings fairly well, but she knew she had to do better.

"It's just stress, baby. I know I said we had to get back to our schedules today, but I wasn't really ready. Thanks for not giving me a hard time this morning."

"It'll be alright," Colton told her.

She smiled at him. "You think so?"

"We got the lawn mowed, didn't we?"

"Yes we did," she replied. She still had blisters on her dainty hands to prove it.

●●●●●●●

The first week of getting back to normal went a lot better than expected. Donna had to admit that Nolan cheating on her changed her grieving process dramatically. Rather than weep each time she thought of him, Donna thought of Miss Bettye Sanders, which replaced her sorrow with irritation.

When she saw Nolan's house slippers on his side of the bed, she didn't feel like they were sacred, and she should leave them there. Now they were that cheating dog's shoes, which made it easy for her to toss them into the closet.

She wondered if it was healthy to go from one extreme to another, but the alternative didn't seem any better. What was she supposed to do, break down in tears at the drop of a hat whenever someone mentioned Nolan's name? *Oh my poor husband! I miss my baby*! Hmph. He might have deserved such reverence before his whore started making calls. But Donna refused to let him walk all over her feelings in life and in death.

If she was wrong, then she could get some input from her friends. That's what they were for. Donna usually met up with her two besties on Friday nights for happy hour at various eateries throughout the city. On Friday, April 4th, they met at the Mamacitas restaurant on Meacham Boulevard.

Donna knew Tricia from their college days at Texas Lutheran. Intelligent and fiercely competitive, Donna always knew her friend would do great things. Tricia was now the director of eight dialysis clinics in the area. She was married with two kids. She was still the skinniest of the bunch, but she recently announced that she was several weeks pregnant. Donna couldn't wait to see her new godchild.

Kendra was a middle school teacher, like Donna. They met at Wedgewood, but Kendra moved to Arlington eight years ago to be with her boyfriend at the time. She stayed in the city after their breakup and had been living the single life ever since. Kendra was fair-skinned and very attractive. She wasn't as curvaceous as Donna, but her short stature made her appear to have more breasts and booty.

By seven p.m. the ladies were on their second round, and they were already boisterous because of Donna's recent revelations. She handed her cellphone over the table, so her friends could weigh-in on the pictures Mr. Atwell sent her.

"What is this?" Tricia asked. She leaned close to Kendra, who had the cellular in her hands.

"I don't know," Donna said. "Let me see it."

Kendra turned the screen towards her, and Donna sneered.

"That's the bracelet I bought Nolan for his 37th birthday. Asshole said he lost it."

"Did he give it to her, or did she steal it?" Tricia asked, staring at the photo.

"I don't know," Donna said. "I didn't ask her."

"You talked to her?" Kendra asked.

Donna shook her head. "No. Not yet."

"Are you going to?"

"I'd like to meet her in person, before this is all said and done," Donna acknowledged.

"This picture doesn't mean anything," Kendra said. "Anybody can take a picture of a bracelet."

"She's wearing it," Donna pointed out.

"It's just some random arm," Kendra said. "That could be anybody."

"Girl, she got the man's bracelet on her wrist," Tricia argued. "Unless that's Donna's arm, then nobody else has an excuse for wearing it."

Donna nodded in agreement.

"Where are the other pictures?" Kendra asked. She swiped the screen and said, "Who's this? This is Colton?"

"I don't know," Donna said. "Show me the picture, girl. I don't have a crystal ball."

Kendra laughed as she turned the phone towards her.

"You went the wrong way," Donna said. "Yeah, that's Colton cutting the yard. It was his first time doing it without Nolan's help."

"That boy's getting big," Kendra noticed. "And muscular. He lift weights?"

"Just naturally athletic," Donna said with a dash of pride.

"What's this?" Kendra asked. "These Nolan's shoes?"

"Yeah, she has a picture of his shoes over at her house," Donna said.

"That doesn't mean anything," Kendra said. "Anybody can take a picture of somebody's shoes."

"That's not my house, and that's not my bed," Donna argued. "Nolan's shoes have no reason being off his feet in somebody's bedroom."

"How does that even work?" Tricia asked. "He went over there and left his shoes? I know he didn't come home barefoot, did he?"

Donna laughed. "Girl, you crazy. No, he never came home barefoot. But Nolan does come home with new shoes sometimes. I don't get all in his business, asking where his old ones are. Maybe *she* bought him some new shoes."

Donna caught herself speaking about him in the present tense, and she sighed. "He *used to* come home with new shoes sometimes."

"I still don't see how this is proof of an affair," Kendra said. But then she swiped to the next picture. "Oh. Okay, this will do."

"Yep, that's it," Tricia agreed.

Donna knew they were looking at the one picture Bettye took of Nolan at her home. He was asleep in her bed, and he was topless. He might have been fully nude, for all Donna knew. The picture was cropped from the belly up.

The first time she saw it, Donna suffered a major meltdown. How dare he sleep at that whore's house? And he looked so damned comfortable. Donna couldn't stop her brain

65

from racing, imagining all of the dirty things he did in that bitch's bed prior to falling asleep.

And it was clear that Nolan was very careful with his affair. Apparently he wouldn't take any pictures with his girlfriend, and he wouldn't allow her to take pictures of him. She had to wait until he was asleep before she could snap that shot – which made Donna wonder exactly what her motives were all along.

Why did she need a picture of Nolan so badly? Did she plan on exposing him all along, or was she madly in love, desperate for some sort of validation of their relationship, upset that she didn't have anything to prove that he was a part of her life? Did she stare at his sleeping picture longingly, praying for the day when Nolan would leave his wife for her? Did Nolan tell her he would leave his wife for her?

Whatever the reason for the pic, it was the most damning piece of evidence Bettye presented thus far. But she had something even more damning steadily growing bigger and stronger in her womb. Donna knew it was wrong to hate an unborn child, but she couldn't stand that fetus. She wondered if Nolan ever asked her to abort it.

"Is that it?" Kendra asked, returning her phone.

"That's it as far as the pictures," Donna said.

"You said you got her phone number," Tricia said. "Did Nolan call her a lot?"

"No." Over the past week, Donna investigated his cellphone records thoroughly. "He saved her number as 'Paul,' and they rarely talked on the phone. He never called her on Saturday mornings, when he was supposed to be playing golf, and he already deleted all of the messages they'd been sending. They did more messaging than anything, but it's all gone."

"How do you know he deleted them?" Kendra asked.

"The cellphone bill shows there were some messages sent between them, not every day, but just about. But the bill doesn't show what the messages said; just the date and time. The only messages from her that were still on the phone were from the day he died. I guess he was on his way over there, and she got worried when he didn't show up. I can tell he had her trained, too, because she sounded scared to even ask what was taking him so long."

"That is so messed up," Tricia said.

"For real," Kendra said. "I don't know how you can sit there and be so calm about it."

"I think this whole thing has changed me," Donna ventured. "And not for the better. When I found Bettye's messages, I was sitting there happy that she was worried. She's asking him, 'Where are you? Are you okay? Please call me.' And I'm thinking, *Yeah, bitch. He's dead. You'll never see him again.*"

"Wow," Tricia said.

"Yeah, that's pretty bad," Kendra chipped in.

"But you're hurting," Tricia said.

"*I know*," Donna cried. "I am so messed up right now. I gave Nolan everything he wanted. I tried to be everything he needed, so he'd never have to cheat on me like this. I feel disgusted and *used*."

"You should feel that way," Tricia said.

"I just wanna know *why*," Donna said. "But he's gone, and I can't ask him, and that makes me so mad! And now this bitch is asking for money, and I have to wait three months before I can find out if Nolan is that baby's father or not. *I'm so mad, y'all.* I wanna throw away everything in the house that has anything to do with him, but I can't because I don't want Colton to see me acting like that."

Her eyes welled with tears. Her friends wished they could make the pain go away, but there was no easy fix for this.

"Maybe it'll help if you remember the good times," Tricia suggested. "Y'all were together for fifteen years. You didn't find out about any of this until after he died. I know this is fucked up, but there had to be a lot more good times than bad. Do you ever think about it like that?"

"Yes," Donna said. "And that makes me sad. And then I realize the good times were all a big lie, and I'm mad all over again."

"So you're saying one affair taints the whole marriage?" Tricia asked.

"Who said it was only one affair?" Donna asked. "Do you really wanna go down that rabbit hole with me? 'Cause, trust me, I've been thinking about it a *whole lot*."

Tricia sat back in her seat. She definitely didn't want to start thinking about that. One affair was bad enough.

Their handsome waiter approached with a bright smile, totally oblivious to the bitter mood at the table.

"You ladies doing okay? Ready for another round?"

"Yes," Kendra said. "A shot of Tequila for everybody – except Tricia."

Tricia smiled and placed a hand over her growing bundle of joy.

"Sounds good," the waiter said and disappeared just as quickly.

"So, what's next?" Kendra asked. "Y'all just sitting around, waiting for that baby to pop out?"

"That's all we can do," Donna confirmed. "That lady and her lawyer agreed not to do anything stupid until we get the paternity test. At this point, my only hope is that she's as big a whore as I think she is."

"She *was* sleeping with a married man," Tricia said. "That says a lot right there."

"Lord Jesus," Kendra joked, "we pray that Bettye's bedroom is so busy, each new guy has to take a number before he can get in."

They all laughed.

"Let us pray that her coochie runs so deep," Tricia said, "that there's at least *one* brother hiding in there from the police!"

That cracked them up even more.

"Y'all going to hell, you know that right?" Donna said. But she had to admit that she'd been wishing for similar feats of whoredom.

●●●●●●●

The talk with her friends made Donna feel better about her unfortunate situation. She still felt like the butt of a very ugly joke, but she didn't feel like she was alone anymore. Even if the baby turned out to be Nolan's, Donna knew that her friends would help her get through it. They wouldn't let Nolan or his mistress drive her bat shit crazy.

The rest of April seemed to drag by, but Donna put the affair out of her mind by May, and she did enjoy that beautiful month. Colton didn't return to the school's basketball team after his father's death. Donna didn't fault him or push him too hard.

She hoped he wouldn't give up on sports altogether without his biggest mentor in the picture.

Nolan's brother Brandon came by the house a lot. He truly was a Godsend. He got Colton excited about going to the Mavericks games again, and he even scooped the leaves out of the storm drains when Donna realized they were clogged to the point of overflowing. Nolan was supposed to take care of that chore after winter, but he was too busy with politics (and his girlfriend, apparently).

The only real drama came from some of Colton's teachers, towards the end of the school year. They said he'd been lackadaisical as of late, and he smarted-off to one of them when she lectured him about his missing homework. Donna feared that he was acting out because of his father, but it turned out Colton had a new girlfriend he was subconsciously trying to impress with his new "bad boy" image.

Of course it was silly of him to try such a stunt while his mother taught at the same school. To drive the point home, Donna gave up her planning period for the next few days so that she could sit in on his Science class. Colton was quite the opposite of a *bad boy* with his mommy sitting right next to him, watching every move he made. By the third day he begged her to give him another chance.

"I'll be good, Mama. I promise! Please stop coming in there!"

Donna relented, and Colton kept his word. He graduated from middle school with honors on Friday, June 6th. Donna didn't like the fact that he'd be away from her watchful eye when he started high school in the fall, but that was small potatoes compared to the joy she felt at his graduation ceremony. Her little boy was becoming a man! She wished Nolan could've been there to watch him walk across the stage. But Nolan lost his life while going to visit his girlfriend (who he most likely impregnated).

And there was no need for Donna to feel bad about that.

69

CHAPTER SEVEN
DADDY'S MAYBE

On Tuesday, July 8th Donna's lawyer called to tell her that Bettye Sanders gave birth to a healthy baby girl. They were now ready to perform the paternity test, but there was a hang-up.

"We, uh, there was a problem with the DNA sample you gave me, Nolan's toothbrush..." Mr. Atwell said.

Donna sat in her car in a Walmart parking lot. She suddenly had no idea why she was there. She stared at the people walking around the entrance, a hard lump forming in her throat. Something in her stomach felt cold and slimy. She'd been anticipating this day for a long time, but secretly she hoped for a miscarriage. A fall down a flight of stairs could do it. Was that wrong? Damn Nolan for making her wish for the death of an unborn child! She truly detested him.

"Did you hear me?" the lawyer asked. "They had a problem with the sample you left."

"What, what's wrong with it?" Donna managed. It was 98 degrees outside, but her arms were speckled with goose bumps.

"They couldn't get a useable sample," Mr. Atwell said. "We need something else, a hairbrush maybe. It's been a few months, so everything you have is deteriorating rapidly. Do you think you could find another toothbrush, or a hairbrush? If not, we're going to need a sample from one of Nolan's relatives, preferably a parent or sibling."

Oh God. Donna brought a hand to her face and sighed softly. So far she'd kept the affair secret from everyone but her best friends. She couldn't imagine how the conversation would go, if she had to ask Nolan's parents for DNA. This is not the kind of problem a grieving widow should have. *Damn you, Nolan!*

"I'll look again," Donna said. "I know there's another toothbrush. A hair brush, too."

"Okay," Mr. Atwell said. "Let me know when you have it. I'll be at the office all week, but you don't have to come to the firm. I'll meet you on Camp Bowie."

Donna appreciated everything the lawyer was doing to keep Nolan's reputation intact, but she was starting to feel sick every time she heard his voice. He only brought one kind of news: Bad.

"Thank you," she said. "I'll call you tomorrow."

●●●●●●●

Nolan had three toothbrushes in total and two hairbrushes. The toothbrushes were completely dry, and Donna didn't see a lot of Nolan's hair snagged in the bristles of the hairbrushes. She knew they needed a strand of hair that was pulled out at the root, if they were to extract DNA from it. Nothing in either of the brushes looked promising.

Donna packed them up anyway, along with the toothbrushes, and took them to the lawyer on Wednesday morning. On the way there, she cursed herself for being such a fool. How could she let this happen? Bettye was six months pregnant when Nolan died, which meant he'd been seeing her for at least that long. But he wouldn't get her pregnant on their first date, would he? Surely not. Donna figured Nolan would have to be very comfortable with her to have sex without a condom. So maybe they'd been seeing each other for a year or more.

Donna thought of all of the things she did to make her husband happy. Her motherly duties aside, she always prided herself on being an unselfish, fulfilling lover. She convinced herself that she could be Nolan's mistress and his wife, so he'd never have to seek love in the arms of another. What more could she have possibly done? She would go as far as to categorize herself as a *freak* for Nolan, but that wasn't enough.

And where was his discretion when he was sticking his raw dick in some other woman? Nolan wouldn't let his wife give him a blowjob while they were stopped at a traffic light. He never broke the law, not even by littering. Apparently he was living a completely different life outside of his home. How could Donna not see any of this? How could she be so blind?

When she got to the lawyer's office, he told her, "I talked to Bettye's attorney, and they're willing to settle for one fourth of Nolan's net worth, if the child is his. That's pretty typical. I told them he wasn't worth a million dollars, or even a quarter million. They said that was fine. As long as we disclose the financial documents, they'll agree to one fourth. Is that okay with you?"

Donna nodded vaguely. She didn't really need Nolan's money. It would be nice to pay off the house. She'd have an easier time juggling the bills by herself if the mortgage wasn't one of them. But she'd be okay either way. They'd just have to be a little more thrifty.

"I should get the paternity results back in about a week," the lawyer said. "Hang in there. We're almost done."

Donna nodded. She'd been waiting three months so far. Another week wouldn't kill her.

●●●●●●●

Mr. Atwell called again on July 17th with more bad news.

"I'm sorry, Donna, but we didn't get any useable DNA from your new samples. I'm afraid we're going to have to go to plan B. We need a relative. I hate to ask, but what about your son?"

Donna's mouth fell open at the same rate as her eyes. She had to catch herself before she cursed him out.

"Absolutely not!" She lowered her voice, because she was home at the time, and she had no idea where Colton was in the house. "He doesn't know anything about this," she explained. "And I'm not telling him."

"Okay. Well, have you told Nolan's parents? Could one of them do it?"

"No. I'm not telling them, either."

"Does he have a brother or sister? I'm sorry, Mrs. Hodge, but you're gonna have to tell someone what's going on – unless you simply want to pay them. If you want to give them the money without knowing for sure, that's your other option. I would highly advise against that."

Donna almost instructed him to give them the money, but she thought of how much Ms. Bettye Sanders had taken from her already. Donna couldn't even grieve her husband properly because of that skeezer. Nolan was mostly at fault, but Bettye knew he was married. *No*, she decided. *That bitch doesn't deserve a goddamned thing!*

"I'll talk to his brother," Donna said. The thought of telling Brandon all of this was disturbing, but not nearly as bad as telling Colton or Nolan's parents. They were damned near inconsolable at the funeral.

"Okay, let me give you the address to the testing facility," the lawyer said. "He can go there to leave his sample. It'll be quick and easy. All they need is a buccal swab."

Donna shook her head in disdain.

Damn you, Nolan. You selfish sonofabitch.

"Alright," she said. "I'll call you tomorrow, to let you know when he's going."

She disconnected and called Colton's godfather. Brandon managed a small restaurant chain, so Donna wasn't surprised when her call went to voicemail.

"Brandon, this is Donna. There's, um, there's a problem. I need to talk to you. Can we have lunch tomorrow? Call me back."

He returned her call within the hour. "Hey, Donna. What's wrong?"

"Can we meet somewhere?" she suggested. "Tomorrow I–"

"What about tonight?" he said. "I can pick you up."

"No. I don't want you to come here. I don't want Colton to know."

"Okay. I can meet you wherever you need me to. Is this *real* bad news? Will I even feel like eating afterwards?"

"No," Donna said. "Probably not."

"How about the Starbucks on Hulen then? I can be there in an hour."

"Okay," Donna said. "I'll be there."

●●●●●●●

An hour later she sat across from Nolan's big brother at a small table in the mostly empty coffee shop. Brandon was taller and wider than Nolan. Rather than an athletic build, Donna would say he had more of a lumberjack physique. He was also a few shades darker than his brother, but their resemblance was unmistakable. The sight of him made Donna feel weak and forlorn.

From stories she heard during her marriage, Donna knew that Brandon was well respected in their family, and Nolan held him in very high regards. Brandon listened quietly while Donna told her tragic tale from start to finish. When she was done talking, he placed his forearms on the table and leaned towards her. His eyes were soft, filled with empathy. Nolan always said his brother was a gentle giant. Over the years, Donna had confirmed that to be true.

"How are you dealing with all of this?" he asked.

She shook her head. "My brain is totally fried," she admitted. "I've been stressed since Nolan died. This woman, she took everything I had left. Sometimes, I don't even want to get out of bed in the morning. If not for Colton, I'd probably be in a mental hospital by now."

"How's he doing?" Brandon asked. "You haven't told him any of this?"

"No. You know he thinks the world of his father. Unfortunately I know what it's like to find out your king is really a toad. Colton doesn't deserve that."

Brandon nodded and then sighed. "Nolan was a dog back in his college days. But I thought he left all of that behind."

Donna never knew that, but she wasn't surprised. When she first met Nolan, he gave her the impression that he was a player. She almost didn't go out with him, because she feared she'd become another one of his conquests and nothing more. But Nolan didn't display any playboy characteristics when they got together. He didn't even stare at beautiful women, let alone pursue them – as far as Donna knew.

"You didn't know he was cheating?" she asked.

Brandon frowned and shook his head. "No. Hell no. I would've kicked his ass, if I knew. You're a great woman, Donna. I would never stand by and let him mistreat you."

"The woman lives on the east side," she told him. "I looked it up. He was on his way to see her when he got into the accident."

Brandon sighed, still shaking his head.

"I'm so hurt," Donna said. "I miss him terribly, but I never would've known about her if it wasn't for that accident. I'm so mad at him, Brandon." Her eyes welled with tears. She plucked a tissue and tried to catch them before they fell.

"The wages of sin is death," Brandon said, quoting the bible.

Donna thought about that verse after her husband's death, but she wouldn't dare say it out loud.

"Sometimes karma doesn't wait until you have a chance to fix things," Brandon continued. "Sometimes karma happens immediately."

Donna brought a fist to her mouth. Her features contorted, and she began to cry in earnest.

"I didn't want him to die."

"I know you didn't." Brandon reached across the table and held her hand. "I wish he was still here. This is the kind of thing he should've been forced to deal with personally. It's not fair to leave you with this mess."

Donna agreed wholeheartedly. She was glad that Brandon was so understanding.

"What do you need me to do?" he asked.

"Give a DNA sample," Donna said. She let go of his hand so she could look through her purse. She found the address for the testing facility. "Just go there, and they'll do a buccal swab. It won't take five minutes. They're expecting you."

"Okay," Brandon said. He took the paper from her. "Are you gonna be alright, Donna? What happens if it is his child?"

"I have to give them a quarter of Nolan's money."

"Do you need help with the bills? I could give you—"

"No," Donna said. "It's not about the money. I just want it to go away. I don't want anyone to know."

Brandon nodded. "Okay. I'll stop by the place tomorrow. How long will it take to find out?"

"About a week."

"Jesus. You have to wait that long? I don't think I could take it, if I was you."

"I've been waiting three months for her to have the damned baby," Donna informed him. "Another week won't matter."

"I'm, I have to say I'm amazed," Brandon said. "If I was in your shoes, I don't think I'd be so composed. I'd be calling Nolan all sorts of bad things right about now."

"Don't worry," Donna said with a half-smile. "That happens quite a bit. I'm trying to keep it cool now, for your sake."

"Don't worry about me. You can say whatever you want."

"I'll always love Nolan," she told him. "But right now I hate him, too. I just hope that a year from now, I'll love him more than I hate him."

"Me too," Brandon said. "I hope you can reach that point."

●●●●●●●

Donna knew the next week would pass terribly slowly, and she was not mistaken. But it was worth the wait. On Thursday, July 24th, her lawyer called with good news for a change.

"We're good," he said. "Brandon is in no way related to Bettye Sanders' child. Nolan is not the father."

Donna's heart was so light, it threatened to float out of her chest. She nearly screamed with joy. Never in a million years did she think she'd be happy to hear about her husband's girlfriend's baby.

"Oh thank God! Oh my God, thank you!"

"I'm about to call her lawyer and set up a meeting for Monday. Do you want to come?"

Donna's heart stopped at the thought of seeing the mistress for the first time. She definitely wanted to, but at the same time, she was afraid. Did she really want to meet the woman who gave her husband something that his wife couldn't? The thought alone made her feel inadequate. But looking Bettye Sanders in the eyes was the only way to get true closure.

"Yes," she said. "I want to be there."

"Okay," Mr. Atwell said. "I'll call you back with the exact time. Congratulations, Mrs. Hodge. I know this has been hard for you."

Again Donna found amusement in how far her life had sunk. She was actually being congratulated for not taking any further losses from her husband's scandal. She couldn't help but laugh.

"Thank you, sir. Thank you very much!"

• • • • • • •

On Monday morning Donna got dressed with butterflies in her stomach. Today was the big day. At nine a.m. she'd sit across from Nolan's girlfriend and have a good, old-fashioned stare-down. Bettye could throw the affair in Donna's face, but Donna would have the last laugh because the child that initiated this whole debacle wasn't Nolan's. Donna couldn't wait to see the mistresses face crack after that revelation.

She didn't consider herself catty, but as a woman, she was competitive by nature. She and Bettye would size each other up and immediately look for faults. They would wonder what the hell Nolan saw in *her* and convince themselves that *He always loved me more.* Bettye might tell her, "*He only stayed with you for his political career,*" and Donna might tell her, "*You were just a dirty, little secret that he swept under the rug, with all the other junk,*" and they'd hiss and arch their backs.

No, none of that was likely to happen. But Donna would be ready if it did. She had to be prepared for virtually anything.

Colton was still asleep when she got ready to leave, so she left him a note on the kitchen counter.

Be back soon. Think about where you want to go for lunch!

Thirty minutes later she walked into Mr. Atwell's office with her chin high, her face hard and unreadable. Bettye and her lawyer were already there. Donna had to walk past them on the way to the only other seat in the room, which was positioned next to Mr. Atwell's desk. He had the chair turned so that he and Donna would be facing the unwelcomed guests.

Donna felt like all eyes were on her as she moved. She took her seat and finally got a chance to look Nolan's mistress in the eyes. That was a hard thing to do. She felt her blood pressure rising as her face flushed with heat. She was glad for her brown skin tone. Bettye wouldn't see much of the devastation she brought to the Hodge family.

Nolan's other woman was tall and thin. Even though she was sitting, Donna saw that her body was ridiculously awesome. Her hips were wide, her waist slim. Her breasts were big and perky. Of course they were. The girl was no more than 25 years

77

old. *A twenty-year old, Nolan? Seriously?* What the hell was he thinking? Nolan officially climbed over the hill on his last birthday. Is that what this was about? Did turning 40 mess with his head, make him seek out this pretty, young thing?

How fucking selfish was that?

Bettye had long, cinnamon colored hair. Her lips glistened with pink lipstick. She wore a skirt and a conservative blouse, but she looked out of her element. Donna thought she'd be more comfortable in booty shorts or a freakum dress. She was pale, barely had any melanin at all, which, combined with all of her other attributes, made her the true definition of a high-yellow heifer.

This was the woman Nolan risked his marriage, his career and eventually life and limb for. Bettye looked young and immature and as dumb as a box of rocks, but her bedroom feats were surely supernatural.

Donna's eyes burned. They itched to cry, and that made her so angry, she wanted to run over there and slap the shit out of the home wrecker. The only thing that kept her butt planted in the seat was the fact that Bettye's lawyer was looking through the paperwork that would shut this case down. And his client looked extremely worried, too.

That's right, bitch. You're not getting a goddamned thing. You whore! Do you have any idea who your child's father is? You slut!

"Thanks for coming, Mrs. Hodge," Mr. Atwell said. "We were just discussing the results of the paternity test. I believe Mr. Summers was about to tell us how he'd like to proceed..."

All eyes went to Bettye's lawyer, who looked very professional and capable. He looked up from the papers at Donna and then her lawyer and said, "Excuse us, please. We need to step out into the hallway for a moment."

He rose to his feet, and Bettye did as well. She looked back at Donna before following her attorney out of the office. Donna stared her down, making sure Bettye looked away first. The mistress' ass was awesome. She had legs for days. And Nolan went swimming between them. Donna shook her head and blew out a pent-up breath. Her nostrils flared. Mr. Atwell leaned towards her, almost to the point of whispering in her ear.

"You doing okay?"

Donna didn't know why he was speaking so softly, but she did the same. "Yes. No. I'll be fine. What's happening?"

"They're trying to save face at this point," Mr. Atwell said. "I know her attorney doesn't want to leave empty-handed. He's worked on this case on and off for three months."

"But it's not Nolan's child," Donna said. "What can they do?"

"Nothing," Mr. Atwell said. "I'm sure they'll realize that in a few minutes." He sat back in his chair and reached to pat Donna on her arm. "Don't worry. This will all be over shortly."

Donna sat back in her seat as well. They waited a full five minutes before Bettye and her lawyer re-entered the office and sat down. Bettye looked mad as hell. Donna couldn't stop a slight smirk from curving her lips.

But Mr. Summers wasn't going down without a fight.

"We're going to request an exhumation."

The smile fell from Donna's face. Mr. Atwell's eyes widened, and he lost his composure for a moment.

"What the hell? Are you out of your goddamned mind?"

"Without Nolan's DNA, this test is inconclusive." Mr. Summers managed to keep a straight face while he spoke.

"We got DNA from his brother!" Mr. Atwell reminded them. "Nolan's brother is in no way related to this woman's child, therefore Nolan isn't either. That will stand up in any court, and you know it!"

Donna's lawyer was getting red about the cheeks and ears. She didn't know what to think anymore. Could they really dig up Nolan's body? The idea was revolting and scary. The mere thought almost made her burst into tears.

"That's your opinion," Mr. Summers said.

Mr. Atwell's eyes grew even larger. He tried to calm himself. "Sir, there is absolutely *no way* a judge is going to okay that. Exhumations can only be done in cases of *unsolved murders*. You know that the results from this paternity test are accurate. I don't know what you're trying to pull here–"

"Even if it gets thrown out, it will make it to a courtroom," Mr. Summers said, revealing his cards. "I was under the impression that you didn't want this to make it to a courtroom."

Mr. Atwell stared angrily at his opposition. If looks could kill, Mr. Summers would've burst into flames.

"So, is that your game? You want to threaten to expose the affair in an attempt to blackmail us? You'll be disbarred for this."

Mr. Summers stood firm. "Again, that's your opinion. All I know is I've worked too hard on this case to simply let it go. I'm going to fight to the bitter end, for my client."

Mr. Atwell was fighting mad. Literally. Donna saw his hand ball into a fist on his desk. But she saw things differently. Bettye's lawyer didn't give a damn about his client. He was merely another selfish, greedy asshole, like Nolan. And it was actually Nolan who helped Donna figure out a way to end this mess. Nolan taught her that money was the root of all evil. There wasn't a squeaky wheel in the world that couldn't be greased with greenbacks.

Donna sneered at Bettye and then spoke to her lawyer directly.

"We'll pay your attorney fees, up to four thousand, and we'll pay for the paternity tests that were performed as well. In return, you drop this case and leave us alone."

The two lawyers in the room said, "Oh no we won't," and "I'll take it," at the same time.

Donna turned to Mr. Atwell. "Yes we will. Get the papers written up, please."

Mr. Summers grinned. His client looked around the room in confusion.

"So what that mean?" Bettye asked.

"It means you're not getting a goddamned thing," Donna told her. It felt good to say that to her face. "But I'm paying your lawyer fees, so you won't owe him anything."

Bettye had a hard time letting go. She pleaded with her lawyer.

"But I thought we were going to court anyway?"

Mr. Summers shook his head as he gathered his things. "You don't have a case," he told her. "It's over. The test says it's not his child."

"But, but I thought we were gonna dig him up."

Donna shook her head in disappointment.

You see this, don't you? she said to her dead husband. *Your girlfriend wants to dig you up for nothing. You sure know how to pick 'em, don't you? You selfish bastard.*

Mr. Summers looked Bettye in the eyes. "It's over. I'm sorry. It's not his child." He returned his attention to Mr. Atwell. "So, can I get that check now? I'd like to deposit it on the way back to my office."

Donna's lawyer didn't respond. He continued to stare at the man furiously.

"Either cut him a check, or I'll do it," Donna said, reaching for her purse.

Mr. Atwell relented. Donna watched his expression soften as he gave up the fight.

"I have to get some papers drawn up first," Mr. Atwell said. "It'll take half an hour."

"I'll wait," Mr. Summers said, grinning smugly.

"Is there anything else you need from me?" Donna asked her lawyer.

He shook his head. "No. I'll put a clause in their paperwork that will prevent Mr. Summers and Ms. Sanders from trying this stunt again..."

He shot both of them a stern look. Bettye's lawyer continued to grin arrogantly. Bettye still looked perplexed.

"I'll call you later, so we can finalize Nolan's will," Mr. Atwell told Donna.

She nodded and stood and walked to the door. Before she exited, she asked Bettye, "You coming?"

The girl looked around fretfully before saying, "Nuh, no. I'll wait, too."

Donna chuckled and continued on her way. *Damn.* She must have had that *Bitch, please come outside, so I can whoop your ass* look in her eyes. She decided Bettye wasn't as dumb as she looked.

When she got in her car and had a bit of privacy, Donna laughed and she cried. She felt like the weight of the world had been lifted from her shoulders. Her husband was gone, his mistress was gone, and the love child wasn't his. Donna's life could officially start anew. This wasn't where she thought she'd be at the age of 38. She knew she'd need counseling, maybe a whole year worth. But all things considered, things weren't that bad. It could certainly be a helluva lot worse.

•••••••

81

When she got home, Colton was up and playing video games already. Donna started to chastise him, but it was the summertime, and he was a good kid. She went to his room and took a seat on his bed. She watched the television over his shoulder.

After watching his life-like character suffer multiple horrendous deaths on the virtual battlefield, she said, "You're not very good at this game, are you?"

"Actually I am," he said. "But I'm trying to do a challenge right now."

"What kind of challenge?"

"Dual pistols," he said. "That's why I have a gun in each hand. They don't have much range, so I have to get pretty close to people. Everybody with a regular gun kills me before I can get them, unless I'm really sneaky."

"So what do you get for accomplishing the challenge?"

"A patch. Or maybe it's an emblem. I forget."

Donna had no idea what he was talking about. "Is it worth it?"

"Dad said successful people try to accomplish at least one goal every day," Colton said.

A few days ago, that would've made Donna sick to her stomach. But now she smiled at Nolan's memory.

"I don't think he meant for a video game challenge to be your goal."

"Tomorrow I'll start a software company from the ground up."

Donna threw a pillow at the back of his head. "Smart ass."

"Where'd you go this morning?" Colton asked.

"Nowhere. Running some errands. Did you see my note?" He nodded. "Yes."

"So what do you want to do for lunch?"

"You can pick, Mama. I always do."

Donna was surprised and pleased with the courtesy. She knew that she had an excellent chance of molding him into a smart, respectful young man. Colton was only thirteen. Donna had five good years to influence him before he went off to college.

For the first time in the past three months, she looked forward to what their future held, rather than cringe at the thought of it.

CHAPTER EIGHT
MARCEL

One year and six months after a child named Jeremiah Walton slammed his step-father's SUV into a sleek black Infinity, killing one of Overbrook Meadows' brightest stars, Marcel Webber went to the Chili's on McCart Ave and ordered a cheeseburger with fries. He ate the meal slowly. The date was Friday, August 28th. It was six p.m., and the sun was starting to fade, leaving a beautiful cinnamon hue in the western sky. The restaurant smelled like grilled steak and salsa and family.

Marcel sat alone at a table, but he didn't play on his phone or read a newspaper or do any of the other things his waitress was accustomed to seeing lone diners do. Marcel didn't look upset, but he was definitely deep in thought. His waitress didn't want to disturb him, but his plate was empty, and the drink she served him earlier was gone as well. Her customer cradled the glass in his huge paw. He brought it to his lips and sucked a few small ice cubes into his mouth.

Tam, his waitress for the night, pasted a smile onto her face as she made her way to his table. She was nineteen years old. She had only been working as a waitress for a few months, but that wasn't what made butterflies take flight in her tummy as she moved. It was the customer. There was something about him.

He was a big guy. And tall. Tam would guess six-feet-five or better. He wore a tee shirt and jeans. His chest was huge. Tam thought each of his pectorals was the size of her head. His stomach was flat. He wasn't excessively muscular, but his biceps seemed to explode from his shirt, as did his strong neck and shoulders. His skin was dark, his hair short. He was clean-shaven.

He looked up at her when she drew near. His eyes were dark and uninviting, but he smiled at her.

"Can I get another drink?"

Tam's legs became weak, and she nearly stumbled forward. *Damn.*

His voice was deep and bass-filled. This man had so much testosterone, it seeped from his pores. Tam thought she could *smell* his pheromones. It made her nipples harden under her blouse. She knew that she was too young for him. The customer looked to be approaching forty, if not a few years older than that. But, damn. She couldn't stop her body from reacting to his overwhelming masculinity. By the time she got her head together, she realized he said something else.

"And you can bring my check, too."

"Oh, okay. Did you, how was your burger?"

"It was nice, thanks."

"Can I, do you want me to take your plate?"

She reached for it. Marcel noticed that her fingers were slightly trembling. He almost asked what was wrong with her, but he knew that it wasn't her. It was him. He was eating alone on a Friday evening, staring into space, nursing a Crown Royal on the rocks. She was probably afraid that he'd pull out a gun and shoot up the place. Marcel had a gun, a few of them actually, but he wasn't the criminal type. He tried to lighten the mood.

"I haven't been here in a while. The food keeps getting better. And you have great specials."

That didn't help. His deep voice rumbled through Tam's chest and made her heart go pitty-pat. She wondered what her mom would think if she dated a man who was older enough to be her father.

Yeah, right. It wasn't like she had a shot with this one. This guy was serious business, and Tam was quite the opposite. She wouldn't have made it through high school without copying worksheets from every nerd available. And she didn't even make it through a semester of junior college before dropping out. Not to mention her period was two weeks late, as of today, and her sperm donor still chose to live with his *other* baby-mama.

Tam's life was about as messed up as it could get, but still, it didn't hurt to daydream. She thought she could get things on track with a man like this in her life. For real this time.

She smiled and took his plate. "I'll be right back."

She returned five minutes later with his drink and his check. The customer was back to his brooding by then. Tam thought about flirting with him, but thankfully common sense kicked in, and she realized how silly she was being. The most she could hope for was a good tip, and he delivered. He finished his second drink and left her $40 for the $31 ticket.

Tam was at another table when he stood to leave. But he didn't leave. Instead he went to the bar and took a seat on one of the stools. Tam hoped to get him off her mind, but it would be hard as long as he was still in the building. She could *feel* his presence. She cursed herself for being born ten years too late and returned her attention to her new customers.

The bartender approached Marcel moments after he sat down.

"What'll it be?"

"Crown on the rocks."

"Gotcha."

Marcel watched the man prepare the drink. The auburn-color liquor looked delicious as it splashed over the ice. Marcel knew he should go home, but he couldn't. Not right now. He did promise himself not to get drunk in the restaurant, but sometimes the liquor had other plans. He checked his watch.

When he looked up again, he saw a woman approaching the bar. She was talking on her cellphone. Marcel didn't mean to stare, but he was immediately attracted to her style and her figure. She was tall and curvy. Her skin was dark and pure. She wore slacks with a sleeveless blouse that didn't show off much cleavage. Her hair was nothing fancy, pulled back in a ponytail. Her smile was what really caught Marcel's eye. And her laughter. She seemed full of life. Truly happy. She took a seat next to him, and Marcel looked away. But she was talking loudly enough for him to hear her conversation.

"Girl, what the hell does *almost there* mean? You said that ten minutes ago."

There was a pause, while her friend responded.

"On the freeway? Tricia, I'm in the restaurant *right now*! And I'm about to order my first drink. You know what, screw you heifers. Kendra said she's on the other side of Hulen, so I know she won't be here for at least five minutes."

Another pause.

"It's my nerves, girl. I gotta tell you what this boy did in my class today. You won't believe it. And his mama had the nerve to call up there, trying to defend him. I had a long day, and I'm about to get my drink on."

Another pause.

"I'm at the bar, girl. We can get a table when y'all get here. And you're paying for this first drink, too. It's your turn." She laughed. "I don't care if you're not here. I'll save the receipt for you!" She laughed again and said, "Alright, Tricia. Hurry up. Bye!"

She disconnected and slipped the phone into her purse. She was still smiling brightly when she looked at the bartender.

"What can I get you tonight?"

"Margarita on the rocks."

"You want to upgrade that to top-shelf?"

"Might as well. I'm not paying for it."

"Okay. Give me a sec."

The bartender backed away, and Donna noticed the man sitting next to her for the first time. Her eyes widened. *Good God.* How did she not notice this godly creature? He was huge – not fat, but tall and powerfully built, like a pro quarterback. His skin was dark chocolate. His haircut was short, all of the lines were perfect. He didn't wear a moustache or goatee.

He turned and locked eyes with her.

Donna smiled. He did too.

"Hi," he said.

Donna wasn't aware that her mouth fell open. *Oh no he didn't hit me with that baritone!* She didn't have a particular type of man she was interested in, but if she did, this handsome stranger would surely fit the bill. He had nice, suckable lips. His smile was warm and inviting.

Somehow she found the wherewithal to say, "Hi."

"Had a hard day?"

"I had a *typical* day," she replied. "It's always something new."

87

"You're a teacher?"

She knitted her eyebrows, but her big smile remained intact. "Yeah. How'd you know?"

"I heard you when you sat down," the man said. "You were talking about something that happened in your class. I wasn't eavesdropping. I swear."

She stared into his eyes, and all sins were forgiven. The man had dark eyes, clean teeth and a perfect nose. Donna was sure there was *something* about him that she wasn't attracted to, but so far she hadn't found it.

"I'm Marcel."

He offered a hand to shake. Donna took it. His grip was firm, but not too strong. He knew how to be gentle with a lady.

"I'm Donna."

"Where do you teach?" he asked.

"Here you go," the bartender interrupted and placed Donna's drink in front of her.

"Thank you! I teach at Wedgewood Middle," she told her new friend.

"Let me guess, English?"

"No. Math. Why'd you think you could guess?"

"I'm usually a good guesser."

"Well, your guesser might need some tinkering," she said with a laugh. "Why'd you pick English?"

"You look like an English teacher," he said. "You're not dressed for P.E. You seem way too lively for science. And you don't have any chalk dust on your fingers, so I didn't think you'd been at a chalkboard all day, doing math problems. Plus you talk like someone who has an English degree."

Donna was impressed. "That's some pretty good reasoning," she said. "But we use dry-erase boards nowadays, and I have plenty of ink from those markers on my hands."

She displayed her fingers and palms. Her hands were smooth and dainty. Marcel had a strong desire for her to touch him. He didn't care where.

"I saw that ink," he said, just as he saw that she didn't have a ring on her third finger. "Still made me think of English."

"I minored in English."

He grinned. "See. My guesser isn't that far off."

"So, what are you, some kind of detective?"

88

He nodded and took a healthy sip of his drink.

"Seriously?"

"Well, not anymore. I was in homicide for six years. I work drugs now."

"You're a cop?"

"I am."

"That's a hard job. I'll bet you see a lot of stuff."

He raised an eyebrow. "You have no idea."

Donna took her drink and sipped from the straw. Marcel downed another third of his glass. The way he watched her made Donna feel self-conscious.

"Why are you looking at me like that?"

"Like what?"

"I'm worried that you're doing more detective work on me," she said with a giggle. She reached and rubbed her hair, making sure it was still in place. "I need to go to the beauty shop."

"You look fine," he said. "I think you're beautiful."

Donna's face flushed with heat. She took another drink in an attempt to cool down.

"Does teaching keep you pretty busy?" he asked.

"Yes. And my son. I try to get him involved in stuff, even though he doesn't want to do anything."

"How old is your son?"

"Fifteen. He's a sophomore this year."

"He play sports?"

"Not as much as he used to."

"Are you divorced?"

"No. My husband got himself killed in a car accident."

"Oh, I'm sorry to hear that."

"Don't be. He was on his way to see his pregnant girlfriend at the time."

Marcel opened his mouth, but he didn't know how to respond to that.

Donna laughed. "Everybody looks at me like that when I tell that story."

Marcel smiled too. "So you're serious?"

"Yes. Very."

"Wh, how long has it been?"

"A year and a half since he died," Donna said.

"And his girlfriend's baby?"

"Wasn't his. She probably told him it was, though."

Marcel chuckled. "I like you."

Donna felt the temperature rise again. This time it was accompanied by goose bumps. She didn't know how to reply, so she said, "Thanks."

"So, was your husband deaf, dumb or blind?" Marcel asked.

"None of the above. He was a great man. He was flawed as hell, but still a good guy."

"I'm sorry," Marcel said. "I didn't mean to bad mouth him."

"That's okay."

"But I don't understand why he would cheat on you. I've only known you for a few minutes, but you seem like a wonderful person."

"Maybe that's your faulty detective skills again."

"No. I don't think so."

His expression was so serious, Donna began to feel heated again. She wasn't sure why he affected her like that.

"How about you?" she asked. "Divorced or forever single?"

"Divorced."

"Any kids?"

"I had a son," he said. "Jaylen. He died, about eight months ago."

"Oh. I am so sorry." Donna felt like an ass for bringing it up.

"No need. We're just talking. You had no way of knowing."

"Yeah, but–"

"It's okay. Really."

Marcel finished his drink and told the bartender, "Gimme another."

His inner voice warned him not to drink excessively, especially in front of this woman, but he convinced himself that it was okay. Donna wasn't there when he got his first two drinks with dinner. As far as she knew, this was only his second one.

"This was Jaylen's favorite restaurant," he said. "I was driving by today, and I decided to stop. I shouldn't have. The nostalgia is starting to get to me."

Donna brought a hand to her mouth. "Oh, you poor soul."

Marcel caught himself. What the hell was he doing? He didn't want to come off as some lonely, depressed weirdo. "I'm sorry," he said. "I didn't mean to start talking about him."

"No, it's fine. It's just sad, that's all."

"I barely know you. I'm not the type of guy to dump my sad story on whoever will listen. I promise, I never do this."

"You don't have to apologize."

"I'm glad I came in here today," Marcel said. "If I hadn't come, I wouldn't have met you."

Donna smiled, but she thought the downward turn of their conversation had caused irreparable damage to the chance encounter. This man was irresistibly handsome, but he was hurting. Badly.

Marcel was fully aware of his depression, and he had a good feeling what Donna must think of him at that moment. But he wasn't willing to let this beauty walk out of his life so easily. As a matter of fact, he felt like he needed someone like her in his world. Donna lost her husband under terrible circumstances, but she was a fireball of energy. She was a beacon of light and happiness in his otherwise dreary day.

She changed his mood significantly the moment she sat down. Marcel realized Donna was at a place that he desperately wanted to be. She smiled and joked about her husband's death, rather than become downcast. It may have taken her a year and a half to get there, but the bottom line was she was there. She was a survivor. She was proof that life does go on, and it can even get better.

Marcel was physically attracted to her – in a strong way. But it wasn't her looks that had him yearning for more. Not right now, at least.

"You're looking like you'll say no if I ask you out," he said. "But I have to ask. It's not likely that I'll ever see you again, if I don't get your number now."

"Well, um..."

"If you're taking this conversation into consideration," Marcel said, "try to remember everything that happened *before* I mentioned my son. I think we were getting along really well."

Donna's smile returned. "We were. We still are. And I'm not upset with you for bringing him up. Trust me, I can understand what you're going through."

91

"I know you can."

Donna looked through her purse for a pen and paper, but she was distracted by another woman who approached the bar.

"Oh shit, girl. You were serious!" Tricia took a seat on Donna's other side and reached for her drink. "What is this you got here?"

"It's *mine*, is what it is," Donna said and laughed. She snatched her drink from her friend's greedy hands. "But you are paying for it."

The bartender was Johnny-on-the-spot that night. "Hey, how you doing this evening," he said to Tricia. "What can I get for you? Are y'all together?"

"Yes, we are," Donna told him. "And you can give her the bill."

"No problem."

"I want what she got," Tricia told him.

"Okay. You want top-shelf, too?"

Tricia gave her friend a look. "Bitch, you got me paying for top-shelf?"

"Is that what I got?" Donna asked innocently. She leaned forward and took another sip. "Yep. I guess so!"

Tricia laughed. "Yeah, I'll take that, too," she told the barkeep. "I thought we were getting a table," she said to Donna. "Or at least a booth."

"We are. I was just waiting for y'all. You ready?"

"Yeah, 'cause I wanna order some of those onion string things, with the jalapeños."

Tricia hopped off her stool, and Donna did the same. Marcel thought she was giving him a convenient brush-off, but she said, "Oh wait, hold on," and turned back to the bar.

Donna found a pen in her purse and a receipt from Family Dollar. She checked to make sure she didn't buy anything personal that day before she turned the receipt over and scribbled her cell number.

"Here you go," she said and handed it to her new acquaintance.

"Thanks," Marcel said. He folded it and slipped it into his pocket. "I'll talk to you later. Y'all have fun."

"Okay," Donna said. "You too."

She and her friend walked away, and Marcel realized how much he was attracted to her physical beauty. Her figure was perfect. She wasn't skinny, but her waist was slim and her hips and ass... *Lordy*. He wondered how her male students learned anything in her classroom. If he was a kid, he would've failed repeatedly, *on purpose*, to stay in her presence another year.

"Ooh, do tell!" Tricia said before they were out of earshot.

"Girl, shut up!" Donna told her, and they both laughed.

CHAPTER NINE
BROTHERS

Kendra arrived at the restaurant a few minutes later, and the threesome ordered onion strings and chicken wings to go with their $4 margaritas. The restaurant was nearly packed by then, mostly with couples, but there were a lot of parties of families and friends.

Donna loved kicking it with Kendra and Tricia. Her friends got her through some of the worst times of her life, and she was always there for them as well. Tricia was usually more well-grounded, and Kendra was known to fly by the seat of her pants.

That Friday night they talked about their work and their kids. Tricia had two girls who were into everything from ballet to music lessons and another one who just finished potty-training. They were constantly making their mother proud. Donna wished she could say the same about her son. She worried that she and Colton were going to have a big fall-out before he made it through his sophomore year.

"What's he doing?" Kendra asked her. "Being mannish?"

Donna nodded. "I hope that's all it is. His grades aren't that hot, and his teachers say he doesn't seem interested some of the time. He does enough to pass, though. I almost made him sit out of basketball this year, but I don't think that would've mattered, either. He doesn't even have the same drive for sports, like he used to."

"What is he, a C-student?" Tricia asked. She lifted her frosty mug, and Donna did the same. The alcohol was delicious. The company was even better.

"He makes B's and C's," Donna said. "In middle school, it was A's and B's."

"You think high school is too much of a distraction for him?" Kendra asked. "Maybe it *would* help if he didn't play sports for a year, until he can get focused."

"Do you think it's because of Nolan?" Tricia asked.

"That's what I'm worried about," Donna said.

"Is he still in counseling?"

Donna shook her head. "No. He completed his sessions. The counselor said Colton's still upset, but that's to be expected. She said he's not depressed or withdrawn, and he's learned to cope with his father not being there."

"Maybe you should take him to a different counselor," Tricia suggested.

"Every time he does something wrong, I worry that it's because of the accident," Donna said. "It's been over a year and a half, and I'm still doing it. But I know some of this is teenage rebellion. I can't keep blaming everything on Nolan."

"That's good," Kendra said. "Make him be responsible."

"You need to whoop his little tail," Tricia said. "A boy ain't never too big to get popped by his mama."

"I know that's right!" Dona laughed, but she knew that her son's problems might be serious. She regretted taking the backseat while Nolan acted as the primary disciplinarian for Colton over the years.

"Lemme see your bracelet," Tricia said to Kendra. "You been flashing it in my face all night. I'm surprised you haven't taken it off and slid it over here by now."

Donna laughed.

"What you talking about?" Kendra said, grinning brightly.

"I see your new bling," Tricia said. She reached for her hand. "Come on. Let me see it."

Kendra extended her arm over the table, so her friends could admire her newest courtship offering.

"Patrick gave you that?" Tricia asked.

Kendra nodded. She was beaming.

"You think an engagement ring might be next?" Donna asked.

"I'm not ready to get married," Kendra said quickly.

"Did you tell Patrick that?" Donna asked.

"Yes, I tell him all the time."

"And in the meantime he keeps giving you pretty, shiny things," Tricia noticed.

"And expensive, high-heeled things," Donna added, and they all laughed.

"By the time you realize what a catch Patrick is, he'll be gone," Tricia warned good-naturedly. "He won't chase you forever."

"That's fine," Kendra said. "Patrick ain't the only Patrick out there. And he ain't the only one who can afford bracelets and bags and trips to the salon."

"*Woop!*" Donna said. She reached over the table and gave her friend a high-five. "That's what I'm talking about!"

Tricia cracked up too and then asked, "What about you, Miss Donna? How'd things go with Randall?"

Donna grinned and gave her friend a look. "Alright, I guess."

"Just *alright*?" Tricia said. "You said he was taking you to the movies. How'd it go?"

Donna shook her head, but her smile remained. Tricia was responsible for the blind date. Tired of seeing Donna wallow in (what she referred to as) an unfortunate state of abstinence, she hooked her up with a friend of the family. Donna didn't consider her state of abstinence to be *unfortunate*. She was simply single. She was young and vibrant and still had a healthy interest in men. She just so happened to have not been involved with anyone for more than one year and six agonizingly long months. That's all. Nothing wrong with that.

"Bitch, please," Tricia had told her. "There is too something wrong with that!"

Kendra had agreed, and after a little encouragement, Donna agreed a little bit, too.

Randall was a car salesman for a Mercedes dealership. Donna looked him up on Facebook and thought he was nice-looking. She gave Tricia the okay to give him her number, and now, after nearly two decades, Donna had a man – who was not Nolan – calling her house and asking what she was doing and how her day was and if he could take her out. Donna found the experience to be a little surreal, and not in a good way.

She wasn't sure if she wasn't ready to go out with someone new, or if it was this particular man she was opposed to, but something about it was not quite right. But then again, Donna was 39 years old (for a few more months at least), which was far too young to be an old maid.

"I shouldn't have gone to the movies with him," she told her friends. "Back in the day, when I did go out, I would never let them take me to the movies on a first date. It's so dark in there, you can barely see them, let alone talk long enough to see if you like them."

"Why didn't you go get something to eat afterwards?" Tricia asked.

"Because he took me to a late show, and it was after ten by the time we left."

Kendra laughed at her. Tricia did, too.

"What?"

"Ten o'clock is not late," Kendra said.

"Yes it is," Donna countered. "I'm not going to stay out 'till midnight with some man I just met. Nothing good happens after midnight. My daddy told me that."

"So, you don't like him?" Tricia asked. She looked like she might pout.

"I didn't say that," Donna said.

"Well, *do* you like him?" Tricia persisted.

"I don't *dis*-like him," Donna said. "But I don't think it was a good first impression." Thankfully her friends let her leave it at that.

"What about your friend at the bar?" Tricia asked. "You like him?"

Donna frowned at her. "You messy."

"What friend at the bar?" Kendra asked. She rose out of her seat, so she could get a look. "What friend?"

"They were all hugged-up when I got here," Tricia said. "Donna gave him her number."

"Just messy," Donna said, shaking her head. "For no reason at all."

"Who was Donna all hugged-up with?" Kendra's smile was ear to ear as she scanned the bar.

"That man over there," Tricia said. She rose to her feet as well, so she could point him out.

97

"Will y'all please sit down?" Donna said, feeling embarrassed. "I was not hugged-up with anyone," she told Kendra. "Why you believe this girl?"

"*Who*?" Kendra squealed, nearly exasperated.

"That man with the black shirt," Tricia said. "And jeans. The big guy."

"Oh, *okay*," Kendra said when she spotted him. "That's you, Donna?"

"No that's not *me*! Will y'all please sit down, before he sees you staring at him? *Jesus*. Grow up."

"Whatever," Kendra said, but she did sit down. "So, your tall, dark and sexy over there... Do tell."

Donna rolled her eyes. "I just met him."

"I'm going over there," Kendra said. "I wanna see his face."

Donna looked back at the bar. Marcel was still there, his back to them. "You are not going over there," she told her friend.

"Is he cute?" Kendra asked Tricia.

She nodded. "That man is fine."

"Go head, Donna!" Kendra exclaimed. "You go from *no prospects* to *two men* in a couple of weeks."

"Sorry to burst your bubble," Donna said, "but Randall is nowhere near my man. And I don't think I'd go out with that one over there."

"Why?" Kendra asked. She looked in Marcel's direction again.

"He's been at the bar by himself since we got here," Tricia said. "There may be something up with him."

"What's wrong with him being here by himself?" Kendra asked.

"I think he's been drinking the *whole time*," Tricia continued. "He could be a *lonely drunk*."

Donna wasn't sure why, but she didn't like for her friend to come down on Marcel like that. She didn't watch him throughout the night, but he had only nursed a couple of drinks, as far as she could tell.

"His son died eight months ago," she told them. "He said he was thinking about him, because this was his favorite restaurant; his son's."

98

"Oh," Tricia said. The smile slipped from her face. "Well, he probably wouldn't be any good for you anyway. If he's depressed, he needs to deal with that *first*."

"Yeah," Kendra agreed. "You remember how you were, after what happened to Nolan. Sometimes people need time to heal."

Those were Donna's thoughts exactly.

"Hey, check it out," Tricia said. "Tonight they must be having a special on dark chocolate..."

Her friends followed her gaze to another tall, burly brother who had entered the restaurant. Just as Donna bunched her eyebrows, thinking the new arrival looked strangely familiar, he walked to the bar and greeted Marcel. Marcel turned and smiled warm-heartedly, and the two of them struck up a conversation.

"Guess he's not lonely," Kendra remarked.

"What are the odds of two men built like that knowing each other?" Tricia asked. "I wonder if they played football together, or something."

"They look like brothers," Donna said. Her curiosity was definitely piqued. She turned back towards her friends, after she realized how long she'd been staring at them. For the next few minutes, she managed to fight strong urges that compelled her to look Marcel's way again.

●●●●●●●

"Hey, big bro."

Marcel checked his phone before he acknowledged the unwelcomed guest. The last message he got from Terrence read: I'm on my way

That was sent fifteen minutes ago. Marcel rose from his barstool and gave his little brother a brief hug before returning to his seat. Terrence was younger by three years. He was a hulk of a man, like Marcel, but not quite as big. He wasn't quite as handsome either, in Marcel's opinion. But Terrence did excel at one thing his brother had failed at. He was an excellent family man.

"Man, you weren't kidding, were you?" Marcel told him as he lifted his glass to his mouth. He drained the last of it before Terrence could do something stupid, like try to take it away.

"I told you I was coming."

"I didn't think you'd drop everything to get over here."

"Nothing more important than my family," Terrence said and slapped him on the back. He rubbed his shoulder comfortingly as he took a seat. "How you doing, man?"

"I'm good."

The bartender looked their way. Marcel nodded and tapped his glass. Terrence shook his head.

"How many you knocked down?" Terrence asked him.

"That was my third," Marcel said. "This is my fourth coming up."

That was only partly true. He did have three drinks at the bar so far, but he conveniently left out the two he had with dinner before migrating to the bar.

"What are you doing here?" Terrence asked. "Why you by yourself?"

"Just thinking," Marcel replied.

"About what?"

"Can't a man be alone with his thoughts?"

"If you were truly alone, I'd be fine with it," Terrence said. "But you're not alone. You got that liquor keeping you company."

As he spoke, the bartender came and took Marcel's glass. He brought it back full of the brown stuff. Marcel reached for it, but Terrence stayed his hand and took it himself.

Marcel gave him a look. "You told him you didn't want one."

"I don't. Not really. But I don't think you should have it, either."

Terrence proceeded to sip Marcel's favorite drink in front of him, which was a serious buzzkill. He winced from the strong alcohol.

"What is this? Straight Crown?"

"Nobody told you to mess with it. You can't steal a man's drink and then complain about the taste of it. *This porridge is too hot, Mommy.*" He laughed.

Terrence noticed his brother's speech wasn't slurred. That was good. Marcel didn't smell like liquor, either, and his eyes were keen and focused. He still didn't believe Marcel had only three drinks tonight, though.

"You wanna come home with me?" he asked.

Marcel frowned at that. He really did want to be alone with his thoughts, not in a house full of people. He loved his nieces and nephews dearly, but there was no peace at that place.

"We can watch a game in the den," Terrence told him, reading his mind. "I won't let nobody bother you."

"I can watch a game right here," Marcel commented.

Terrence sighed. "But you can't stay sober here. Why you want me to come out and say it?"

"Because you're a man," Marcel said. "When men talk, they should be able to say what they really feel."

"I feel like you lied about cutting down on your drinking," Terrence said. "And I feel like you lied to your counselor about how well you're doing. And you're lying to yourself, too."

"Alright, that's enough," Marcel said with a smirk. "I don't need you sharing *all* of your feelings. You're starting to sound like a woman."

Terrence chuckled and grimaced as he gulped down another mouthful of Marcel's toxins.

"Why didn't you get some coke in this?" he asked.

"Do I go to your house telling you what to put in your cup?" Marcel said. "Gimme that."

He reached for his glass.

"Hold on." Terrence quickly finished it off before setting it down. The look on his face as he tried to convince his taste buds to ignore the fire water was priceless.

Marcel laughed at him.

"Don, don't order another one," Terrence said, when he regained his ability to speak. "We finna go."

"Says who?"

"Come on, man. Don't give me a hard time. It's Friday night. You don't need to be in here drinking by yourself. We can order some pizzas and watch the game – or we can watch some fights on cable. I got all the channels. Whatever you want."

Marcel shook his head. It was clear his loving brother wasn't going to let him wallow in grief tonight. He knew that Terrence had his best interests in mind, so he relented and agreed that he'd had enough. When the bartender asked if he wanted another, Marcel told him, "Just the check."

While waiting for it, he told his brother, "Today's Jaylen's birthday."

Terrence was surprised by that. He knew it was near the end of August, but he had forgotten the exact date.

"I used to bring him here," Marcel went on. He was looking straight ahead, lost in some distant memory. "This was his favorite restaurant."

Terrence's heart sank as he watched him. What do you say to someone who's lost everything? The ink wasn't dry on Marcel's divorce papers yet before Jaylen was murdered in his own home. If Terrence was in his brother's shoes, he figured he'd lean heavily on the bottle as well.

But it wouldn't be the same. He had a wife and five children. He'd still have a house full of people to support him if someone died tragically. Marcel had a support system as well, but no one stayed with him 24/7. It had been eight months since Jaylen's death. Terrence knew that his brother shunned most people, telling them he was better now. But every day he went home to a painfully quiet house and woke up to the same emptiness.

"He would've been thirteen," Marcel said. He wasn't crying. Terrence thought that was good; a sign of progress, but he wasn't so sure. Maybe it would be better if he did cry.

"You talked to Coleen?" Terrence regretted the question right away.

"She said I should've had a security system," Marcel told him. "She said that's what cost Jaylen his life – that and me making him a latch-key kid. She never did feel good about that."

Terrence grimaced. What the hell was wrong with that woman? Were all ex-wives this vindictive? She blamed Marcel for everything, but did their son's death have to be his fault as well?

"That's stupid," he told his brother.

"No, she's right," Marcel said. "If Jaylen didn't go home by himself that day, it wouldn't have happened."

"You don't know that."

"If I had an alarm system, nobody would have gotten in the house."

"*You don't know that,*" Terrence insisted. "I can understand why Coleen's wondering about all that stuff. I can understand why you're wondering about it, too. But for her to throw it in your face like that is wrong, man. That's the lowest thing she could do. They say hurt people *hurt* people, but she's taking it too far."

Marcel didn't respond. He continued to stare blankly at the many bottles of liquor behind the bar. They all looked absolutely beautiful.

"You two can *what if* yourselves forever," Terrence said. "You can *what if* yourself right into a crazy home."

Marcel didn't speak for what felt like a long time. "I'm not crazy," he finally said.

"I know you're not."

"Today's Jaylen's birthday, is all. I came to his favorite restaurant and had a few drinks. Nothing wrong with that."

"No," Terrence agreed. "I guess there's not."

"I miss him," Marcel said, and his eyes did well with tears then. He was quick to wipe them away.

"I miss him, too," Terrence said. "You ready to go?"

Marcel shook his head and sighed. "You're one persistent bastard. You know that?"

"I do," Terrence said. "Did I ever tell you Michelle hated me when we first met? Now look at us. You'd never believe she used to roll her eyes when she saw me coming."

He stood, and Marcel eventually did too. He didn't stagger or stumble, so Terrence knew he wasn't loaded. He watched him carefully while he paid his tab. Marcel was the strongest SOB he knew. He never cried when Coleen left him, but Jaylen's death took all of the light out of him. Terrence used to think his big brother could get through anything, but he wasn't sure this time. Marcel was so different now.

"You okay to drive?" Terrence asked as they exited the restaurant.

"You really can be a worrisome little punk," Marcel grunted.

"I love you, too," Terrence said and followed him into the fresh, nighttime air.

CHAPTER TEN
BOY TROUBLES

On Wednesday the following week, Donna received a phone call at school while she was teaching second period. She didn't get the message until her planning period a couple of hours later. She was surprised to see that the vice principal from Finley High School wanted to speak with her. She used to have nothing but praise for Colton's scholastic feats, but now her first thought was *What the hell did he do now?*

She waited until she got back to her empty classroom before she returned the call. It took a nerve-racking seven minutes to get Mr. Farris on the phone.

"Hi. Mrs. Hodge?"

"Yes," Donna said with a sigh. "I got a message from you regarding Colton..."

"Oh, yes," the vice principal said. "We had to suspend him today."

Donna's eyes flashed open. She was feeling a little mid-day fatigue, but not anymore. "What? What are you talking about?"

"There was an outburst in his Math class," the administrator said. "He told another student to..."

Donna heard papers rustling.

"I'm sorry. I just made it back to my office. Let me see here... Oh, okay. Here it is. He cursed at another student."

"What did he say?" Donna nearly growled.

"He, um, he told him to shut the 'F' up. But he used the actual word. It was in the middle of class. Quite an outburst. Mrs. McMillen says he didn't whisper it to him. He yelled rather loudly."

Donna pursed her lips. She tapped a pencil on her desk so hard the point broke off.

"We have a zero tolerance policy for fighting and use of profanity," Mr. Farris told her. "Colton's been suspended for the rest of the day. He can return tomorrow, but a parent or guardian has to accompany him."

Donna's teeth were clenched. She and Colton had to report to school at virtually the same time. The suspension was bad enough, but his behavior causing her to be late for work compounded the problem significantly. She was so angry, she could barely sit still.

"I'll be there in the morning," she told the vice principal. "Where do I need to go?"

"To my office," he said. "The three of us will sit down and talk about this briefly, and then you can continue with your day. I'm sorry for the inconvenience."

"It's not your fault," Donna said. "I understand how hard your job is. I'll see you in the morning."

●●●●●●●

Donna was thankful that her planning period was right before her lunch break, because it gave her the option of leaving the campus if she needed to. She had a lot of worksheets to copy that day, but Donna decided she could stay after school for that. At 11:45 she hopped in her car and headed home. She didn't call Colton on the way, and he still hadn't called her. They only lived a mile away from his school, so she figured Colton chose to walk rather than face her wrath.

Halfway home she began to contemplate what she'd do if Colton didn't go straight there after he got kicked out of school. All of his friends were still in class, and he didn't have a car. She supposed he could wander the streets aimlessly or take the bus to the mall. Donna realized she didn't have a solution for that scenario, so she pushed the thoughts from her mind.

Thankfully Colton was home when she got there. He was in his room playing video games. Donna was so upset, she didn't ask him to turn it off. She stormed in and started yanking plugs from the wall willy-nilly. Colton rose from his seat to stop her.

"Mama, what you doing?"

105

She spun on him. "Boy, you better sit your silly ass down!"

"You coulda just told me to turn it off!"

"Don't raise your voice at me!" Donna closed the distance between them and pointed a rigid finger between his eyes. "You'd better watch your mouth!"

Colton looked like he wanted to push her hand away, but he tossed his game controller onto the bed and sat back in his chair angrily.

For a moment, Donna was taken aback by how big he was. His arms and legs were long and thin, but there were small muscles developing. He wasn't as tall as his mother, but at the rate he was growing, he'd surpass her before his senior year. Colton hadn't cut his hair in months. He sported a small afro that actually looked pretty good on him. He had a slight moustache and a little hair on his chin.

Most notably was his serious eyes and deepening voice. Colton didn't sound like Mama's little boy anymore. He had the beginnings of a deep, manly voice, which totally unnerved Donna when he shouted at her. For the life of her, she couldn't remember when her son started raising his voice when they argued. It certainly never happened before Nolan died. He would've skinned Colton's hide for such disrespect.

"What the hell happened at school?" she barked.

Colton folded his arms over his chest and stared at her fiercely. From the psychology classes she remembered from college, Donna knew that he was being defensive, and this argument probably wouldn't get them anywhere. But she was too upset to calm down and try a less aggressive tactic.

"You already know what happened," he grumbled, "or you wouldn't be here."

Donna's eyes darted quickly. She stopped herself when she realized she was looking for something to hit him with. She hadn't spanked the boy since he was eight. She knew that it was much too late to regress to that level of discipline, but she was nearly at her wits' end.

She took a step back and took a few deep breaths. She knew that she needed help, and she knew where to find it. When she spoke again, her voice was smooth and steady.

"Alright, son, here's how's it's gonna go. You will respect me in my house, or you will get your ass beat."

Colton had the nerve to *hmph* at that.

"No, I'm not gonna whoop you myself," she continued. "I'm going to call your uncle Brandon over here and tell him how you've been acting."

Colton's eyes widened for a second, and he lost a good deal of his composure. Donna didn't know if he was worried about Brandon physically hitting him, or if he didn't want to lose favor with his godfather, but she was grateful that it worked. She had his attention now.

"Tell me what happened at school," she demanded.

Colton's face flushed with crimson. He looked around irritably, and his eyes filled with tears. "I was just trying to do my work," he reasoned. "This boy kept talking, making jokes when the teacher wasn't listening. He got on my nerves, so I told him to shut up."

"That's not what you told him."

"I told him to shut the 'F' up," Colton said.

"You told him to shut the 'F' up, or you said the actual word?"

"I said the word. That's what I meant."

"The principal says you didn't just say it," Donna reported. "He says you yelled it in the middle of class and caused a big disruption."

"I got mad," Colton said, "because I was frustrated. He kept talking, and nobody would do anything about it." A tear spilled from his eye. He was quick to wipe it away.

"Having good intentions doesn't make what you did right," Donna said. "You know better than to yell at somebody in the middle of class – especially a curse word. What's gotten into you? What do you mean you got mad?"

"I just be mad sometimes, Mama. I don't know why."

Donna was still upset, but as a mother, her heart ached for him. She wanted to chalk this up to him being a moody teenager. But since Nolan's death, every emotion Colton had was suspect. Donna hated that there was no way to look inside his heart to find out which problems were related to his father not being there.

"You think you need to go back to counseling?"

"No," he said right away.

"Why not?"

"Because I already went for a long time. I'm not crazy, Mama."

"I know you're not crazy. Nobody said that."

"I don't need to talk about my feelings, just because I got mad today."

"It's not only about you getting mad," Donna said. "You're not doing that great in school *overall*. You don't even have the same interest in sports, like you used to. Colton, I can't figure all this out on my own. I can't figure *you* out. I think we need some help."

"Mama, I'm fine. I'm not going back to counseling."

Donna raised an eyebrow, but he didn't back down.

"If I sign you up for counseling, your ass will be there," she stated. "Until you turn eighteen, you'll be wherever I tell you to be."

"Mama, I don't need counseling," he whined.

Donna wished he wasn't so stubborn, but she actually preferred this type of disagreement, compared to the anger. Whining was what she expected from a child his age.

"If you don't need counseling, then you're acting out for no good reason," she said.

Colton looked away. He didn't want to acknowledge that, but he didn't want to return to counseling even more.

"Okay," Donna said. "Unhook this game and bring it to my room. Turn your cellphone off and bring that, too."

She thought he'd reconsider his stance on counselling at that point, but Colton stood and began to pack up his gaming console.

"Hurry up," Donna told him. "I need to drop you off at your grandmother's on my way back to work."

He was stunned. "What do I have to go over there for?"

"Pulling weeds," she said. "And mowing the lawn. If you get done before I get off work, I got some Algebra worksheets for you to do."

Colton's jaw dropped. Donna knew he hated that she was a teacher sometimes. She had access to an endless supply of school work. Even worse, Donna was a math teacher, so she could check the accuracy of his work when he got done. It was impossible to bullshit his way through one of her assignments.

"You might wanna change your clothes, too," Donna advised him. "You'll be on your knees for quite a while, and I don't want any grass stains on your school pants."

Colton's head and shoulders slumped in resignation. Donna returned to the front room to wait for him.

●●●●●●●

When she picked him up after work, her mother said Colton was a perfect gentleman. He didn't display any of the attitude he had earlier in the day. Grandma couldn't imagine him using bad language in a classroom.

"He's a little angel," she said and planted a kiss on his cheek. "Are you sure they're talking about *this* Colton?"

"He already admitted to saying it," Donna informed her. "But I'm glad he didn't give you any trouble today. Thanks for watching him."

"Anytime," Grandma said. "It was a pleasure having him."

Regardless of her mother's glowing report, Donna didn't let up on her son when they got home. She instructed him to do his homework and then clean his room from top to bottom. He wasn't allowed to turn on the television or even the radio. If he finished before bedtime, he had to get started on re-organizing the garage.

Donna graded papers while he worked. They took a break for dinner and then returned to their tasks. The house was unusually quiet that night. Donna relished the tranquility. She almost didn't answer her phone when it rang at seven o'clock from a number she didn't recognize.

"Hello?"

"Hey, Donna?"

The voice was deep and authoritative. It sent an unexpected chill down her spine.

"Who's calling?"

"This is Marcel."

Donna racked her brain but couldn't place the name.

"Do I know you?"

He chuckled. "No. Not really. I met you last Friday, at Chili's. We talked at the bar..."

Donna's eyes widened. *Oh. It was Mr. Big, Strong and Sexy.* But that thought was quickly followed by the fact that

109

Marcel was grieving for his son. She didn't want that to be his defining attribute, but for now it was. Her friends told her not to talk to this guy. Marcel was hurting, and he needed time to heal.

Or maybe he wasn't as depressed as she made him out to be. Donna decided that the only way she'd know for sure was to talk to him and see how often he brought up his son. If that was the only thing on his mind, then she had to cut him loose. She knew that was cold-hearted, but she didn't have room in her life for another man with issues. Dealing with her mini-man was hard enough.

She put her work aside and leaned back against her bed's headboard.

"Since when did the two-day rule become the five-day rule?" she asked him.

"I don't know what you mean."

"Isn't that how it goes?" she said. "You're supposed to wait two days after you get a girl's number before you call her?"

He chuckled. "If that's a rule, I wasn't aware of it. I would've called you Friday night, but I knew you were out with your friends. And then I was embarrassed because I felt like I made a fool of myself when we met. I did put off calling you, but not for some silly rule. I was afraid you'd think I have some emotional issues."

Donna raised an eyebrow. "Oh, well, um..."

He chuckled again. It was a rich sound that made Donna smile as well.

"So, I take it you do feel that way," he said.

"No. Not necessarily. I can understand what you're going through."

"I'm not going through anything," he assured her. "It was just a thing that happened that day. You caught me at a bad moment, but I'm thankful that we met, even if I did come across as a blubbering idiot."

"Stop saying that," Donna said with a giggle. "You looked fine." *Really fine*, she thought. She remembered Marcel's cool, brown eyes and his smooth, dark skin, his solid neck and pectorals. Marcel was built like a warrior. His sensitivity deepened, rather than detracted from his character.

"I thought about you a lot this week," he confided. "I'd really like to see you again."

The declaration made her heart rate increase, but Donna hadn't decided if that was going to happen or not, so she simply said, "Thank you."

"Oh. Well, hell. That was awkward."

She laughed. "I'm sorry."

"Don't apologize," he said. "I like that. It's kinda humbling, but it's okay."

Donna grinned but didn't respond.

Marcel changed the subject. "Did you have a nice day? You don't sound like the kids stressed you too much."

"My students were fine," Donna said. "But my child did give me some trouble."

"What'd he do, if you don't mind me asking?"

"He got himself suspended," Donna said. "He cursed some boy out in the middle of class."

"How old is he?"

"He's fifteen. A sophomore." Donna thought that would be the moment when Marcel brought up his own son, but he didn't.

"Why'd he curse him out?"

"He said the boy was interrupting class."

"And they suspended him for that? Sounds like the teacher should be happy for the help."

"He yelled at him to shut the 'F' up," Donna explained.

"He probably just said what the teacher was thinking," Marcel reasoned. "I'm sure you've gotten to a point where you wanted to tell a student that yourself."

"Yeah, but Colton knows the difference between appropriate and inappropriate classroom behavior," Donna said. "If he doesn't, he gon' learn today."

"Damn, I don't envy him right now. You sound like a pretty strict disciplinarian."

"I wish," Donna said. "To be honest, I feel like he's getting away from me sometimes. He hasn't been the same since his father died."

Donna caught herself, and she had to smile. Here she was about to condemn Marcel for bringing up his dead son, but she brought Nolan up both times they talked. Maybe she was wrong about that being an indication of his level of depression, because she wasn't depressed at all.

111

"I'm still blown away by what you told me about your husband," Marcel said.

"What do you mean?"

"I know you're gonna think I'm trying to butter you up, but I find it awfully hard to believe that a reasonable and sane man would cheat on you. And you don't strike me as the kind of woman who would marry an idiot."

"You're *totally* trying to butter me up."

"No, I'm genuinely baffled. If I was trying to butter you up, you'd know it."

Donna felt tingles in her belly. "Hmm. What does that mean?"

"What's that?"

"Never mind. My husband was a selfish, power-hungry butthole," she said. "He wanted everything. He almost had it, too."

"How long were you married?"

"Fifteen years."

"Did he cheat on you the whole time?"

"I don't think so. I didn't find out about it until he died."

"Wow. I'll bet that messed you up pretty bad."

"You have no idea."

"But you're better now."

"I am."

"You're bright and happy and confident. Fine as all get out."

Donna's face flushed with heat. "Are you trying to butter me up now?"

"I am," he said. "Barely."

Barely? "Oh, it gets better?"

"Are you flirting with me, woman?"

"Yes, I think so. It's been so long, I'm not sure if I'm doing it right."

"Well, if your goal is to make me feel like I might have a chance to take you out one day, then you're doing it right."

Donna liked this light-hearted banter, but she was glad when her phone beeped, indicating she had another call. Marcel was starting to make her feel things she wasn't sure she was ready for. She checked the caller ID and told him, "Sorry, but I have to go."

"Whoa. Now that's some *terrible* flirting!"

She laughed. "I'm not flirting right now. I have to take another call."

"What? That's even worse! You're not supposed to tell me you're pushing me to the side to talk to someone else."

"Oh. Damn. See, I told you I don't know what I'm doing."

"That's fine," he said. "I'll be your chopped-liver. Talk to you later, beautiful."

His compliment made Donna's heart flutter. She almost told him never mind, she could continue talking to him. But Randall was the closest thing she had to a boyfriend, so she stuck with her initial decision. "Okay, Marcel. Bye." She accepted the other call. "Hello?"

"Hey, sweetie pie. What took you so long to answer?"

Donna's smile was quickly replaced with a frown. "Excuse me?"

"What took you so long to answer?" Randall said. "I been sitting here, waiting, listening to the phone ring. I can't lie, though. Absence does make the heart grow fonder."

Donna rolled her eyes. "We've only been out on *one date*," she reminded him. "Don't you think it's too soon to be calling me *sweetie pie*?"

"No, I don't think so."

"I'm not your sweetie pie."

"I feel like I can speak things into existence."

"You're so full of it."

"I'm full of feelings for you," he replied.

Donna sighed. She still wasn't sure if she liked this guy. He was the first man she dated since Nolan's death. She complained about Randall to her friends, and they said she was being too judgmental. They said she had an idea in her head of what she expected from a man, and it was unrealistic.

In the past few months, Donna read a lot of magazine articles that backed up her friends' theory. A lot of single women did expect too much. So she took their advice. Maybe Randall wasn't over the top. Maybe this is how men courted women nowadays. But that didn't mean Donna had to settle, did it?

"Guess what happened to me at work today?" Randall said.

My day was interesting, too. Thanks for asking.

"Ummm. I don't know," she said. "You sold a car?"

"Yeah, but it's not the cars I sold, it's *how* I sold them. The first lady that came in swore up and down that she didn't want a new car. She said her son told her it was a *bad investment*, because once she drove off the lot, she'd have a *used* car. But you think I let that stop me?"

"It–"

"Hell no!" he said, before Donna could offer her opinion.

She looked at her fingernails and then found a nail file when she saw that there was a slight inconsistency between her two pinkies. She wasn't aware that she was zoning Randall out until a couple of minutes passed, and she found herself thinking about Marcel. His flirting was similar to Randall's, but it was totally different at the same time. Or at least it made Donna feel differently. She wondered why.

She wondered how badly her friends would respond if she told them she went out with Marcel. They already made it clear that they were not in favor of her seeing him. But what if Donna told them he wasn't the depressed loner they thought he was. He was only upset that one day. But was that truly the case?

Donna had to admit that she had no idea what was going on with either of her suitors. Marcel could very well be irreparably heartbroken, trying his best to hide it from her. And Randall might be the man of her dreams. Maybe he'd treat her like she was the only woman in the world, if she let down her guard and invited him into her life. All she could say for sure was she regretted getting off the phone with Marcel to talk to Randall.

She was not upset when her son's sullen mug appeared in the doorway.

"Hey, uh, I gotta call you back," she told Randall.

"But I was just getting to the good part," he complained.

"Sorry. I gotta go."

"Okay, I'll finish up later, pretty lady."

Oh goody. There's more to come!

"Okay, bye."

"Hey, before you–"

Donna disconnected, knowing he would think she didn't hear the last part. *She totally heard the last part.* "What's up?" she asked her son.

Colton took a step into the room. "Who was that?"

114

Donna's eyebrows knitted, and her head tilted to the side. "Who are *you*, questioning me about who I'm talking to?"

"I just asked a question. Why you getting defensive?"

She realized he was right, but Donna wasn't about to let him use psychology against her.

"I don't like the way you asked me," she said, "like you're *checking* me, or something."

"You got a boyfriend?"

"I'm still getting those vibes, Colton. It's not what you're saying, it's how you're looking at me, and how you're saying it. You're making me feel like you'd have a problem with it, and you think you're in a position to do something about it."

Colton wiped his nose and kept his next thought to himself.

"I finished cleaning my room," he said instead. "Can I watch TV now?"

"No, you cannot watch TV now. You haven't even been grounded for a full day yet. What makes you think you're off the hook?"

"Then what am I supposed to do?"

Donna smiled. She loved it when a bored child asked her that.

Colton's eyes flicked to the stack of worksheets on her bed, and he said, "Never mind. I'll just read a book."

Before he took off, Donna told him, "Bring me your homework, so I can check it. And bring me the book you want to read."

Colton sneered, briefly. He knew she'd want to approve his book selection. And before he went to bed, she'd probably ask him about the pages he told her he read. His mother had been doing that for years.

"You'd better watch yourself," she told him. "All of those little faces you're making are getting on my nerves. I talked to your Uncle Brandon today. He's itching to come over here and set you straight. He said I could call him any time before ten, if need be."

She checked the clock mounted on her dresser. It was 8:45. Colton checked the clock, too.

"Do we have a problem?" Donna asked him.

He lowered his gaze. "No, Ma'am."

"Then go do what I told you to do." She kept a mean glare in place until he was out of sight.

Maybe they didn't have a problem tonight, but she felt like things would come to a head soon. The boy was getting to be too damned mannish.

And Colton didn't want her to have a boyfriend, but maybe that was for the best. Clearly she already had her hands full with him. Donna didn't think she needed any additional testosterone in her life.

CHAPTER ELEVEN
S-CLASS

That Saturday Donna called her friend Tricia at five p.m. to let her know she was about to cancel her second date with Randall.

"Why?" Tricia wanted to know.

"Because I'm not feeling him," Donna said.

The date was September 5th. It was beautiful outside. She and Colton spent most of the afternoon raking leaves from the huge pecan trees that were already starting to shed in her backyard. Donna wasn't that tired, but after taking a long, hot shower, it felt good to lounge on her sofa. She wore shorts and a tank top and had a pint of Blue Bell homemade vanilla in her lap.

The thought of leaving the coziness of her den and doing her hair and putting on makeup and finding a sexy outfit for the evening was not appealing – especially considering she'd be doing it for the likes of *Randall*.

"You've only gone out on one date," Tricia complained. "What exactly don't you like about him?"

"I don't know," Donna said. "If I could put a finger on it, believe me, I would tell you."

"Maybe you can't put a finger on it because it's all in your mind," Tricia ventured. "You've been single for a long time, Donna. You could be subconsciously trying to sabotage things with Randall."

"If I wanted to remain single, I think I'd know it," Donna said. "I'm not trying to sabotage anything subconsciously. I'm telling you, there's something up with him. He's too... I don't know. *Too much.*"

Tricia laughed. "You're probably sitting over there with your hair tied back and a bowl of ice cream in your hand. That's why you don't want to go."

"You have no idea what you're talking about."

"Give him one more chance," Tricia urged her.

"What is it to you?" Donna asked. "I thought he was just a friend of the family."

"He's my brother's best friend. I've known Randall since he was in middle school. He's a good dude. I like him. I think you two would be good for each other."

"Alright," Donna conceded with a sigh. "I'm gonna get up and put this ice cream away and do my hair, and if something goes wrong tonight, you owe me *big*."

"I knew you had some ice cream," Tricia said. "What kind is it? Butter pecan?"

"No, vanilla," Donna said with a chuckle. "Like I said, you have no idea what you're talking about."

When she got off the phone, Donna was surprised to see her son standing in the doorway.

"Boy, what are you doing?"

"Nothing," he said. "Walking around. Are you going on a date tonight?"

Donna was getting frustrated with this little eavesdropper, but she tried to take his feelings into consideration.

"Come here," she told him.

Colton entered the room reluctantly.

"Sit down."

He did so.

Donna studied his face and smiled. "Eavesdropping on my phone calls is a bad thing to do. Do you understand that?"

Colton nodded. "But I asked you if you had a boyfriend, and you told me, 'No.'"

"I don't have a boyfriend," Donna said. "But I was talking to Tricia about a guy she wants me to go out with. Does that bother you?"

He didn't respond.

"I know it does," Donna said. "I can see it in your eyes. Do you wanna talk about it?"

"What about Dad?"

Donna reached and rubbed the hair on the top of his head. "Colton, you know your father has been gone for over a year. It's been a year and a half."

"He's not gone, Mama. He's dead."

"Yes, baby. I know that."

"But you're already ready to go out with another man?"

"I have to move on," Donna said. "It's a part of life."

"But why do you have to do it *now*?"

Donna's heart bled for him. She feared that no matter what she said, he wouldn't understand.

"Baby, I'm 39 years old. I'll be forty soon. How long do you think I should wait before I see someone else?"

"Can't you wait until you're fifty?"

Donna frowned. "How about I don't see anyone at all, for the rest of my life? Would that be good for you?"

"That would be cool."

"And in the meantime, you can wait until you're fifty before you go out with any girls. Does that sound like a fair trade?"

He nodded. "Okay."

"You are such a liar," Donna said and laughed.

"Well, if you are going out with some guy, why is it such a secret?" her son asked.

"It's only a secret because you're sneaking around, picking up bits and pieces of my conversation."

"That's because you haven't told me anything."

Donna saw the truth in that statement. "Listen, Colton, just because I don't talk to you about something doesn't mean you have to do whatever you can to figure it out. If you walk by and see me on the phone, you need to keep it moving. You can ask me about it later, and if I *choose* to talk to you about it, I will. Otherwise you have to understand that I'm the mom, and I don't have to explain myself to you if I don't want to. You got it?"

Colton sighed and nodded.

"But since you asked," Donna said, "I have been talking to a man named Randall, and I'm going out with him tonight. Would you like to meet him?"

The boy nodded again, but he didn't seem sure of himself.

"Okay, I'll tell him to pick me up from here tonight," Donna said. "But for the record, Randall is not my boyfriend. I'm not sure how I feel about him yet."

119

"Randall's a stupid name," Colton said. "He's probably stupid."

Donna laughed, thinking he might be right on both points. "Here," she said and gave him the Blue Bell container. "Put this in the freezer, so I can go get dressed."

Colton took the ice cream. "Can I have some?"

"Yes, but make sure some of it gets put back in the freezer."

"There's not that much left," he said as he rose to his feet.

"It's more than half full," Donna countered.

Colton had left the room by then. "It's half empty," he called back to her.

"That's you being pessimistic," Donna said. "And *greedy!*"

●●●●●●●

Two hours later Donna was dressed in a black evening dress she hadn't worn in years. It was mostly loose-fitting, but it did get a little snug around her hips. Donna thought her curvy figure looked great in her bathroom mirror, and she was glad that she took Tricia's advice and didn't cancel her date. It felt good to get dressed up for a man. She wore her hair down in loose curls. She didn't use a lot of makeup, but she did apply lipstick and mascara.

Her heels were only three inches, but they made her long legs appear even longer. Donna felt like a model when she strutted out of her bedroom and into Colton's room down the hall. After their talk, she thought they had reached a level of understanding. But the boy's eyes bugged when he saw how his mother was dressed for the night.

"You're wearing *that*?"

"What? What's wrong with it?"

"Where are y'all going, that you have to dress like that?"

Donna laughed. "Boy, quit tripping." But she saw that he was serious. "Colton, it's just a dress."

"But, but you got your legs all out."

Donna looked down and saw that her dress stopped just above her knees. "I'm not showing a lot of legs. You're being silly."

"And your chest."

120

Donna did have some cleavage showing, but it wasn't an absurd amount.

"Colton, you can't be serious. This dress isn't even tight on me."

He opened his mouth, most likely to complain about something else, but the doorbell rang. They both looked in that direction.

Donna suddenly regretted her decision to let Randall pick her up. She thought it would help Colton feel better about the situation, if he was aware that she was going on a date, and he had a chance to meet Randall himself. But judging by his reaction to her outfit, Donna knew he wouldn't respond well – regardless of who she was seeing.

"Is that him?"

"Yes, Colton. But you don't have to meet him, if you don't want to. I'll be back in a few hours."

He didn't respond, and he didn't make any moves to get up.

"Okay," Donna said. "Be good. Don't go looking for your cellphone, and, you know, be good. If there's an emergency, you can use the house phone to call me."

The boy still didn't respond. He continued to stare at her dress like she was leaving the house in a bikini.

"I... We're gonna have to talk about this later," Donna said and backed out of the room. She had frantic butterflies flitting around in her stomach by the time she made it to the front door.

She plastered a smile on her face when she opened it. Randall stood on the porch looking handsome and eager in a short-sleeved button-down that wasn't tucked in.

"Hi," she told him.

"How you doing?" Randall asked and smiled pleasantly.

He really was a good looking guy. Randall was tall and fair-skinned, with a completely bald head and one of the most perfectly trimmed moustache/goatee combos Donna had ever seen. He was thin, not skinny, but not particularly muscular either. His eyebrows were bushy, his lips thin and pink. His shoes were shiny and without a scuff.

"Mmm mmm mmm," he hummed. "Girl you look good enough to eat!"

As Donna's face registered horror from the comment, Randall looked over her shoulder and said, "Hey, little man. Didn't see you there. How's it going? My name is Randall."

Donna looked back in time to see Colton walking away. She was both surprised that he followed her out and embarrassed by Randall's comment.

"Well, that was rude," Randall said, the smile slipping from his face.

"You just said I look good enough to eat," Donna murmured. "I wouldn't want to meet you either, if I was him."

"I'm sorry," Randall said. "I didn't know he was there."

"Whatever. Lemme, lemme get my purse. Wait here."

She left him in the foyer and disappeared down the hallway. Donna retrieved her purse from her bed and then stopped by Colton's room on the way back. She stepped inside and found him sitting at his desk with a huge scowl distorting his features. She was surprised by how nervous she felt, as if *he* was the parent, and she was the ungrateful child going out with a boy her dad didn't approve of.

"You alright?" she asked him.

"I don't like him." He kept his eyes on the desk, refusing to look up at her.

"I know that wasn't the best first impression–"

"He's a dog, and you can do better."

"Colton, you can't completely judge someone you've only known for two seconds."

"Then I don't wanna talk about it anymore."

Donna folded her arms over her stomach and held back much of what she wanted to say to him. "We'll talk about this when I get back."

"I'm still gonna feel the same way."

"I said we'll talk about it when I get back," she said sternly but quietly.

When she got back to the front room, Randall was smiling again.

"Is everything okay?"

"Yes," Donna said, and she forced a smile. "Where you taking me?"

"Anywhere you wanna go. I'll get tickets to the *moon*, if it'll make you happy."

Ugh! She was getting tired of his stupid come-ons. She would've ended the date right then if it wasn't for Colton. She didn't want him to think that his tantrum led to her rejecting Randall, lest he try it again and again.

"Listen, chill with all of those cheesy lines," she told him. "It's already got me in trouble with my son, and I personally don't think it's flattering. Just be yourself, and let's try to get to know each other. Okay?"

His mouth fell open. "Uh, oh, okay. My bad. I didn't mean to cause any trouble. I think you look really good tonight, and I wanna take you to Manhattan."

Manhattan was one of the hottest restaurants in the city. Donna had never been, and she was eager to check it out.

"That sounds nice," she said flatly. "Thank you. I'm ready to go."

●●●●●●●

Manhattan was as nice as Donna imagined, but the company was subpar, as expected. Midway through the meal, Donna was kicking herself for agreeing to go out with such a loser. This was her life, not Colton's and not Tricia's. She knew she should've followed her gut instincts. Now she was bored out of her mind as Randall went on and on about his job, the bright future that lay ahead of him at the dealership and the fully loaded automobile he drove them there in.

Even one and a half margaritas couldn't stop Donna from staring at him blankly, with her lips parted, her cheek resting on her fist, wondering how long it would take for him to notice that she was contemplating walking out of there at any moment.

"That S-Class has a 449 horse power V8. It can go from zero to sixty in 4.8. Smooth as a seal swimming in the ocean. Got a built in GPS. The best sound system money can buy. And I know you saw those LED lights glowing in the wood panel. Nobody else is doing it like that. That's one of the best cars on the road. It's over 120 thou' fully loaded. Even at a nice restaurant like this, the valet was looking like we were Jay Z and Beyonce. You see him?"

Donna sighed loudly. "Don't you get to drive any car on the lot, since you're a car salesman?" she asked.

123

Randall's smile slipped. "Well, yeah. But they don't let *anybody* do that. I've been working there for twelve years. I'm a *senior* salesperson. Aside from me and the owner, and two other guys, no one's driving a mean machine like that off the lot – unless they pay for it first."

"But it's not your car," Donna said. "Why do you keep bragging about it, like it's yours or something?"

Randall's frown intensified. "I didn't say it was mine. I love cars. I can appreciate their power and beauty. Sorry if I'm boring you. It's just something I'm interested in."

"That's cool," Donna said. "But it's starting to sound like you're trying to sell *me* a car."

He grinned. "No. I don't mix business with pleasure. But if you'd like to get yourself an S-Class, I can certainly make that happen for you."

Donna rolled her eyes. She finally put a finger on exactly what she didn't like about Randall: He was cocky. Too damned cocky. He reminded her of another cocky sonofabitch who built a perfect life for her and Colton and then ruined it all by having an affair and getting himself killed in the process.

And to make matters worse, Randall wasn't even as successful as Nolan. If you're going to walk around thinking you're God's gift to the planet, at least get your shit together. *Car salesman* was a good job, but it wasn't good enough for him to be strutting like a peacock. And the more she thought about it, he wasn't event that handsome.

"You know," Randall said. "I think we got off on the wrong foot."

That's because you have nothing but left feet! Donna thought. "Yeah, *constantly*," she said.

"Are you still upset about your son?"

Donna hadn't thought about Colton since they got to the restaurant. She shook her head. "No."

"Good," he said.

"I'm sorry for the way he acted."

"Thank you. It did ruffle my feathers a little bit."

"Really?" Her voice was drenched with sarcasm, but he didn't notice.

"Yeah," Randall said. "He was kinda disrespectful, don't you think?"

Donna chuckled. *You got some nerve.* "All he did was walk away from you," she said.

"And you don't find that disrespectful, for a boy to walk away when a man is talking to him?"

This argument was escalating quickly. Donna felt like she should back down, but she was sick of cocky men running off at the mouth whenever they felt the need to. Maybe everything Randall said wasn't the *end-all be-all*. Did he ever think about that?

"Colton's not a *boy*. He's fifteen years old."

"He's a juvenile. An adolescent."

"And you two have about the same level of maturity."

"Oh, you got jokes. Does that make it better for you, to laugh it off rather than deal with your *boy's* problems?"

"He didn't have a problem until you walked into my house and disrespected me with your dumb ass catcall, like it was a strip club or something. I'm not going to get mad at my son, when he deserved to get an attitude with you."

"You didn't seem to have a problem with it when I said it," Randall said. "It didn't stop you from hopping in that S-Class."

Donna didn't have a comeback for that because he was right. She forced herself to come on this date, and now she was paying the price. She could be at home right now, lounging in the den with an empty pint of Blue Bell.

"Thank you for a lovely evening," she said and tossed her napkin onto the table.

Randall watched her with a half-smile. "You gon' walk out on me?"

Donna nodded. "Yup." She saw that her margarita was still half-full. No need to waste that. She downed it quickly while he watched.

"But I'm not ready to go yet," he said.

"That's okay," Donna replied, rising to her feet. "I'll call a cab."

He chuckled. "You gon' waste all that money on a cab, when you can just wait for me?"

"Yes. I'd rather get in a car *with a complete stranger* than step foot in your Mercedes Benz S-Class – that isn't even yours."

"You don't deserve to be in an S-Class," he grunted. "You probably used to niggas that drive lowriders and shit. I don't know what Tricia was thinking, trying to hook me up with somebody like you."

"That's the first thing we ever agreed on," Donna said. "What the hell was Tricia thinking?"

She left the table and went to the lobby to call for a ride. Instead of a cab, she phoned Tricia, but she didn't answer. She called Kendra instead, and she said she'd be there in about thirty minutes.

Donna was still waiting for her friend when Randall strolled by on his way out of the restaurant. She pretended to be deeply involved with an app on her cellphone, but she felt Randall staring at her, and she heard him snickering as he walked past.

A class act all the way. Tricia was going to get an earful for this one!

●●●●●●●

When she got home, Colton emerged from his bedroom and stood stiffly in the hallway.

"Why you back so early?"

"Me and Randall didn't get along, so I left."

Donna went and plopped down on the couch. She kicked off her shoes and popped a few kinks out of her neck. It felt good to be home.

"Come here," she said, patting the spot next to her.

Colton entered the room and sat down with her. He expected to be reprimanded for the way he behaved earlier.

Donna surprised him by saying, "I appreciate you for trying to stick up for your dear, old ma."

Colton still looked angry, and he didn't respond.

"However," Donna said, "you're not old enough to decide when to be respectful to adults or not. Until you talk to me first, you need to be respectful to *all* adults – no matter how wrong you think they are. Do you understand that?"

He nodded.

"I know you don't want me to go out with anyone," she continued. "I've always been with your father, and I know it's hard for you to wrap your mind around anything past that. All I ask is that you try to understand my side of it, too. I'll be 40 years old in a few months, and your dad has been gone for a long time. I know

126

you love me, but I need more than you can offer. Just like even though I love you, you still like girls at your school, right?"

He nodded.

"So if I do go out with another man, you're gonna be understanding and nice to him, right?"

He scratched his head. "Can you wait until I go to college?"

Donna chuckled. "Is that what you really want?"

"Parents are supposed to put their children's needs in front of their own," Colton said.

Donna laughed. "Where'd you hear that from?"

"TV."

"Don't believe everything you see on TV."

Colton chuckled. After a few moments he asked, "Do you miss Dad?"

"Of course I do."

"I think that's why I got mad," he said. "I keep thinking about how he would feel, you know, about you going out with another man."

Donna understood that. But she wondered if Colton would still have such reverence for his father if he knew about Ms. Bettye Sanders. Unfortunately, she would never know.

"I'm sure your father would want me to be happy," she said, "just like you should. Anyway, I was thinking that since my date is over, me and you could watch a movie tonight. Want me to make some popcorn?"

Colton's eyes brightened. "Yeah. Can I pick the movie?"

"Sure. But no blood and guts, please."

"Can I have my phone and Xbox back?" he asked as he rose to his feet.

"No. Not for another week."

"Even though you're mean, I still love you."

"Why thank you," Donna said with a laugh. "Then I guess I must be doing this parenting thing exactly right."

CHAPTER TWELVE
DRY ERASE

For happy hour the following Friday, Donna and her friends went to the Blue Mesa Grill near the university and had blue margaritas with free quesadillas until 6:30. Donna hadn't seen Tricia since their last outing, and she was eager to tell her about Randall's foolishness. But Tricia had already talked to Randall, and he had a story of his own.

"He said you're bougie."

Donna's eyes widened, but she had to finish the food in her mouth before she could respond. "*What?*"

The restaurant was mostly full at that hour. The sound of sizzling fajita plates coupled with the smell of onions and salsa and bell peppers gave Donna a voracious appetite. She'd already eaten more than she planned on. But she wasn't officially on a diet, so she kept scooping tortilla chips in the salsa bowl on their table.

Donna and her crew weren't the only black women in the restaurant, but they were the sexiest. A few handsome patrons had been trying to get their attention for the past half hour, but no one at the table was interested. Tricia was happily married, Kendra's latest boy toy had a seemingly endless supply of money, and Donna had a new friend that she had taken a liking to.

"He said you complained about *everything*," Tricia reported. "He said he picked you up in a brand new Benz, and all you were worried about was whether he owned it, or if he just got to drive it because he worked at the dealership."

Donna gave Kendra a look. "Does that even sound like me?"

Kendra shrugged. "I don't know."

"*Girl, you do know!*" Donna said with a laugh. "You know I'm not like that!"

"Did you ask him if he owned the car?" Tricia asked her.

Donna shook her head at her. "It's funny how the story gets all discombobulated, depending on who you get it from."

"You gonna answer the question?" Tricia said. "Sounds like you stalling."

"No, it sounds like you believe that *creepazoid* over me. I am so disappointed in you."

Tricia looked at Kendra with a grin. "You notice how she's not answering the question, right?"

Kendra laughed.

"I did ask him that," Donna said finally. "But only because he was throwing it in my face so much. *Ooh, look at the wood panel. Ooh, you know how many horses there are under the hood? Ooh, did you see how they looked at us when we pulled up, like we're Jay Z and Beyonce? Did you see my ride? Tell me you saw my ride!*"

They all laughed.

"So, yeah," Donna said. "I got so sick of hearing about that damned car, I finally told him, '*Is this even your car? Why are you bragging so much about it, if it's not even yours?*'"

"Maybe he was trying to sell you one," Kendra offered.

"That's what I said!" Donna exclaimed. "I told him that he was either trying to impress me with a car that wasn't his, or he was trying to sell me one. He said, '*Naw, but if you want to get one, I can hook you up.*'"

Tricia found this whole story amusing. "That doesn't even sound like Randall."

"Obviously you never went out with Randall," Donna said. "And when he wasn't talking about that stupid car, he was saying a bunch of other inappropriate shit that started to get on my nerves."

"Like what?" Kendra asked.

"Well, when I first answered the door for him, he said I looked so good, he wanted to eat me up, or something like that."

"No he didn't," Kendra said.

"Girl, yes he did. And the worst part about it was Colton was standing right there."

Tricia and Kendra's eyes widened.

"Yeah, and you know he was pissed," Donna said.

"Why'd you let him come to your house?" Tricia asked.

"Good question," Donna said. "But let me get this straight; you tried to hook me up with a man who you *know* I shouldn't give my home address to...?"

"No, I didn't say that. I just thought you wouldn't want a man you don't know around your son."

"Well I know that now," Donna said. "But this is the first man I ever dated since I had Colton. Forgive me for not understanding the rules right away."

"What did Colton say to him?" Kendra asked.

"Nothing. Randall told him, '*What's up,*' and Colton just walked away."

"Damn," Kendra said. "*Awkwaaard.*"

"*Incredibly,*" Donna agreed. "And then Randall had the nerve to complain about it at dinner, like Colton did something wrong."

"Wow," Tricia said. "He didn't tell me all that."

"Of course not," Donna said.

"So you left him at the restaurant?" she asked.

"No, technically he left me. After we argued about that stupid car, we argued about Colton, and then I got up and left. But I had to wait for Kendra to come pick me up because the person responsible for the whole thing wouldn't answer her phone!"

Donna gave Tricia an accusing look.

"Sorry. You know I would've been there for you," Tricia said. "If I would've known all of that went down, I definitely would've come. But Richard took me out for our anniversary."

"Where'd you go?" Kendra asked.

"He took me to the Bass Hall to see The Color Purple, and then we went out to eat. And he got us a room at the Hilton."

"Damn, big spender," Donna said.

"It was nice," Tricia said. The memory made her glow with delight. "No kids all night. Richard can still be very romantic, when he makes the time for it."

Donna was happy for her friend. After more than a decade of marriage, her and Richard were still going strong and very much in love. But their happy marriage made her think about Nolan. They would've been married seventeen years now, if he hadn't died en route to an ongoing affair. Or maybe Donna would've eventually found out about Bettye Sanders, and she and Nolan would be divorced by now.

"Is Colton still mad about Randall?" Kendra asked.

"No, I think we're good," Donna said. "I told him I agreed that Randal was disrespectful. But Colton was disrespectful, too. He said he doesn't like the idea of me going out with men."

"That's understandable," Tricia said. "Nolan was the only man he ever saw you with."

"Yeah, but he's holding Nolan in such high regards because he doesn't know about the affair," Donna said.

Tricia disagreed. "Even if he knew, he still wouldn't want to see his mama with another man."

"Are you ever going to tell him?" Kendra asked.

Donna shook her head. "No. Nolan's memory is all he has left. It would break his heart, if he knew."

Her cellphone rang. Donna dug it from her purse and smiled when she saw the incoming number. She answered and told Marcel to, "Hold on," as she rose from her seat. "I gotta take this call," she said to her friends before stepping away from the table.

"Where you going?" Tricia asked.

"To the bar for a second." When she got there, Donna sat with her back to her friends' table and gave her new friend her full attention. "Hey. What's going on?"

"Nothing much," Marcel said. "Are you busy? Am I disturbing you?"

"No. I'm at the Blue Mesa with my friends."

"Your Friday night happy hour?"

"Yeah. It's kind of a ritual."

"I don't want to keep you from your friends," Marcel said. "I can call you later."

"No, it's alright," Donna said. "They're not talking about anything. I got a few minutes."

"How was your day?"

Even over the phone, Marcel's deep voice gave Donna chills. But at the same time, he made her whole body feel warm. She sat with both elbows on the bar, grinning like a school girl.

"It was fine. How about yours?"

"It was okay," Marcel said. "I'm working on a pretty big case, but at the end of the day, I think it's a waste of resources."

"Why do you say that?"

"Because the mayor only cares about numbers. The chief has to deliver a bunch of arrests each week, even if it's only low level players. I wanna take down the big fish, but they don't think it's worth the surveillance. It can get frustrating."

"Sounds like it."

"I've been thinking about you," he said. "A lot."

Donna blushed.

"Even your hands intrigue me," he said. "I wonder if you have ink from your dry erase markers on your fingers right now."

Donna couldn't stop smiling as she checked.

"Do you?" he asked.

"I do. It's real hard to get off."

"Is your hair still in a ponytail?"

"No. It's down. It's pretty frizzy today."

"I would ask for a run-down of your whole outfit," Marcel said. "But you know what would be better?"

Donna had an idea, but she said, "What's that?"

"If I could see you for myself."

"That would be nice."

"Tell me the truth," he said. "Are you avoiding me?"

"No. Why do you say that?"

"I don't know. I feel like I'm getting conflicting signals," Marcel said. "We seem to have a good connection when we talk, but sometimes you say you'll call me back, but you don't. And you were noncommittal when I asked you to have dinner with me."

Donna's heart sank. Marcel's complaints were valid, but she didn't mean to make him feel that way. The problem was not him, it was Colton. After the Randall disaster, Donna was not eager to tell her son that there might be *another* man in the picture. She didn't want him to think that she was so desperate for companionship, she'd go from one to another so quickly.

It was really a timing issue. Again Donna kicked herself for not cancelling that second date with Randall. If she hadn't let him come to her house, then Marcel would've been the first man Colton knew about. And she was sure things would have gone a lot better. Marcel wouldn't have made a wolf call the moment she answered the door for him – or at least he didn't strike her as the kind of guy who would do that.

But now she couldn't make any major or minor moves until she was sure. She couldn't invite Marcel to her home, and she didn't even feel comfortable talking to him on the phone when Colton was there. That boy had ears like a bat. As a result, Donna only talked to Marcel sparingly, which was why she readily put her Friday night with her girlfriends on hold to take his call.

"I do want to see you," she said. "And I'm sorry I didn't call you back last night."

"Do you really want to see me?"

"I do," Donna said, grinning broadly. She closed her eyes and imagined all of his chocolaty sexiness.

"I'm sure I want to see you *more*," Marcel said. "Can we plan a date? Are you free tomorrow?"

Donna didn't have anything planned, but unfortunately Colton didn't either. He had his Xbox back now, but it wouldn't keep him busy enough to not notice his mother getting dressed for a date.

"How about lunch on Monday," she offered. "I have a planning period right before my lunch break, so I can leave for an hour and a half."

"I'll take it," Marcel said quickly. He was actually scheduled to do surveillance on a drug house that afternoon, but he was pretty sure he could get someone to cover for him. "What time can you leave?"

"Eleven-fifteen."

"I'll be dressed for work," he said. "Is that okay?"

"What do you wear for work?"

"Tee shirt and jeans."

Donna thought about how good he looked in that outfit when she met him two weeks ago. She knew she might be distracted by the way his muscles rippled under the thin fabric of a tee-shirt, but that was a risk she looked forward to.

"That's fine," she said. "I won't be wearing anything special, either."

"Nothing special like that sexy outfit you had on when we met?" he asked.

"Yeah, I guess so. That wasn't sexy."

"I disagree. I thought you looked very nice. Very."

Her face flushed with heat. "Thank you."

"Do I make you nervous?" he asked.

133

She giggled. "A little."

"You make me nervous, too."

"Yeah, right. A big, strong guy like you?"

"My heart's the same size as anybody else's."

Donna thought about how he talked about his son when they met at Chili's, and she knew that was true. That was actually one of the things she found most endearing about him.

"Go ahead and get back to your friends," he said, "and I'll find something to do tonight *other* than think about you."

"You can think about me, if you want," Donna flirted.

Marcel chuckled. "Yeah. I better go, before I say something inappropriate. Have a nice evening."

"You too. Bye."

When Donna got back to her table, her friends wanted her to spill the beans.

"Who was that – that you had to go *waaaay* over there to talk to?" Tricia asked.

"I saw you twirling your finger in your hair, like you're in high school," Kendra said.

"I was not twirling my finger in my hair."

"Yes you were," Tricia confirmed. "What's his name? Was that Randall?"

"Eww! No. It – *eww*!"

Tricia laughed at her.

"Who was it?" Kendra asked.

"I was talking to Marcel."

"Who's Marcel?"

"Sounds sexy," Tricia said.

"He is, and y'all already met him. Well, you saw him at least. Remember when we went to Chili's a couple of weeks ago?"

Kendra's jaw dropped. "That man at the bar?"

Donna nodded.

Tricia frowned. "I thought we agreed not to talk to him."

"No, *you* said I shouldn't talk to him."

"Right," Tricia said. "We came to an agreement."

Donna laughed. "I don't know if you got the memo or not, but your word is not law."

"But wasn't he depressed?" Kendra asked. "Didn't you say his son died?"

"And he was drinking alone," Tricia recalled. "We said that's a bad sign."

"He's not depressed," Donna said. "I talk to him all the time. It makes me happy, whenever I see his number on the caller ID." Her smile was deep and rich. "He's fine. He was feeling a little down the day we met, but he's not like that every day. And he wasn't at the bar by himself the whole time. His brother met him there, remember?"

"How long ago did his son die?" Kendra asked.

"Eight months ago."

"What happened to him?"

"He got killed," Donna said. "It had something to do with a burglary that went bad. I don't have all the details, because I try not to bring it up when we talk."

"You think he's ready to get in a relationship so soon?" Tricia asked.

"It was his son that died," Donna said. "Not his *wife*."

"He's divorced, right?" Kendra said.

"Yes."

"Do you know why he got divorced?" Tricia asked.

Donna shook her head. "No. We haven't talked about it."

"Don't you think you should find out?"

"No. It's not a big priority," Donna replied. "People get divorced all the time. That doesn't mean they're damaged goods."

"But if he got divorced, and then he lost his son, he's probably going through a lot," Tricia argued.

"Okay, but that still doesn't mean he's damaged goods," Donna said. "I like him. He's smart and he's funny, and he's not full of himself like *some people*." She paused to give Tricia the evil eye. "He makes me feel special," she said and her smile returned.

"What does he do for a living?" Kendra asked.

"He's a cop."

"He is fine," Kendra acknowledged. "That was his brother he left the restaurant with that day?"

Donna nodded.

"He's fine, too," Kendra said. "That's awesome, Donna. I hope it works out for y'all. Have you told Colton yet?"

"No. I can't tell him yet because of what happened with the last guy I went out with..." She shot Tricia another look. "I'm not telling Colton anything until I think it might be serious."

135

"I'm happy for you, too," Tricia finally decided. "But if he starts crying the next time he brings up his son, you'd better start running."

"He didn't cry the first time he told me about him," Donna said. "And it's only been *eight months*. I wouldn't leave him high and dry if he did cry. What's wrong with you? Why you being so cold-hearted?"

"I don't know," Tricia said. "But I got some *bad vibes*."

"You have bad vibes about a man you know nothing about," Donna said. "But you had *good vibes* about a man you've known since you were in high school? What does that tell you?"

"Randall never acted like that, the whole time I've known him," Tricia said.

"Well consider yourself lucky. He walked off *laughing* when he left me at the restaurant. I was so embarrassed."

"Yeah, she was pretty upset when I picked her up," Kendra told Tricia. "She said you and her weren't friends anymore."

"*Oh, I'm so sorry, Donna*," Tricia said. If she wasn't smiling, they might have thought she was really forlorn. "What can I do to make it better?"

Donna picked up her menu. "You're gonna have to feed me. They stopped serving free quesadillas already. How much money you bring?"

Tricia laughed. "None. But I got my bank card, and I just got paid."

"Good," Donna said as she scanned the delectable dishes. "'Cause tonight, I think I'm gonna be an *expensive* date."

136

CHAPTER THIRTEEN
EVERYTHING ON THE TABLE

On Monday afternoon, Marcel called Donna on her cellphone at 11:20 am, rather than enter the school and sign in at the front desk. Donna suggested that for his convenience, but also because the front office crew at Wedgewood Middle was sure to start gossiping if a fine man like Marcel signed in as a visitor and left the building with her.

Donna spotted his car the moment she exited the main entrance. Marcel drove a black Dodge Charger with racing wheels, racing stripes and dark tint on the windows. He hopped out to open the door for her, which was unexpected. No one had done that for her in years.

"Good afternoon, Ms. Hodge."

Marcel wore the jeans and tee shirt he promised. Donna was sure his shirt was at least XXL, but the fabric still had to stretch over his shoulders and chest. His arms looked massive as he held the door open for her. He had a fresh haircut, and his face was still clear of stubble.

Donna considered herself tall for a woman, but she was dwarfed when standing next to Marcel. He looked strong enough to pick her up and cradle her next to his chest. The thought made her giggle inwardly. Donna caught a whiff of his cologne as she stepped by him. She wasn't sure what brand it was, but she liked it.

She took a seat in the plush interior of his car and watched as Marcel walked around the front on his way back to the driver's side. Donna took advantage of the opportunity to admire him openly. Marcel was light on his feet, despite his size. His jeans fit him well. She never knew that she liked a nice ass on a man, but she found herself staring at Marcel's. Her smile was infectious when he took a seat next to her.

He looked into her eyes and told her, "You look very nice today."

Donna wore a black skirt with a white blouse. She took Marcel into consideration when she got dressed that morning. The blouse wasn't anything special, but the skirt hugged her hips and accentuated her small waistline. She wore her hair down and straight. She even put on a little make-up for him. A few of her peers already commented on how nice she looked today, but that didn't make her feel as good as when Marcel said it.

"Thank you," she replied.

"I've never met a teacher as pretty as you," he said. "When we met, I was thinking about how hard it would be to concentrate, if I was in your class."

Donna grinned. "I'm sure you would've been fine. I've had a few crushes, but nothing out of control."

"Do you offer any after school tutoring?" Marcel asked as he started the car.

The bass in his voice made Donna's heart kick pleasantly in her chest. The Charger roared to life, and they rolled slowly out of the parking lot.

"You need tutoring?" she asked.

"Yes," he said. "I forgot how to figure out the value of x."

She chuckled. "It depends on the equation."

"I think I need help with all of that stuff. Are you willing to teach me?"

She knew he wasn't serious, but it sure sounded like he was. She blushed and had to look away for a moment.

"Sure."

"Do I still make you nervous?" he asked.

"No. A little."

"You make me nervous, too," he said. "But I like it."

Donna smiled. "I do too."

Marcel's smile was mischievous. Donna felt her palms becoming moist.

"So, where to?" he asked.

"There's a Subway on Altamesa."

"Okay. I know where it is. You sure you don't want to go anywhere fancier?"

"No. Subway's fine. Did you have a good day so far?" she asked. "You worked today, right?"

"Yeah. It was okay; just watching a bunch of corner kids ruin their lives."

"What's a corner kid?"

"The youngsters who sell dope for the big boys. They handle all of the hand-to-hand transactions. The bosses leave them out in the open, usually on street corners."

"Is that who you're after, the corner kids?"

"Yes, unfortunately," Marcel said. "But I think I told you, I consider it a waste of time. The corner kids are mostly juveniles, so we can't keep them off the streets for very long. And they're easily replaceable. I wanna take down the bosses, but we have to arrest the corner kids to make the numbers look good. Supposedly it makes the neighborhood look good, too."

"When do you get to go after the bosses?"

"That's the million-dollar question," Marcel said. "I've been asking for years. When I get an answer, I'll let you know."

"That must be frustrating," Donna said. She heard about similar problems from Freddie, back when Nolan was in the city council. She wasn't surprised that nothing had changed since then.

"Were you busy yesterday?" Marcel asked.

"No," Donna said. "I'm sorry I didn't call you back."

"That's okay."

"No, really it's not. I've been meaning to talk to you about my son."

"Let me guess. He doesn't like me."

"It's not that. He doesn't even know about you. I know he doesn't like the idea of me going out with anyone, so I haven't said anything to him yet. I saw that you called after church, but I spent most of the day with Colton, and I didn't have a chance to call you back. I'm sorry."

"That's fine. I understand."

Donna was surprised that his response was so different than Randall's.

"It's nice of you to say that, but I know it's not fair to you."

139

"Your family should always come first," Marcel insisted. "That's important."

"It won't be like this for long," she said. "I do want you two to meet, at some point."

"Whenever you're ready. I understand that these things take time. I'm not pushing you, and I'm glad you explained the situation to me. Now it won't feel so bad when you don't call me back."

"You're *too* understanding. Are you sure I didn't make you feel bad?"

"Just a little. But I feel a hundred percent better now. I'm glad you agreed to have lunch with me."

"Me too," Donna said. She sat back and relaxed. It felt good to get that off her chest. But there were a few more things they had to discuss before she reached the next level of comfort and trust with him.

●●●●●●●

At Subway they dined on salads rather than the sandwiches the chain was best known for. Donna hoped to put all of their issues on the table during the date, because there was no need for them to go any further if there were any serious red flags.

Sitting across from him at a small table made her feel a little loopy in the head, but Donna tried to overlook his serious, brown eyes and his unreal physique and focus on the matter at hand. She used Marcel's complaints about the police department as a transition to her bad luck story about Nolan. She told him about his death and his cheating and the trouble she had with his mistress afterwards. Marcel listened quietly. He held his peace until the very end.

"You're a strong woman, to get through all of that right after losing your husband. I commend you."

"Thank you. I didn't feel like a strong woman at the time, but I do now. The experience changed me, I think for the better. But I'm a lot less trusting now. I'm not sure if that's good or not."

"I think it's a good thing," Marcel said. "You have to be careful nowadays. You never know what people's intentions are."

"I agree. What about your ex-wife? Do you mind telling me about her, why y'all broke up?"

Marcel sat back in his chair, and his expression changed slightly.

"I'm sorry," Donna said. "I was just curious. You don't have to if–"

"No, it's alright," he said. "I was just thinking of where to begin with her. Coleen, she was my first real love. I tried my best, but I think our relationship was doomed from the beginning."

Donna leaned forward with her elbows on the table. "Why do you say that?"

"She wanted to be a stay-at-home mom," Marcel said. "I knew that before we got married, and I was okay with it. I didn't make very much money as a cop, in the early years. But I worked a lot of overtime, and I took a second job working security overnight at Walmart."

"I'll bet that was hard."

"It was, but I was willing to do whatever I could to make her happy, to provide for our family. But when our son was born, things were different. I was never there for his first *anything*, and it started to get to me. I re-did our budget, so that I could pay for everything without the second job, but we had to make a few cutbacks. I didn't think it was that big of a deal, but Coleen did. And that's when we started arguing a lot.

"After a while I started to wonder if we were really arguing over money, or if we were arguing because I was home a lot more than I used to be. Sometimes she'd make me feel like my presence irritated her."

"I'm sure that hurt a lot," Donna said. Her eyes were filled with compassion.

"It did," Marcel said. "But I had my son there, and most of what Coleen did didn't bother me. My son loved me, regardless of how she felt, and that's all that mattered."

Donna nodded. She understood that very well.

"When I got promoted to homicide," he went on, "I thought that would solve our problems. I made more money, and I wasn't home as much. I knew Coleen wanted me out of her hair sometimes. But then she started complaining about my work schedule. I was on-call almost every night. I had to leave the house at three am sometimes.

"I started to get upset because I explained the situation to her before I took the job. I told her there's no time table on when

141

someone gets killed. I didn't understand how she could get mad at me for leaving but still treat me like she didn't want me there when I came home. She couldn't give me a good explanation for that.

"That's when I began to realize that it wasn't me, it was her. There was something she wanted that I probably couldn't provide. But I still tried, though. I tried to make our marriage work for the next ten years. It broke my heart when I found out she was having an affair, but it wasn't the end of the world for me. I knew we'd been simply going through the motions for a long time.

"I didn't look for revenge when she filed for divorce. Coleen knew she was wrong, so she didn't do anything stupid, like try to take the house or my car. She did try to get full custody of our son, but that's where I drew the line. I wouldn't let her leave me for another man and take Jaylen, too.

"We agreed on joint-custody, but that didn't stop the fights. Coleen tried to micromanage everything. She took me to court, complaining about how Jaylen got home from school and who looked after him when I had to work late. The judge sided with me, but in retrospect, I think Coleen was right about some of the things she said. My son got killed in my home while I was at work. That, that was the most devastating thing that has ever happened to me."

Donna's heart bled for him. Marcel maintained composure up to that point, but mentioning his son took a lot out of him. His shoulders slumped. His expression became downcast. Donna wanted to end the conversation, but if they were to continue dating, she had to know how badly he was hurting.

She could probably handle it either way, but she wasn't the only one she had to look out for. At some point she'd have to introduce Marcel to Colton, and she could not do that if he had emotional problems that were unresolved. She knew that might be a little insensitive, but Marcel was right about family being the most important thing to her.

She took a deep breath before asking, "How did he die?"

Marcel sighed and cleared his throat. "There were two burglars. They broke into my house, around the time Jaylen got out of school. They were both kids. One was sixteen, the other one was seventeen. Jaylen surprised them when he got home that day. One of them had a gun. He panicked and started shooting.

142

Jaylen got hit in the chest. They said he died instantly, but I know that's not true."

Marcel swallowed roughly. He looked to the ceiling, in an effort to keep his tears in. It worked, but in his mind's eye the restaurant was now covered with blood. He saw the blood on the carpet in his home. He saw the drag marks and the small, bloody handprints. Initially the homicide detectives who worked Jaylen's case thought the killers moved his body from the kitchen to the front room. It was later determined that Jaylen crawled there himself, in an attempt to reach safety outside the front door.

He never made it, but it wouldn't have mattered if he did. The one bullet that entered his body severed an aortic artery. Only God could've put him back together in time, but it was God's will that Jaylen die at the age of twelve. Marcel blamed a lot of people for Jaylen's death, including himself and the man upstairs. But his counselor taught him that blame wasn't an effective response in situations like this. Marcel should focus his energy on acceptance and mourning and hopefully one day healing.

"The boys who killed him were both tried as adults," he said. "They could've been sentenced to death, but they got life without parole. I didn't want that, but the DA said it had to be one or the other. So now there's three little boys gone forever, instead of only Jaylen. I hated both of those punks for a long time, but I think they're too young to be locked up forever."

Donna was surprised to hear that, and she was heartbroken over his story. She looked more distressed than Marcel did. He didn't shed a tear, but Donna had to pluck a few tissues to blow her nose.

"I'm sorry."

"It's alright," he said.

"How are you doing?" she asked. "How has your recovery been?"

"It's slow," Marcel admitted. "Some days are better than others. The day I met you, that was one of my bad days. But thankfully I have more good days now."

"What about your ex-wife? You're not upset about the way she treated you, the way she left you?"

Marcel shook his head. "I never had to grieve for her. Well, I did, but that grieving started long before she asked for a divorce. By the time she left, I was good. All I cared about was

Jaylen. Losing him is what hurt me. They took away every..." His throat got stuck. He cleared it and closed his eyes for a moment.

Donna knew he was fighting back tears. In a way, she hoped he would let it out. But she knew he had to deal with this on his own terms.

"When I lost Jaylen, I lost everything I had. He was the only bright spot in my marriage. He was the only thing that made it feel like the time I spent with Coleen was actually worth something. Now... Now there's nothing."

Donna's expression seemed to collapse on itself as tears squirted from her eyes. She plucked more napkins. "I'm sorry."

"It's okay," he said.

"I don't know how you can get past that," she said. "I don't think I could."

"You'd be surprised what you can do, if you're put in a bad situation."

She knew that was true. When her lawyer first told her about Bettye Sanders, she thought she'd go crazy for sure. Yet she persevered. But Marcel's story seemed so much worse. Donna didn't think she would survive if something happened to Colton. She couldn't even bear to think about it.

"Are you sure you're okay?" she asked.

"Yes. But I think I ruined our first date with all of this heavy stuff." He forced a smile. "I don't wanna talk about this every time I see you. This is twice in a row. I'm worried about what you must think of me."

"I think you're strong," she said. "I think you're honest and compassionate. I think life dealt you a bad hand, but you made the most of it. You're stronger than I could ever be."

"I appreciate that, but I definitely don't want you to feel sorry for me. I'm glad we got all of this out in the open, and I hope we can move past it. I want you to treat me like a regular guy and stop worrying about how much I'm hurting."

"I don't mean to. You're right. I know that's not fair."

"I think you're a wonderful person," Marcel said.

He looked into her eyes. Donna found his stare to be hypnotizing. She couldn't look away.

"I hope I can see you again," he said. "And I'm okay if you hide me from your son, for now."

He smiled. Donna did, too.

144

"You're one of the most understanding men I've ever met."

"You're the prettiest woman I've ever gone out with," Marcel replied.

Donna's face flushed with heat. "You're just saying that."

"No. I'm serious. My ex-wife looks like a mud duck, compared to you."

She laughed. "I can't imagine you marrying anyone who looks like a *mud duck*."

"I love to see you smile," he said. "I like it a lot better than when you cry."

"Thank you. You have a nice smile, too."

He checked his watch. "Is your lunch over with?"

Donna checked her phone and was upset to see that it was. "Yeah. I guess I'd better get back to work."

"Will I see you again?"

Donna had a few reservations, but she didn't want to end their date on a bad note. "Yes. That would be nice."

"Awesome."

He stood and offered a hand to help her up. Even in the early days, Nolan was never that chivalrous.

"Thank you very much," she said, loving the feel of her hand in his.

●●●●●●●

"I don't look forward to these afternoon classes," Donna said as they pulled into the school's parking lot.

"Why not? The kids are too hyper?"

"Either that, or they've eaten too much, and they try to fall asleep on me. The closer it gets to the last bell, the more antsy they get. It's hard to keep them focused."

Marcel pulled to a stop near the main entrance. He felt good about their first date, but he didn't feel great. He wondered why Donna wanted to know so much about Jaylen and his ex-wife. She felt sorry for him, that much was clear. But Marcel didn't want her sympathy. He didn't need a shoulder to cry on. He had plenty of those already. And he definitely didn't want Donna to push him into a platonic bubble.

He appreciated her caring nature, and he appreciated the fact that she could relate to his loss. But the more time he spent around her, Marcel realized there were many more things he liked about Donna, like her eyes and her lips and the way she smiled at his mediocre jokes. He *really* liked her figure. Donna wasn't a thin woman. She was just right. The skirt she wore today hugged her hips pleasantly. Each time he touched her hand, a fire lit in his belly, and he longed to touch other parts of her body.

Marcel was respectful of women by nature, but beneath his warm smile and soft touch beat the heart of a lion. The lion had needs that hadn't been satiated in a long time. He could tell Donna that she was the woman he'd been looking for, but sometimes actions spoke louder than words.

She gathered her purse in her lap and said, "I really appreciate–"

Marcel cut her off with a hand that slipped smoothly behind her neck and implored her to come closer. A moment later his warm lips were on hers. Donna was so startled, her heartbeats stopped altogether. This did not seem like the Marcel she'd gotten to know thus far. This new creature was determined and demanding. Whether she would kiss him or not was not up for debate. She inhaled sharply, and as he lightly sucked her bottom lip, and her heart started to beat again – very quickly – she decided that she liked this side of Marcel very much.

She closed her eyes and gave in to the moment as a whirlwind of hope and doubt and longing and fear swirled around in her chest. She was vaguely aware that this was the first man she'd kissed since Nolan. That felt like a long, long time ago. Donna wasn't aware that parts of her body had been hibernating until the kiss awakened them. She felt her nipples harden. The swirling in her chest sank lower. It made her stomach tighten, and then it descended a little lower.

A sensation between her legs made Donna gasp. Marcel deepened the kiss, but he did not insert his tongue. Thank God! Donna was sure she'd go crazy if he did that. She nearly squirmed in the bucket seat as her clitoris woke up, bright-eyed and anxious.

Oh my God! Is this really happening?

In her wildest dream, Donna never imagined a kiss that could hit her from head to toe. She wanted to savor it. She wanted to leave with him. She wanted him to drive away and take her somewhere secluded, so she could experience the kiss over and over again.

But just as unexpectedly as it began, Marcel backed away. He looked over her shoulder, reminding Donna that she was, in fact, at her place of work. She looked back as well, blinking furiously. She used the momentary lack of eye contact to get her breathing under control and try to adjust the stunned look on her face.

There was no one outside the school at that moment. Even if there was, they wouldn't have been able to see anything past the dark tint on his car. But still. She was glad that he stopped when he did. She didn't think she would've been able tc.

When she turned back to Marcel, he was as cool as a cucumber. He didn't look like a man with issues. Even if he did, Donna was willing to work with those issues. She wasn't sure if she felt the same way before the kiss.

"You have to isolate x," she told him.

His eyes narrowed. "Say what?"

"To find the value of x, you have to isolate it; get it on one side of the equation, all by itself."

Marcel smiled.

Donna's body went weak. She wanted to kiss him again. There was no way it would hit her like a wrecking ball two times in a row, was there? Couldn't be.

"I'll call you later," he said.

She nodded. "Okay. I better go."

"Enjoy your day." He would've gotten out and opened the car door for her, but his pants were a little compromised at the moment.

Donna got out of the car and had to concentrate on her first few steps to keep from wobbling. Marcel watched her hips sway until she was halfway up the steps. He drove away with a whirlwind in his chest as well, but his was a little different.

Rather than elation at the prospect of a new love, Marcel had a depressed, lonely person inside him that told him he was a liar. *A dirty, stinking liar.* Donna wanted to clear the air today. She wanted to know how messed up his life was. Marcel told her most of it, but he didn't tell her the worst of it.

But it wasn't that bad, was it? It was just a hump, a little hurdle that he had to get over. He could do it. With a woman like Donna in his life, he could do anything. But if he truly believed that, why didn't he tell her?

A dirty, stinking liar.

Marcel's fingers began to tremble on the steering wheel. His expression was anxious, and fearful. He had to return to work, but a twisting in his gut told him that he wouldn't make it. Not unless...

"Oh shit, man. Damn," he whispered aloud in the quiet car. He knew that he could spend the next ten minutes trying to talk himself out of it, and then end up doing it anyway when he got to the stakeout. Or he could do it now, get it over with, and stop beating himself up. Stop feeling bad. Stop caring for a while.

He pulled over and found his stash in the car trunk, under the spare tire. Back inside the car, he held the mostly empty bottle of Crown Royal on his lap, admiring the maple syrup colored liquid. There were only two swallows left. He'd be good after that.

Marcel let his seat back and brought the bottle to his lips. Unlike his brother, he wasn't a pansy. Each swallow contained a full mouthful of alcohol. He didn't wince at the taste. The liquor burned so good. It warmed his chest and then his whole body. He felt the rush in every extremity. After two gulps he realized he miscalculated how much whisky was left in the bottle. But there was no sense in leaving such a small amount.

It took three and a half pulls to finish. Marcel didn't feel good immediately, but it didn't take long, only a few minutes. He didn't fret about Jaylen's bloody face or Donna after that. He was good. He was ready to take on the world.

CHAPTER FOURTEN
COLEEN

Donna made a clear effort to call Marcel more during the week. He was appreciative each time he got a chance to talk to her, and he didn't push it. The situation with Colton was delicate, and it wasn't something that should be rushed into. Donna never told him that she was waiting to make sure things worked out with them first, but Marcel figured that out on his own. Surprisingly, he agreed with her.

Marcel knew that his problem was getting the best of him, and he felt guilty for keeping it from Donna. His excuse was that they barely knew each other, and he told her enough sad stories already. She would surely head for the hills if she knew that he was having trouble cutting down on his drinking.

Marcel's other excuse was that he could fix himself on his own, if he took the time to seriously work on it. It wasn't like he was a raging alcoholic. He only started drinking heavily when Jaylen died. It was the only thing that helped him get to sleep those first few nights. But then he had to drink to get through the funeral. And he had to drink when he went back to his normal life in his empty home that reminded him of Jaylen at every turn.

He had to drink then. But he was better now. Nine months had passed. He didn't break down on a regular basis, and sometimes he even smiled when he thought of Jaylen. He only drank now to get to sleep. And after meals. Occasionally during work, but not that much. He didn't wake up and reach for his bottle. But if he was off that day, he did start drinking around noon.

Who are you kidding? his inner voice chided. *You drink every day, multiple times a day. You haven't gone one day without drinking since Jaylen died. You go to different liquor stores so the ladies at the register won't figure you out and call you what you are. You're a drunk. An alcoholic. Why don't you get some help, instead of dragging more people into your madness?*

The hell with you, Marcel told that annoying little voice. *You don't know shit. I'm alright. I can stop. Maybe not right away, but I can start cutting down. I can be completely sober in a month.*

You know you don't believe that.

Marcel grabbed the bottle of Crown Royal on his nightstand and checked the time on the digital clock behind it. It was 2:42 am on a Thursday night. He had to get up at 6:30 for work. But he couldn't work if he couldn't sleep, and he couldn't sleep if he kept talking to himself.

That was another good thing about alcohol. It shut down the voice in his head. It shut everything down. He took four healthy pulls of the brown stuff, loving the way it coated his insides with golden warmth. Clearly today wasn't the day he'd quit, but that didn't mean he couldn't quit. It was all about timing. Tomorrow he could start anew.

●●●●●●●

Donna couldn't get out for another date that weekend.

Marcel joked that she had another man in her life, but he wasn't really upset about it. Donna was the kind of woman worth waiting for, and Marcel could use the alone time to work on himself.

On Sunday he woke up bright and early and hit the gym. He didn't have to go far. He had everything he needed to stay fit and lean in his own home. One of the bedrooms had nothing but workout equipment; an elliptical machine, a weight bench and an exercise bike.

He got warmed up with three miles on the elliptical. Marcel was glad that smoking wasn't one of his vices, because he never would've made it. His powerful arms and legs cut through the air as he pushed his magnificent body further and harder. He was sweating steadily by the end of the second mile. It was a good sweat. He felt his body ejecting many of the toxins he forced upon it.

After the warm-up, he hit the weight bench, hoping to shred and tone, rather than make any gains. He was already big enough. He did a lot of reps with smaller weights to add definition to the muscles in his arms and chest and shoulders.

There was a tall mirror in the room. Marcel checked it when he was done. The torture he put himself through was already visible in the reflection. The only part of his body that he wasn't happy with was his stomach. He hadn't had a six-pack in years, but lately his belly wasn't as flat as it used to be. He didn't have a pudge yet, but things could get out of hand if he didn't keep an eye on it.

He knew that he'd lose the weight a lot quicker when he stopped drinking, which was another good reason to put the bottle down. So far he thought he was doing fairly well. He only had two beers when he went out with his brother yesterday. He drank more when he got home at midnight, but he knew that was the last stronghold. So far nothing helped him catch up to Mr. Sandman like Crown Royal did. Denying himself during the daylight hours was the main goal. If he could accomplish that, then he could honestly say he was not an alcoholic.

The doorbell rang before Marcel could start on his crunches. He wiped his face, neck and chest with a towel before he went to answer it. He wore a tank top with basketball shorts. The date was Sunday, September 20th. Technically it wouldn't be fall for a few more days, and the sun was still holding on to the fierce summer temperatures. It was 92 degrees outside. Marcel opened the door to find his ex-wife standing on his porch, looking like a ray of sunshine.

"Good afternoon," he told her. "Come in."

Coleen stepped inside hesitantly. She looked around the front room like she'd never been there before.

Coleen was 38 years old, four years younger than Marcel. She was a beautiful woman, tall and curvaceous. She was brown-skinned, with a touch of red, like cinnamon. She was dressed for church, which made sense because it was a little after one. Her dress was not form-fitting, but Coleen's figure could not be contained by normal means. And she did have too many buttons open on her blouse, exposing quite a bit of cinnamon cleavage.

Marcel chuckled inwardly. He didn't think his ex-wife was a hypocrite, but he always felt she was misguided. He wondered how she could be such a faithful member of her church while not subscribing to many of the things the bible and her pastor taught them.

They were separated for nearly a year before Coleen filed for divorce. Before that, she had an affair that lasted several months. That put the amount of time she lived in sin at one year and four months. That number could be stretched even more, if you counted the years Coleen didn't support her husband or try to adhere to the marriage vows she made before God. Through it all, she never missed a day of church.

But Marcel couldn't point fingers, because deep down, he was glad when she finally told him about the affair. He was relieved when she announced that she was leaving him for another man. Marcel became weak to the point of complacent during their marriage, and he needed Coleen out of his life. Next to the birth of their son, her moving out was the best thing that had ever happened to him.

She looked him up and down slowly and told him, "You look good. Been taking care of yourself."

Coleen had no idea how wrong she was about that, and Marcel didn't bother informing her.

"You look good, too," he said. "How's everything?"

"Good," she said.

"How's Paul?"

"He's alright."

Marcel did not press for more. He was past the point of hoping her new relationship would fail. Even when he did wish for that a year ago, it wasn't so that he could have her back. He simply didn't want her to continue winning. Coleen's dream of being a stay-at-home mom with unlimited spending on her credit card was the main catalyst in their divorce. There was a time when Marcel wanted to know what Paul did for a living and how he could provide for her so much better than her husband could.

Thankfully none of that mattered now. Marcel wouldn't go as far as saying he wished his ex-wife the best, but he could say that he didn't harbor any ill will. He considered that progress.

"You got new carpet," she said, looking around again. "Everything in here looks different. Is that a new couch?"

Marcel nodded. The front room had a new couch, new entertainment center and a new coffee table as well. The carpet was now a darker shade of beige. Coleen knew that their son died in this house somewhere, but she would never know the exact location.

The blood stains were the main reason Marcel started drinking. He should've turned his back on the house after the murder and never set foot inside again. But he was a reasonable man, and he knew that a house was just a house, regardless of what happened there. And more importantly it was still his home. His whole life was in there. He could sell it, but that could take months. In the meantime, he needed somewhere to lay his head.

He ripped all of the carpet up in the front room by hand two days after Jaylen's death. He scrubbed the floor to clean up all of the blood that had seeped through. He threw out the couch and coffee table and anything else that had blood on it, even if it was only a few drops.

But he still saw blood sometimes. Even with the new carpet and new furniture in there, if he stood in the hallway and stared at the floor in the front room, he could see all of the blood, exactly where it had been. The same photographic memory that made him a great detective turned his home into a forever crime scene.

"I got that stuff you wanted," Marcel said. He went to a corner of the room where a large box was filled to the top. There was a saxophone sticking out of it. A little football helmet. A Yamaha keyboard.

Coleen didn't make any moves towards the box. When Marcel looked back at her, he saw that she was watching him. If he was a betting man, he'd describe the look in her eyes as appreciation and longing. Ten years ago, that look would've led them to the bedroom, quick, fast and in a hurry. Today it did nothing for him. He didn't even acknowledge it.

"Can I, can I see his room?" she asked.

"Nothing in there," Marcel said.

She looked hurt by that. "What do you mean?"

"There's nothing in there. It's all gone. I work out in there now."

153

Coleen couldn't believe it. "Can I see?"

Marcel shrugged. "Go ahead."

He followed her down the hallway, to their son's bedroom. Coleen's hips had a certain sway to them. Surely she wasn't aware of it. Marcel found himself glancing at her round rump as he followed, just like the old days. The only difference now was he knew full well what that nice ass was connected to, and he wanted no parts. There was nothing under Coleen's dress that was compelling enough to make him want to crawl back into the lion's den.

She stopped at the doorway and stood silently. Marcel didn't think she'd go inside, but she eventually did. There wasn't one item in the room that had been there when Jaylen died. Marcel even took the posters off the walls. Coleen looked back at him. Marcel was surprised to see tears in her eyes.

"What happened to all of it?"

"I took the furniture to Goodwill. I still have all of the little stuff. Everything you wanted is in that box out front. I got a couple more boxes in the garage, if you wanna look through them."

"But, but why?"

"Why what?"

"Why'd you get rid of everything?"

"What did you want me to do?" he asked her, "keep it as a shrine?"

Coleen didn't have an answer.

"I did that," Marcel said. "I did it for about two months. I'd walk by this room and start crying. I'd come in here and cry. I slept in his bed. I went in his closet and looked through his things. I stayed in there for hours. But after a while, I knew that it was killing me, this room was. So I cleaned it out. I still have Jaylen's things around the house. His trophies are in the living room. But I couldn't have this room, all of his stuff in here. It was too much.

"But after I emptied it, it was still bad. I'd come in here and lay on the floor. Eventually I decided that if I'm gonna come in here so much, I might as well do something useful with my time. So I brought in all of this workout stuff. That made it better. Now when I'm stressed out and angry, I can vent my frustration with these weights or the bike. It's better for me now. It's a lot better."

154

Coleen understood that. She realized he was a lot stronger than she gave him credit for. "I couldn't do it," she said, shaking her head. "I couldn't live here."

"The house is on the market," he informed her.

"Oh," she said. "That's good."

Marcel thought she'd inquire about the revenue from the sale, but Coleen didn't embarrass herself. She gave up any interest in the house when she filed for divorce. Plus she never worked during their marriage, so Marcel didn't think she deserved to be involved in the sale.

"Where will you go?" she asked him.

"I'll stay here. Overbrook Meadows will always be my home."

"Paul wants to move to New York," she told him. "I don't know if I want to go."

The old Marcel would've been happy to hear that there was trouble in paradise, but Coleen's woes brought him no joy. Regardless of how she treated him during their marriage, she was still the mother of his child. They both lost Jaylen, and they were both irrevocably changed because of it. They would be forever linked by the pain.

"Why not?" he asked.

"Because Overbrook Meadows is all I know," she replied. "There's too much going on in my life right now. I don't wanna start all over again. I don't think I have the heart for it."

"Yes you do. You're stronger than you think. And your family's from Arkansas, so there's nothing holding you to this city. You should leave. You deserve a fresh start."

"But, but that's not the only thing," she said. She looked up at him with beautiful, brown eyes that glistened with agony. "Paul, he's, he seems different now. It started when Jaylen died. I know he didn't want any kids himself. And sometimes I felt like he resented Jaylen. I could be wrong. He never came right out and said anything.

"But when Jaylen died, I, I didn't feel like he, I don't know... It didn't seem like he cared as much, as much as I did. He didn't cry or anything like that. I, I don't know what I'm saying. Sometimes, I feel like I should've been with you. I know you felt the same way I did, when we lost him. And, and I think it

155

would've been better, if we grieved together, if I was with somebody who was hurting. But I felt like I was alone."

Marcel understood what she was saying. His friends and family never left his side after Jaylen's death. But sometimes he still felt alone. He wished Coleen was there, so they could tackle it together. But at the time, he and his ex-wife weren't even on speaking terms. She blamed him for their son's death, which made the horrendous experience much worse. Because of that, Marcel had little sympathy for her problems.

"You got through it," he said. "We both did."

She shook her head. "No. I don't think so. I can't look at Paul the same way now. I don't feel the same way about him, as I did before. I don't wanna go all the way to New York with him. I don't feel like we're gonna make it."

"Then don't go. You can get a job, Coleen, and make a life for yourself."

"I just, I've been thinking about you a lot," she confided. "I know I did you wrong. I know that. But I was thinking about you, even before Jaylen died. I was wondering... I don't know. I wonder..."

Her eyes were hopeful and vulnerable. After all they went through, Marcel should've pounced on the opportunity to tell her to go to hell.

Instead he told her, "You're upset, and you're confused right now. Maybe it won't work out with you and Paul, but that's no reason to dig up skeletons from your past. You don't want me. You know that."

"No, I didn't, I didn't say that. I just..."

She couldn't come up with a better explanation for what she wanted to say.

"Come on," Marcel told her. "I'll take that box to your car."

She nodded. "Oh, okay."

On the way back to the front room, Coleen noticed one area of the house that wasn't as spic and span as the rest. She knew that Marcel was a bachelor, and bachelors, by nature, are usually not good housekeepers. It wasn't the debris that gave her pause, rather the type of mess he had in the kitchen.

She stopped in her tracks and stared at the unwashed dishes and countertops covered with pizza boxes and to-go boxes from other restaurants. All of that was to be expected. What

Coleen did not expect to see were the many empty bottles of Crown Royal scattered about. She counted at least eight of them, without even stepping into the room. When she looked back at Marcel, he was standing there, waiting on her.

"What..." She frowned at him. "Are you drinking all of that?"

Marcel's face flushed with embarrassment. He didn't mind cleaning. He even liked it, at times. But the kitchen was one area that he despised tidying-up. Because of his height, his back got sore if he leaned over the sink for too long. The problem with that is, once you have an area that you've pretty much given up on, it's easy to pile more crap on top of it. Every day he walked by the kitchen and cringed and told himself, *I'll get to that this weekend.* Every weekend he found an excuse to put it off again.

"Not all at once," he said. "Come on. Let me help you with that box."

But Coleen didn't want to leave right away. "Marcel..." She looked around the kitchen in more detail. She saw more bottles on the floor, even a couple in the sink. "How much have you been drinking?"

"Not that much. It's not all me. I've had people over."

That was a lie, but she didn't know that. It wasn't like she believed him anyway. Her eyes were now filled with concern.

"Marcel, if you need help, please talk to me. I can help you. We can get you some treatment."

He scoffed at that. "We? Who is this *we* you're talking about?"

She flinched. "Well, us. Me and you."

"There is no *us*," he told her. "There's no *me and you.* There's you and Paul, and that's who you need to be worried about."

His drastic change in demeanor left her with her mouth hanging open.

"Now come on," he said. "Let's get this box in your car."

Coleen didn't say anything else. She pleaded with her eyes when they got outside, but Marcel had no problem ignoring a pair of eyes, especially a pair of lying, two-timing, adulterous eyes. He put the box of Jaylen's mementos in her trunk and went back inside before she got in her car.

157

Rather than finish his workout, Marcel went to the kitchen instead to tackle a mountain of a mess, which started out as only a mole hill. He sighed, surveying the clutter. He'd never allow this to happen again, that much was sure. The kitchen offered clear evidence of his moral and emotional decline. He was a fool to leave it for all to see. He found a half-full bottle of Crown and took five healthy swallows before he got started.

He was slightly irritated that he went against his plan of not drinking during the daylight hours. But this wasn't a regular day. Coleen stressed him out, so it was okay to indulge this one time.

CHAPTER FIFTEEN
THE ONE THAT GOT AWAY

The next morning Marcel showed up for duty bright and early at the 8th District Precinct on Lancaster. Today was the big day. After weeks of surveillance, mostly done by Marcel and his partner Chaz, they were ready to take down the crack dealers in the downtown housing projects on Chambers Street.

At 7 am their boss, Lieutenant Freddie Mueller, called a department meeting to go over the last minute details of the raid. Marcel was not at his best that morning. His head was pounding, and his stomach felt sour. He didn't perk up until he heard Lt. Freddie mention his name.

"Marcel and Chaz, I want you guys across from apartment 112. You'll provide primary surveillance for the whole operation. When the re-up gets there (which should be arriving in a forest green Isuzu Trooper, driven by Mr. Contrell Beaumont), you'll put the call out to get everyone ready."

"Come on, Lieutenant," Marcel complained. "Me and Chaz have been camped out in that shitty apartment for weeks. I got a hangover. Can't you put someone else in that building today?"

Most of the cops in the room laughed. The meeting was technically formal, but there was always a casual atmosphere. No one held their tongue in the briefing room, and Marcel's complaint was surprisingly common. Even Lieutenant Freddie grinned.

"Detective Webber, you and Chaz will sit in that shitty apartment one last time, and you will notify the jump-out team when that green Isuzu brings the re-up. If you're sick, you need to hit the head, throw that shit up, drink some coffee, throw that shit up too, if you have to, and get your ass down to those projects."

That brought more laughter. If they worked at a school or in an office building, Marcel's colleagues might have viewed his drinking in a different light. But many of the cops in the precinct drank more than they should. It took a lot more than a few hangovers to get labeled an alcoholic.

Marcel shook his head, but he wasn't too upset. He and Chaz knew all of the kids in that area by name, so they really were the best men for the surveillance job.

Marcel did not know that Lieutenant Freddie Mueller was once good friends with Donna's ex-husband, just as Lieutenant Freddie was unaware that Marcel was currently dating Nolan's ex-wife. If Freddie had known, he would've cautioned Donna, because Marcel's drinking was no secret to the department, just as everyone knew that Marcel hadn't been one hundred percent since his son got killed in a burglary gone bad.

"After Marcel and Chaz give the word," Freddie went on, "we'll hit apartment 112 from all directions. There's sure to be guns inside, so be on your toes. We want the re-up before they have time to do anything stupid with it, but we'll have the water shut off just in case. Of course we want the guns and the cook team.

"The corner kids are sure to scatter like roaches when they see us coming. We want all of them, too. But I don't want any long-ass foot chases, though. If it's a boss, we definitely want to get him. But there's no need to chase some ten year old through the creek – unless they're trying to get rid of the re-up. Whoever has the re-up, we'll chase him to the ends of the earth.

"We'll have a birdie in the sky and at least twenty men on the ground, so this should go smooth and easy. If someone pops off a shot, you'd better make sure you're following the rules of engagement," the lieutenant said sternly. He paused for a moment, to let that sink in. "And if someone *does* pop off, I don't want everybody else emptying their clip *just because*. If the person you draw down on don't got a gun, then don't fucking pull the trigger! Is that understood?"

Everyone either nodded or murmured their understanding.

"Alright, boys. Let's get it done," Lieutenant Freddie said.

Several men echoed his enthusiasm as they headed off to their respective assignments.

●●●●●●●

Thirty minutes later Chaz and Marcel sat in apartment 113 at the downtown housing projects spying on the same kids they'd been spying on for the past five weeks. They had peep holes in two walls and false-blinds set up on the main front window.

The peephole of apartment 113 had been removed and replaced with a small camera that pointed directly at the unit across the street. They had enough footage from that camera to arrest at least thirty people. The dealers in these housing projects were a crafty bunch, but there were plenty of vacant units, and they never paid attention to the apartment directly across from them. If everything went well today, they wouldn't realize their folly until they were facedown with an officer's knee on their spine.

Marcel had worked with Chaz for more than three years. The two men got along well, and they always had each other's back, above all else. At thirty-two, Chaz was Marcel's junior by a whole decade. Over the past few years, he learned a lot from the big, burly detective as they fought hard to keep the city safe from drugs. Chaz was short in stature. He was Hispanic with a thick moustache that he only shaved when he went undercover.

The two policemen took turns staring out of the window or one of the other peepholes. Marcel's stomach was a little tight, but he wasn't as sick as he let on at the meeting. He was, however, sick of the city's tactics in regards to the crack epidemic in poor communities. He sat on a metal folding chair chugging a bottled water to neutralize whatever alcohol may be left in his belly.

"You think we'll get Contrell?" Chaz asked. His attention was focused on their targets. He did not look back at his partner as he spoke.

"If we do, it will be the only meaningful bust out of this whole operation," Marcel said cynically.

"Why do you say that?"

"Those youngsters don't know shit, and they're too young to prosecute," Marcel explained. "Who's out there now?"

"Chris, Deshaun, Trey…. Um, I think Jamal just went in the apartment. There's about four more guys already in there. They've been in there all night."

"The trap house is humming," Marcel said.

"There's gotta be at least fifty thou' in there," Chaz mused.

"And a bunch of guns," Marcel said. "And baggies and scales and everything they need to make this look like a big deal."

Chaz looked back at him, grinning. "But it's not big enough for you?"

Marcel chuckled. "What's Contrell gonna get for the re-up?"

"He got priors," Chaz said.

"Yeah, so what's that? Fifteen, twenty years?"

"Maybe."

"And the kids? They're all juveniles. Most of them got priors too, so they can hold 'em a year, maybe a couple of years for the worst ones, right?"

Chaz nodded. "Sounds about right."

"So a twelve year old carries a gun because his boss told him to, we arrest that kid, put him in the system for two years, and then what?"

"He learns his lesson?"

Marcel got a big laugh out of that. Chaz did, too.

"Not hardly," Marcel said. "After two years he'll come out tatted-up, all the way up to his neck. He'll be a real-live monster then, and guess where they'll return him to..."

"Right back here?"

"You goddamned right," Marcel said. "And within a year, he'll either get popped again for selling dope or for shooting somebody, and he'll go right back to juvie. After a couple more trips, he'll be old enough for big boy jail. By then he'll be institutionalized. If he ever sees the light of day again, his offenses will get more and more violent, until we lock him up for good."

"Well, I guess he shouldn't be on the corner with a gun when he's twelve," Chaz surmised.

"You sound like the fucking mayor."

"So what's your solution?"

"Gotta go after the big man," Marcel said. "We gotta go after the one who put the dope and the gun in the kid's hand. You think arresting Contrell will do any good? I mean, yeah, it looks good on paper. But Contrell is just as replaceable as the corner kids."

"You think we should go after Mr. Brown," Chaz said.

"Why the hell haven't we gone after Mr. Brown?" The conversation was getting Marcel more and more heated. "He's

162

been running dope in this city for years. *Decades.* You telling me we got the resources to spy on these little boys for a month, but we can't follow Mr. Brown around for the same amount of time?"

"They tried," Chaz reminded him. "Nothing ever sticks."

"So we should let it go?" Marcel asked. "Give him a green light?"

"That's above our heads, man," Chaz said. "It's above the commissioner's head, too. You heard what Lieutenant Freddie said about our budget cuts."

"Don't get it twisted," Marcel said. "The city has money for whatever they decide to spend it on. The problem ain't money, it's the people in control of the money. And I'll tell you this: The people who control the money don't give a shit about crack in the hood."

"Maybe you should go to a city council meeting and voice your opinion," Chaz joked.

"Please," Marcel said. "Lieutenant Freddie would have my ass."

"You remember that one guy?" Chaz said. "That guy who was running for mayor a couple years back. I think he would've made a difference. I caught a couple of his speeches on TV. Sounded like he actually cared about these poor neighborhoods, could've fixed some of this shit. But he got killed in a car accident. You know who I'm talking about?"

"Nolan Hodge," Marcel said, his mood suddenly deflated.

"Yeah, him," Chaz said. "That was one unlucky bastard. What are the odds, huh? Guy's about to take over the city, and he gets smashed at an intersection, and that's it. Everything's gone."

Marcel's thoughts were of Donna by then, and he didn't respond. Nolan was unlucky, but his misfortune led to Marcel's gain. If he had the power to bring Nolan back to fix the city or leave things like they were, Marcel would choose the latter. He knew that was selfish, but Donna was a helluva woman. Even with their limited dating schedule, he'd grown very fond of her. Donna was more important than a whole city filled with crackheads.

●●●●●●●

Contrell's forest green Isuzu pulled to a stop in front of apartment 112 at 9:14 am. Marcel kept an eye on him through the faux-blinds while Chaz radioed it in to the team. Contrary to his pessimism, Marcel hoped the raid went well. Taking down Contrell wouldn't solve the city's overall drug problem, but he did agree that something had to be done about him.

Contrell had simply gotten too big for his britches. The whole operation on Chambers Street was out of control. The workers made transactions in broad daylight, with seemingly no fear of repercussions. They'd been taking advantage of the fact that the housing project was poorly designed; with one main entrance leading to and from the freeway. Contrell had lookouts there who would tip off the workers whenever a police car entered the premises. The lookouts were so good, they could recognize most unmarked cars as well.

But today they didn't know that they were already infiltrated. They had Marcel and Chaz directly across from them and half a dozen more officers in apartments next to and behind them. The task force sneaked in early this morning in two inconspicuous hoopties that carried three officers each; the drivers looked like junkies, and the other lawmen hunkered down in the backseats.

Marcel watched Contrell exit his vehicle with two other men. One of them carried a duffle bag that contained the re-up. "Re-up" was a street term for *new supply*. The dealers in 112 fed cocaine to the whole housing project, so Contrell had to bring in more product two to three times a day. The first re-up always came around nine in the morning. Today Contrell's meticulousness would be his downfall.

Marcel waited until he slipped inside the apartment before he told Chaz, "He's in."

Chaz immediately relayed the information. "The re-up is inside."

"One went in with him," Marcel said, still watching the apartment. "The other one's standing outside, playing lookout."

"One gun went with the package," Chaz told their comrades. "The other's waiting outside."

"Black male," Marcel said, thinking it was *always* a "black male." "Black jeans, white hoodie. Both hands in the hoodie. He's definitely packing."

Chaz delivered these details as well.

"On my go," someone on the other end of the radio squawked. "Everybody ready?"

"Team one, ready," another voice said.

"Team three, ready," a third voice replied.

"Team two ready," said another.

"Waiting on you," Chaz said.

"Alright," the first voice said. "Be safe. Don't shoot unless you have to. Let's get it. **GO! GO! GO!**"

Chaz put the radio down and hurried back to the window in time to see multiple groups of men, some of them masked, converging on the apartment with their weapons drawn.

"**POLICE! GET DOWN ON THE GROUND!**"

"**DROP IT!**"

"**GET ON YOUR KNEES!**"

"**HANDS ON YOUR HEAD! GET 'EM UP!**"

Chaz and Marcel were instructed to hold their position until the front door was breeched. The moment that happened, they emerged from their apartment to assist the raid in any way they could. Their assistance was definitely needed. Within ten seconds, the scene was already chaotic. There were eight to ten kids standing outside when the police stormed the apartment, and each one of them ran in a different direction.

Most of the task force was inside the apartment, securing the scene. There weren't enough guys outside to catch all of the runners, so Marcel immediately began to sprint after the closest corner kid.

"Hey! Get back here!"

The boy was small, but he was fast. Marcel was used to dealers sagging their pants, which made it difficult for them to run. But this kid had his jeans pulled up properly and secured with a belt. His thin arms cut the air methodically as he ran. After a couple of blocks, Marcel began to wonder if the youngster was a track star or just naturally gifted. He wasn't in school today, so it was doubtful that he partook in organized sports. But damn. This boy could run.

"You're making it worse on yourself!" Marcel yelled at him, not losing any ground.

The boy veered off to the right unexpectedly and hurdled a short fence like it wasn't even there. Despite his size, Marcel was just as agile. His muscles responded to the adrenaline, and he got over the fence just as quickly. The boy ran into an alleyway, jumped another fence and sprinted through two backyards before Marcel finally caught up with him. He reached and grabbed the back of his shirt, bringing the boy's forward momentum to a complete and jerky halt.

"*Let me go!*"

The boy began to dig in his front pocket, which was an ultimate no-no when dealing with law enforcement. But Marcel didn't drive his big fist into the back of his head, like some of his cohorts would've done.

"*Get your hands out of your pockets, boy!*"

He spun him around. The boy threw a handful of rocks to the ground. Marcel saw everything, but something suddenly went terribly wrong. Later, he would describe the incident as a temporary break from reality. But at the time, he had no idea what was happening to him.

When the boy turned to face him, Marcel saw that it wasn't a stranger. Even worse, this was someone he knew very well. It was someone he cared for deeply. His head spun. He held the boy with two hands wrapped around his bony arms. Marcel's mouth fell open as he stared at him. He blinked fiercely, but the vision didn't change.

It was Jaylen.

Even as his brain told him that couldn't possibly be the case, his eyes told him something totally different. The boy was brown-skinned. He was Jaylen's size and Jaylen's age. He had Jaylen's eyes, nose and mouth. Even his haircut. Everything was perfect, but at the same time it was all wrong.

No. What, what the.... What's happening?

Marcel's heart began to hammer. Jaylen stared at him, and gradually his fear of being arrested turned to confusion.

"Man let me go!" he yelled. "I didn't do nothing!"

He fought valiantly, but Marcel had a 150 pound weight advantage. His grip was anaconda tight.

"What are you doing?" He shook the boy as he yelled at him. "Why aren't you in school? What are you doing out here? Don't you know you can end up in jail? Your life will be over!"

The boy (who couldn't possibly be Jaylen) was as confused as Marcel was. Plus the big cops grip on his arms kept getting tighter.

"Please, man! Let me go!" he wailed. "You hurting me!"

"*You shouldn't be here!*" Marcel shouted at him, his eyes welling with tears. "*You're not here! You shouldn't be here!*" His heart thundered. His brain raced. He saw crime scene tape stretched in front of his house. Blood on his living room floor. Blood on the coffee table. Blood everywhere. "*You're dead! You're not here!*"

And, as if he willed it himself, Marcel realized Jaylen wasn't there. The boy he was holding had a different face now. He was brown-skinned, but other than that, he looked nothing like Jaylen. As a matter of fact, Marcel knew this kid fairly well from their surveillance. His name was Timothy Palmer. He lived with his mother, who was a well-known user, one of Contrell's many customers.

In his confusion, Marcel's grip on the child loosened, and the boy took full advantage. Timothy jerked his arms free and turned tail, quickly sprinting through another alleyway and out of sight.

Marcel stood frozen, his chest rising and falling, tears streaming down his face. He looked at his hands and saw that they were trembling.

"Oh my God. What's wrong with me?" he panted. "What's wrong with me?"

His delusion was interrupted by the sound of footsteps approaching from behind. Marcel took a moment to wipe the tears from his eyes and try to get his breathing under control before he turned around.

It was Chaz. Of course it was. Partners always look out for each other. The look on Chaz's face made it clear that he had seen everything.

"What happened?"

"He, um, he got away," Marcel said, trying to sound normal.

Chaz studied his face closely as he approached. "You alright, man?"

Alright? Hmph. Marcel almost laughed at that. Of course he wasn't alright. He just yelled at a boy who looked just like his dead son, but it turned out the boy didn't look anything like Jaylen. His mind was playing tricks on him. And on top of that, Marcel didn't even make the arrest. He was very far from alright!

167

"Yeah, I'm good," he said. "I don't know what happened. I had him. But the little bastard squirmed away." He couldn't maintain eye contact as he told the lie.

Luckily Chaz was a good cop, and he had his partner's back – no matter what. This was the strangest thing he'd seen this month, but it wasn't the strangest thing he'd seen this year. Plus Marcel had been complaining about the futileness of arresting these corner kids. Chaz saw Marcel berate one and let him go, but he would never know that Marcel was yelling at his dead son at the time. He grinned and slapped the huge cop on the back.

"You getting old," Chaz said. "Back in the day, you would've got 'em."

Marcel stared at him for a few seconds before he grinned, too, glad that his friend was willing to play along. "You couldn't have caught him, either, with those short legs of yours."

"Hey, don't try to insult me, just because you're ready for retirement," Chaz joked. "What are you now, 59, 60?"

"I'm 42, asshole. And anytime you wanna take it to the track to see what's up, I'm ready."

"Nah. I don't race *old people*. You're liable to have a heart attack, and they'd blame *me* for it!"

Marcel had to laugh at that. He went to the spot where the kid tossed his rocks and ground them into the dirt with his sneaker. Crack dealers always came back to look for dope they discarded while running from the police. This one would be sorely disappointed.

"They got everybody else?" he asked as they returned to the others.

"Yeah. I think so."

"Good," Marcel said. "A month from now, everything will be just like it was this morning. But today, we can say we did something."

"That's right," Chaz said. "We'll deal with next month when it gets here. Everyone's going to Rusty's when we get off tonight. You down? The first round's on me."

After what just happened, Marcel felt like alcohol was the last thing he needed. But when things got crazy, liquor was also the only thing that leveled him out.

"Yeah, I'm in," he said. "I wish we could go right now."

Chaz laughed. "Yeah. I feel you. Hey, I think I got a few hot beers in my car. We can drink them on the way back to the precinct, if you want..."

Marcel grimaced at that, but he didn't turn down the offer.

CHAPTER SIXTEEN
TRUST

On Friday Marcel picked Donna up at lunchtime for their second date. He was eager to impress her, so he took her to the Red Lobster on Hulen Street, rather than one of the fast food restaurants she suggested. Donna was concerned that they wouldn't have time to sit down and enjoy a full dining experience in only an hour and a half. But the service was speedy that afternoon. They chowed down on crab legs and lobster tails and had a little time to sit and chat after the waitress took their plates away.

"You look nice today," Donna said after she placed her napkin on the table. "You're not working?"

Marcel wore a long-sleeved collar shirt with slacks and loafers. This was the first time Donna had ever seen him in anything but jeans and a tee shirt. She was impressed. Without all of those muscles distracting her, she realized how debonair he was.

"I'm off," he said. "We finished our big case, so they're not offering overtime anymore. You look nice too, by the way."

"Oh, please," Donna said. "My hair's a mess."

Rather than down and straight, she went with a natural look this morning. Her hair was frizzy, so her afro wasn't perfectly symmetrical. But Marcel thought her mane was lovely. He longed to touch it, to run his fingers through the denseness.

"You're beautiful," he told her. "Don't ever think you're not."

"Thank you."

Donna blushed. She thought she should be used to him by now, but Marcel's compliments still put her on cloud nine. She figured it was because he was so handsome, and the serious look in his eyes let her know that he truly meant it.

"What are you doing for the rest of the day?" she asked.

"A realtor is bringing some people by to look at my house," Marcel said. "I don't have to be there, but I feel a little uncomfortable about it. What do you think? Do you think I should make myself scarce? I have a lot of personal items lying around..."

"You're selling your house?"

He nodded. "Been thinking about it for months."

"Why?"

"I, uh... I told you my son died at home, right?"

"Oh. Um, yes. But you didn't tell me you were selling your house."

"I know," Marcel said. He brought a hand to his face and rubbed his forehead. "I try not to talk about those things when we're together."

Donna was a little hurt by that. "Why?"

"Because I don't want you to think I have a lot of problems," he said honestly.

Donna nodded. "You know, I did think that at first."

Marcel waited.

"But, what do you think I would do?" she asked. "Stop talking to you?"

He sighed. "You might, if you knew how bad it was."

Donna felt her heart kick. She realized she was disappointed – in herself. "I'm sorry," she said.

"For what?"

"For making you feel like that. And for thinking like that myself. When I first met you, I didn't want to talk to you, because I felt like you needed time to heal."

"There's nothing wrong with you feeling that way."

"It is if it drives a wedge between us," Donna said. "If you feel like you can't talk to me about Jaylen, it will hurt our relationship. It means you don't trust me with your feelings. I don't want you to feel like that. You should be able to talk to me about anything."

Marcel gasped quietly. His heart swelled with emotion. His mind was stuck on the word *relationship*, but he also processed everything else she said. Could this be real? Did he finally have someone he could talk to, about *everything*?

"I, I wasn't aware that we were in a relationship."

Donna's jaw dropped. She brought a hand to her mouth as hot blood rushed to her face. Did she really just do that? She knew that men hated to put titles on things, especially their *friendships* with women. Donna realized that she jumped the gun and put her foot in her mouth, *big time*. She wouldn't be surprised if she chased him away.

"Oh my God. I'm sorry. I didn't mean... Sorry. Forget I said that."

"No, no, it's okay," Marcel said. "I didn't mean it like that. I would love to be in a relationship with you, Donna. But I didn't know you felt the same way. I'm overwhelmed, to be honest with you. I don't have anyone in my life that I trust enough to–"

"We should take it slow," Donna said, still trying to backtrack.

Now Marcel was the one who felt like he put his foot in his mouth. "Oh, okay," he said. "But for the record, anytime you're willing to give us that title back, I'm ready. I would definitely like to be in a relationship with you, Ms. Hodge."

She smiled, but now she was gun shy. "Okay."

Marcel sighed loudly. "Okay... So are we good?"

She nodded. "Yeah."

"Well, as far as my house," he said, "it has too many bad memories for me. And I have been struggling with my son's death lately."

Donna's face was now filled with concern.

"I'm seeing a counselor again," Marcel confided. "I went back to her this week."

"That's good," Donna said. "I was in counseling for nearly a year when my husband died. When you and I met, I thought it was strange when you said you were done with that."

"Not just strange," Marcel said. "I was being stupid. You know, as a man, I think I can handle anything. I think I can *will* myself to feel better, but it doesn't work like that."

Donna nodded. Her emotions were split between empathy for his situation and exhilaration that he finally trusted her enough

172

to confide in her. She wished they were sitting closer, so that she could hold him – or better yet feel his strong arms wrapped around her.

"This week, I had a little breakdown," Marcel said. He watched to see how she would respond to that.

Donna looked as loving as ever. She didn't even flinch.

"I was chasing this kid," he said. Marcel's voice was a little shaky. He realized his heart was beating rapidly.

Donna noticed it too. "It's okay," she said. "You can talk to me."

Marcel took a deep breath. He told himself that she would either leave him or she wouldn't, but either way he couldn't keep lying to Donna by not telling her what was going on with him. If they were truly meant to be, she would accept him as he was and be understanding as he tried to straighten out his life.

"This kid," he said, "he couldn't have been more than thirteen. He was a corner kid; selling dope for some guys in the projects downtown. I chased him for a good while. When I finally caught him, I spun him around, and, and for a few seconds... all I saw was Jaylen. I felt like I was holding my son. Something... I don't know. Something in my head... Something misfired, I guess."

He watched her some more.

Donna didn't look revolted. Marcel couldn't believe it. Or maybe she was hiding her feelings and would stop taking his calls after this. If that was the case, he might as well let it all out. He was in too deep to stop now.

"I started yelling at him," Marcel said. "I don't know what all I said. I asked him what he was doing, why he was out there, and didn't he know his life was going to be over if he went to jail. I feel that way about all of the corner kids, but I yelled at that particular boy because I couldn't understand why Jaylen would do something so stupid. When I came back to reality and realized it wasn't Jaylen, I felt like an idiot. And the kid took off. He got away."

Marcel put his elbows on the table and rubbed his temples. He looked down at the table. "Okay, so I'm crazy, right? You can tell me how you really feel."

Donna reached across the table and took his hand. She squeezed it tightly. Marcel looked up at her and saw tears in her eyes. But she was smiling.

"You're not crazy. I used to see Nolan everywhere, after he died."

"Yeah, but–"

"I saw him in my home," Donna went on. "Sometimes I heard him in the bathroom, but of course he wasn't there. Crowds were the worst. I thought I saw him at the mall one time. I ran and caught up with a man I thought was him..." She wiped her eyes and chuckled. "I chased him for a couple of minutes. And when I finally got closer, he wasn't even black." She shook her head wistfully.

"That's just something that happens," she said. "I think everyone who loses a loved one goes through similar stuff. You shouldn't hold things like that in, because, as you said, you'll start to think it *only happens to you*, and you're going crazy. Did you tell your counselor? Didn't she tell you it was normal?"

"She did," Marcel said. "But I wasn't sure..."

"You're a big, strong man," Donna said. "But you're not big enough to handle *everything*, Marcel. Next time you should talk to me. I might be able to help you, if you let me."

Marcel's heart was light in his chest. But at the same moment, he was filled with guilt.

Tell her about the drinking. Tell her now.

But he couldn't do that. What he needed was to hurry up and fix that disgusting problem. He was sure he could do it, too. People stopped drinking all the time, all by themselves. Only hardcore drunks had to go to rehab.

He squeezed her hand back. "Thank you for understanding."

She grinned at him. "That's what I'm here for."

●●●●●●●

On the way back to the school, Marcel tried to resurrect their "relationship" conversation. Being open and honest would improve things between them, but there was one more hurdle they had to get over.

"Hey, um, I was thinking about what you said, you know, about us being in a relationship."

Donna couldn't stop smiling, but she said, "I said we should take it slow."

"Yeah, yeah, whatever. So anyway, if we're in a *relationship*, don't you think I should meet your son, at some point?"

She laughed. "So you're just gonna *put* us in a relationship?"

"If you'll let me."

Donna shook her head, but her smile remained. "And you would like to meet Colton?"

"I think it's important."

"It is," Donna agreed.

"And I'd like to take you out at nighttime, one of these days," Marcel said. "I know you can't do that now because you don't want to tell your son about me. But if you tell him, and let me get his permission to date you, then we could go out at night."

"First of all, what's so special about nighttime?"

"Our lunches are great," Marcel said. "Don't get me wrong. But I really want to see you under the moonlight. You might be a werewolf, for all I know."

She laughed. "Okay. And why do you think you need Colton's *permission* to date me? You're not serious, are you?"

Marcel nodded. "Colton is the man of the house, whether you see him as so or not. I think he might be resentful if you make major decisions without giving him any say. I know this is your life, but he's a big part of it. If he feels like he's part of the decision, he'll feel better about you spending time with a man who's not his father."

Donna had to admit that he was probably right. And she was surprised by his insight. "What if he says he doesn't like you?" she teased.

"Then we'll have to remain secret lovers," Marcel said, "until he graduates high school and moves out."

Donna knew he was kidding, but the idea of them being *lovers* made her thighs tremble.

When they got to her school, she knew the kiss was coming, but her heart still shot up her throat when he leaned in for it. She closed her eyes and placed a hand on his chest. It was the

first time she touched him there. The feel of his powerful
pectorals made her feel all kinds of wonderful. The taste of his
sweet lips was even better.

Marcel hadn't been this affectionate with a woman in a
long time. Even with his ex-wife, the love was gone years before
they signed the divorce papers. A mighty erection steadily grew
against his thigh as he sucked her full lips, one at a time. Donna's
perfume filled his nostrils. He hoped it would linger for hours
after she departed. He didn't think it was possible for a woman to
make him this happy.

When she exited his vehicle, he watched her hips and ass
until she made it to the top of the steps. He loved her heart and
mind so much, it was easy to forget how beautiful and sexy Donna
was. He hadn't known her very long, but he was willing to do
anything to make sure things worked out with them. Getting
Colton to like him should be easy compared to the work he had to
do on himself.

Marcel wanted a drink right then, but he refused to give in
to temptation. A few miles down the road, the craving subsided.
It was a small victory, but it was a good start.

●●●●●●●

When Donna got home from work that day, she found
Colton in his room working on homework rather than playing a
video game. She took a seat on his bed and watched him for a few
moments.

"How was school?"

"Fine," he said without looking up at her.

"How's it going in Mrs. McMillen's class?"

"Fine."

"No more problems?"

He shook his head.

"What about the boy you yelled at? Everything good with
y'all two?"

He looked up at her and grinned. "He's scared of me."

Donna didn't find that amusing. "Why?"

"Because I yelled at him and got suspended, so now he
thinks I wanna fight."

His mother's frown intensified. "Have you threatened him?"

"No," Colton said with a chuckle. "It's because I'm taller than him, and I'm on the basketball team and the football team."

"What does you playing sports have to do with it?"

"You know how it is. People think jocks are all dumb and aggressive."

"You weren't a dumb jock in middle school," Donna recalled. "Now you're making all of these C's. You like that image? *Dumb jock*?"

"I'm gonna get my grades up."

Donna wanted to make him go into detail about how he would accomplish that goal, but that wasn't what she came to talk about.

"Listen," she said. "Come sit over here."

Colton gave her a worried look before he got up from his desk and sat next to her on the bed.

"We need to talk about something that's kinda important."

He was certainly wary then. "What I do now?"

She grinned and reached to rub the back of his neck. "Nothing, boy. Why? *Did* you do something?"

"No."

"Okay, then quit being so scary. This isn't about you. It's about me."

Colton was all ears.

"I'm dating a guy," she said.

He frowned and sighed quietly.

"I want you two to meet," she said. "I'm hoping you'll be okay with it – with him. He wants to meet you."

"Why?"

"Because he knows that you're the man of the house, and he doesn't think it's right for me to date him without you knowing about it."

Colton's chest poked out a little. Donna knew Marcel was right about how he'd respond if he had a little say so in the matter.

"Is it that same guy?" he asked.

"No."

"Good. 'Cause I don't like him."

"I know," Donna said. "That guy was disrespectful, and I don't like him either. I told you I wouldn't see him again. My new friend's name is Marcel. He's a cop."

"Where'd you meet him?"

Donna thought that was an odd question, but she appreciated the dialogue. "At Chili's."

"You already went out with him?"

She bit the bullet and said, "Yes. We had lunch a couple of times. But he's the one who said he doesn't want to sneak around behind your back. He wants you to know about him, so... Now you do. I told him you have a game tomorrow, and we usually go out to lunch afterwards. I invited him to your game, and I would like for us three to have lunch tomorrow."

Colton didn't respond.

"What do you say?" Donna asked. "Does that sound okay with you?"

He shrugged. "I guess so."

"Thank you." She gave him a hug. "I appreciate that you're being so adult about this."

"What if I don't like him?"

"Well, I guess I won't go out with him anymore, and I'll be lonely forever. Is that what you want?"

It took so long for him to answer, she thought he'd say *yes*. But he shook his head.

"Try not to be too hard on him," she suggested. "If you go in thinking you won't like him, then you're sure to find something that rubs you the wrong way. But Marcel's a good guy. I can't imagine why you wouldn't like him."

"Marcel, huh?"

"Yes, that's his name."

"If he's *ugly*, I probably won't like him."

Donna laughed at that. *That's one thing we definitely don't have to worry about!* "Boy, finish your homework," she said and left him to his studies.

●●●●●●●

The next day Marcel arrived at noon to take them to Colton's basketball game, which started at one. He was genuinely relieved when he learned that Colton was already at the school; he had to be there a couple of hours early.

"Oh, okay, that's good," Marcel said.

He wore khaki shorts with a white golf shirt. Donna had never seen his legs before. She wasn't surprised that they were as powerfully built as the rest of him. She wore a sleeveless sundress that stopped midway down her thighs. Marcel had never seen so much of her flesh before, but he was too preoccupied with thoughts of Colton to fully admire her.

"Why is that good?" Donna asked as she turned to lock her front door.

"I'm nervous," Marcel said. "Now I have time to get ready for him."

Donna found that amusing. "Get ready for him? What do you think he's gonna do, challenge you to a duel?"

"I just want him to like me."

"He probably won't, not right away," Donna said. "I know he'll be looking for something bad to say."

"But, but what about us?" Marcel asked. They walked to his car, and he opened the door for her. "Oh, wow," he said as she slipped inside.

"What?"

"Your legs are so smooth and shiny."

"I just put lotion on," Donna said, feeling self-conscious. "Did I use too much?"

"Oh, no. You look... Well, you've got legs, and you know how to use them. They're very pretty."

He closed the door and went around to the driver's side. "Don't worry, I'll keep my hands to myself," he said when he sat next to her.

Donna was surprised by the comment, considering he never tried anything past a kiss the first couple of times they went out. "I know you will. You're a perfect gentleman."

"Yeah, but those legs," he said. "I really do want to touch them."

"Oh." Donna felt heat rush to her face and between her thighs. "Are you a leg man?" She crossed her legs slowly as he watched.

"Are you flirting with me, woman?"

"A little bit."

179

He leaned closer and kissed her unexpectedly. Donna loved the way he kissed. He had yet to slip her any tongue, but the way he worked his lips against hers was very sexy.

"I don't know what kind of man I am," he said when they separated. "I really like your hair and your hips, your chest, your face, your, um, *bottom*, and now your legs. I really like your legs."

Donna giggled. She was embarrassed but also pleased to hear that he liked so much about her. "My *bottom*?" she teased.

"I'm trying to keep it PG," Marcel replied.

"Why?" she said. "Colton's not here."

"I don't wanna scare you off. Like you said, I'm a perfect gentleman."

"I don't think there's anything you can say that would scare me off."

"What about my actions?" he asked. "Is there anything I can do?"

"I don't know," Donna said with a grin. "I guess you have to try it and find out."

Her eyes were inviting, and Marcel was no coward. He leaned in again. When their lips touched this time, she felt his hand on her side as well.

"Mmmm." The feel of his warm hand on her bra strap made her moan slightly. And then came the tongue.

Yes! Donna's eyes flashed open for a second as he explored her mouth, licking and claiming it as his own. And then she felt his hand moving.

Oh my.

He touched the side of her breast and then cupped it completely. His thumb sought her nipple beneath the soft fabric. He rubbed it in a circular pattern, and it hardened for him immediately.

Oh wow.

Donna felt a pleasant surge of electricity shoot from her nipple through her entire chest. She gasped slightly, still savoring the sweet taste of his tongue. She arched her back subconsciously, pushing her chest into his hand. Marcel responded by squeezing her breast tighter.

The heat between Donna's legs quickly reached a boiling point. She uncrossed them to alleviate some of the pressure of her throbbing clit. She hadn't been touched like this in nearly two years. She felt moisture in her panties. She wanted Marcel to feel it, too. But she was not upset when he backed away and placed both hands on the steering wheel.

When he could speak again, he said, "I notice you didn't run away."

She shook her head and managed a breathy, "Nope."

Marcel looked past her to the front door of her home. "I, I really don't wanna go watch a basketball game now," he said.

Donna couldn't stop herself from saying, "I don't either."

"We'd better go," he said.

She nodded. "Yeah, we better."

He started the car and reluctantly piloted them to their destination.

•••••••

Colton's game was a blowout. By halftime his team was up by fifteen points. Marcel was happy to see that Donna's son was the best player on the team. He enjoyed watching Colton's athletic prowess, the way he sprinted effortlessly up the court when others were fatigued and couldn't match his hustle.

Jaylen was a pretty good basketball player himself. Thinking about him caused Marcel to experience a few unexpected heartbreaks as he watched the kids play. But each time he felt like he needed a drink to get through the game, he looked over at Donna, and her smile made the urges go away.

Colton didn't acknowledge them during halftime, which upset his mother.

"I'm gonna go get him," she said.

Marcel grabbed her hand and urged her not to. "Don't do that. He'll come to us when he's ready."

"But he always waves at me during halftime," she complained. "Sometimes he'll run over here real quick, to give me a kiss. He's avoiding us, well *you*."

"That may be true," Marcel said. "But he knows I'm here. We made eye contact several times during the game. Let him work this out on his own. It's not like he's gonna leave the gym when the game's over, without saying anything to you."

Of course Marcel was right about that. The game ended with Colton's team up by twenty-four points. All of the players retreated to the locker room immediately afterwards. They emerged twenty minutes later dressed in street clothes. Colton looked nervous when he finally approached the bleachers where his mother sat with an unfamiliar man. Marcel was anxious as well. He stood and cleared his throat. Donna stood beside him.

"Baby, you were awesome!" She hugged Colton and planted a kiss on his cheek. "I thought you were never going to come say hi to us," she chided him. "Well, this is Marcel. Marcel, this is my son, Colton."

"Nice to meet you," Marcel said. He reached to shake the boy's hand.

"Hi," Colton said. "Nice to meet you."

They looked each other in the eyes as they shook hands. Marcel could tell the boy was very protective of his mother. And Colton could tell that Marcel was seriously smitten. He was intimidated by the massive size of his mom's new friend, but he felt like he had the upper hand, so he was able to maintain eye contact.

"Man, you know how to handle that ball," Marcel told him. "How many points you score? All of them?"

Colton grinned. "Eighteen."

"Seemed like a lot more than that," Marcel said. "You're a great player. An *unselfish* player. I'm impressed."

"Thank you."

"You ready?" Donna asked him.

"Oh, um, the coach wants to take us out for pizza," Colton said. "Can I go?"

Donna frowned. "You're supposed to have lunch with us today. We talked about it already."

"I know, but–"

"It's alright," Marcel said. "Let him go celebrate with his team. We can have lunch anytime."

Colton smiled at that.

"Alright," Donna said. "Is Coach gonna bring you home afterwards?"

"If he doesn't, I can get Kevin's mom to take me."

"Call me, if you need me to pick you up," she told him.

"Alright."

Before he could take off, Marcel said, "Colton, your mom and I are pretty hungry. Is it alright if we go out for lunch without you?"

Colton grinned sheepishly and said, "Yeah, that's cool."

"Alright," Marcel said. "I look forward to catching some more of your games."

"Okay."

"Have fun," Donna told him. She gave him another kiss before he took off. Colton looked embarrassed as he pulled away from her.

When they got back to his car, Donna asked Marcel, "So, did you get the approval you needed."

"Yep." Marcel was very happy. "And you know what they say: Once you invite a vampire inside, you give them power to do whatever they want."

"What are you gonna do?" Donna asked. "Bite my neck?" Her smile was devilish.

Marcel started to do just that, but he resisted, knowing Colton was somewhere nearby. "Uh, where do you wanna go for lunch?" he asked.

Donna was too much of a scaredy-cat to say *Your place.* "Wherever," she said instead. "Where do you wanna go?"

Marcel was a scaredy-cat, too. "Um, Chuy's?"

Donna nodded. "Okay." She sat back smiling, thinking everything was finally coming together. Her life was better than it had been in a very long time.

Fire joins moon with dark eclipses
Shading portions of the earth
Distant stars collide without witness
Giving way to miraculous births
For each molecule a mate is provided
The seas burst forth as do the skies
Constantly entities are united
Then why not you and I?

CHAPTER SEVENTEEN
SOFT, WARM AND MOIST

By Thursday the following week, Donna was emotionally and physically drained. The new round of state testing was upon them at Wedgewood Middle, and there was a lot of pressure to get the pass rate up for the school. Donna didn't have to teach much during the testing days, but her paperwork increased. And keeping a whole classroom completely quiet for an hour and a half was stressful.

That Thursday she had to go to one of Colton's basketball games right after school, and they didn't make it home until after dark. Donna made a late dinner, and then took a long, hot bath. She didn't get out of the tub when she heard her cell phone ringing, but she called Marcel back before she went to sleep.

"Good evening," he told her.

Donna stretched out on her bed with a smile stretched across her face. Marcel's deep voice always gave her chills. She hadn't seen him all week, and she wasn't ashamed to say that she missed his strong, physical presence.

"Hey," she said.

"Long day?"

"Yes." She sighed. "I'm glad it's over."

"How did Colton's game go?"

"They won. He scored sixteen, eight assists, eleven rebounds."

"Wow. A double-double."

"He would've had a triple, if he passed the ball more. My voice is a little sore from yelling at him during the game."

Marcel laughed. "You were probably the only parent in the stands yelling at their son to *pass* the ball. Everybody else wants their kid to shoot."

"I know. But I don't want Colton getting a big head. He already has too many girls following him around because of his afro. I should take him to the barber and make him cut it."

"You should let him keep it, so you can threaten to cut it when he starts acting out," Marcel suggested.

"Good idea. I think I'll try that." She yawned.

"You sound really tired. Want me to let you go?"

"I'm in bed," she acknowledged. "But I can talk for a few minutes."

Thinking about Donna in her bed made Marcel smile. He wondered what her bedroom looked like, what color her sheets were. He wondered if he'd ever get to see for himself.

"How was your day?" she asked him. "Did you go to counseling?"

"I did," Marcel said. He was grateful that there was someone in his life who cared enough to ask. "We had a good session."

"What about your house?" Donna asked. "Still no takers?"

"That's actually something me and my counselor talked about. She thinks it's a big hurdle in my recovery."

"I do too."

"Unfortunately the market's not looking good," Marcel said. "The folks who came by to check the place out couldn't get past the lender. Too much recent debt. My counselor thinks I should move *before* I sell the house, but I can't afford it."

Donna thought that was a terrible predicament. A lot of people continued to live in a house where a loved one died, but this was different. Jaylen was violently murdered. Marcel wanted to move on, and everyone thought it was for the best. She hated that financial matters were interfering with his healing, and she hated that she couldn't offer him a solution.

185

"Where do you plan on living, after you sell the house?" she asked instead.

"I would love to move to Long Beach."

Donna's heart froze.

"But I've got too much family here," Marcel continued, and she was suddenly relieved.

"I like the west side of town," he said. "My realtor is already looking at some houses off Alta Mere."

"Why Long Beach?" Donna asked.

"I've been there, only once," Marcel said. "It's been five years, but I still have the city saved on the weather app on my phone. Even when I get a new phone, I plug Long Beach back in there. Sometimes when it's too hot or too cold here, I check the weather in California. It's always nice in Long Beach; seventy, eighty degrees. I guess I'm just fantasizing."

Donna thought that was cute. "Do you like the water?"

"Love it. My mama used to tell me I was part fish. I've been living in the middle of Texas all my life. But in my heart, I've yearned to be near the ocean. I wish I could take you one day."

"Take me where?"

"To Long Beach. Have you ever been?"

"I've been to Anaheim and Pasadena, but not Long Beach."

"Do you like the ocean?"

"I do. Are you asking me to go?"

"I'm just thinking out loud," he said. "But I think it would be nice, if you could go with me."

Donna thought she'd have to lose at least fifteen pounds before she'd feel comfortable enough to strut around with him in a bathing suit. But the thought of Marcel in swimming trunks made her close her eyes and smile longingly. She imagined the baby blue skies, Marcel's dark, chocolate torso on full display, the frothy surf sweeping over their feet as they frolicked, hand in hand.

Frolicked?

She laughed at herself. Grown people in their forties do not *frolic* on the beach. Or do they? As silly as it sounded, Donna would certainly be up for it with Marcel. And she was definitely up for seeing his dazzling arm and chest muscles glistening under the afternoon sun. She was so caught up in the daydream, she didn't realize Marcel was talking about something different.

"Do you have plans this weekend?"

186

"Wait, what about Long Beach?" she said.

"What do you mean?"

"Are you taking me to California or not."

He laughed. "Baby, I will take you wherever you want to go."

That was the first time he called her *baby*. Donna decided that she liked it very much.

"I get two months off every summer," she said.

He chuckled. "Okay. I'll make sure to put it on my calendar."

"Don't forget."

"I won't." The date was October 1st, so he had quite a while before he had to follow through with the trip. "But in the nearer future," he said, "I was wondering if you're available for lunch tomorrow. I know you're going to be tied up this weekend–"

"I'm not busy this weekend."

"Oh. Colton doesn't have a game this Saturday?"

"He does, but I'll be free Saturday night."

"*What*? You're gonna let me take you out at *nighttime*?"

She laughed. "Don't sound so surprised."

"But what about Colton?"

"He's okay with it. Isn't that what you wanted, to get his permission so you can take me out more?" Donna giggled. The whole idea still seemed trivial to her, but it was important to Marcel, and Colton seemed to appreciate the gesture.

"Yes," Marcel said. His heart felt weightless in his chest. This was a small progression in their relationship, but it felt huge. "That is what I wanted."

"Okay," Donna said. "You got it. So where would you like to take me?"

"I don't know. Dinner and a movie?"

"Sounds good."

"Do you want to see anything in particular? I hear that new Angela Bassett movie is pretty good."

"Me too. I wanna see that."

"Okay, I'll check the showings and let you know what time I'd like to pick you up."

"Alright." She yawned again. "Mmmm. Excuse me."

"Get some sleep," Marcel told her. "You sound like you're about to pass out."

"I am," Donna said. "I'm gonna sleep good tonight."

"Me too. And thank you."

"For what?"

"Nothing. For being you," he said. "Sweet dreams, Miss Hodge."

●●●●●●●

On Saturday Marcel picked Donna up at dusk and whisked her away to Saint Emilion on 7th Street. They dined on authentic French cuisine in a small booth that was both cozy and candlelit. Donna found herself staring at his mouth and eyes when he talked to her. She realized she was fascinated by his rugged beauty.

Marcel was captivated by Donna's beauty as well. That night she wore a grapefruit-colored cocktail dress that had spaghetti straps and a cinched waist. It was loose and flirty, the fabric coming to a stop well above her knees. She wore her hair down, in tight curls. Her makeup was flawless. The way the flickering candlelight danced in her eyes made Marcel feel heated, all the way down to the core. He wiped his forehead, expecting to find perspiration.

"Did you enjoy your meal?" he asked.

"I did."

Donna had lobster soufflé, while Marcel enjoyed the Poisson du Jour (which was the fish of the day). Tonight it happened to be roast pike.

"Are you still hungry," he asked. "Thinking about getting some desert?"

"No. Gotta save room for popcorn."

Marcel checked his watch. "We still have forty minutes before the show starts. I think I wanna walk off some of this food."

"That sounds great," Donna said, glad that she wore pumps rather than high heels on their date.

Marcel took them downtown and found a parking spot close to the theater. Just a few days into October, the weather was warm in Overbrook Meadows. The moon was high in the cloudless sky. Marcel took her hand as they strolled on clean sidewalks that were moderately populated at 8:30 pm.

He took her to the Water Gardens, which was one of the biggest downtown attractions. The park was an architectural and engineering marvel, featuring intricate fountains and cascading waterfalls that were colorfully lit and looked absolutely amazing after nightfall. The couple walked hand-in-hand, enjoying the sounds and the scents of tons of water flowing in all directions around them.

Marcel tossed a dime into one of the wishing wells. He pulled Donna closer, before she could inquire about what he wished for. He kissed her slowly, and deeply, beneath the moonlight, next to a wall of flowing water. There were people around them, but Donna lost all sense of place and time when he wrapped his strong arms around her. She placed a hand on his chest and enjoyed the sensations his lips and body brought her. She knew that she had fallen hard for him, and she wasn't afraid of her feelings. She felt safe and appreciated with this man.

The park was so beautiful, she almost didn't want to leave. But going to the movies with Marcel was just as nice. She loved the darkness of the theater, the intimacy of their seats that seemed *very* close together. They sat near the back and quickly abandoned their popcorn in favor of the tastiness of one another. Marcel kissed her neck for the first time. Donna sighed and nearly swooned at the majesty of his lips and tongue on her hot flesh. He was surely the king of all things soft and warm and moist. She was eager for him to reign all over her.

When he began to nibble softly on her earlobe, Donna placed a hand on his thigh to help steady the trembling of her own leg. Bad idea. Her hand came in contact with something hot and hard. She quickly withdrew it, her eyes bright and wide. Marcel continued to trace his tongue down her neck, as if he hadn't noticed.

Gradually Donna's hand returned to the peculiarity between his legs, but of course there was nothing peculiar there at all. It was his dick, and it was rock hard. Rock hard for her. She brushed it with the side of her hand, and then placed her palm over it completely when he didn't protest. Her eyes slipped closed. Her mouth fell open.

Oh, my goodness.

Marcel's manhood extended from the base of her hand to past her longest finger. It was thick. Donna wrapped her hand around it, and her eyes flashed open again – partly because she was surprised by the girth, but also because Marcel nibbled her

189

earlobe with enough force to send a sharp tingle through her head and down her spine.

With his lips brushing her ear, he whispered, "What are you doing, Miss Hodge."

She swallowed roughly. "Um, I don't, nothing."

"I don't think I can take much more of that right now," he confided. He hadn't slept with a woman in so long, he stopped counting how many months it had been.

"I can't either," Donna said. She felt her blood racing through her body, mostly between her legs. The side of her neck was an inferno, each blaze set alight by Marcel's tongue.

She turned and looked him in the eyes. Marcel's orbs were half closed. They closed completely as he leaned in and kissed her again. He sucked her tongue like candy. Donna felt her hand squeeze his thick meat, mostly involuntarily. It jumped beneath her fingers, which made Donna moan softly.

"Colton's away for the weekend," she whispered.

Marcel's body was redirecting a good deal of blood to his manhood, so it took his brain a few seconds to catch up to what she said. He relinquished her tongue so he could respond.

"He's... What was that?"

"You don't have to leave," Donna said, "when you take me home." Her heart was thundering. A part of her couldn't believe she was being so forward. But another part of her, a wet, throbbing part, knew that she could no longer deny herself. Her heart, mind and soul yearned for him in the worst way.

Marcel moistened his bottom lip as he watched the lights from the film reflecting in her eyes. Donna leaned in and kissed the same lip. He moaned quietly as she sucked it into her mouth.

"Do you want to see the rest of the movie?" he asked.

Donna shook her head. They were halfway through the flick. She had no idea what it was about.

"Okay," Marcel said. "If you let me go, and give me a couple of minutes, I should be able to stand up without everyone staring at me."

Donna laughed at that. She gave him a parting stroke and squeeze before pulling her hand into her own lap.

It only took one minute before Marcel told her, "Okay. Let's go."

When he rose to his feet, Donna saw that he wasn't quite ready.

"I'm as ready as I'm gonna get," he said, following her gaze.

Donna giggled, and she managed to keep her hands off of him until they got back to his car.

●●●●●●●

She was in a rush to get home, but Donna was grateful when Marcel stopped at 7-11 to purchase a box of condoms. She was impressed that he was responsible enough to think of it, even though she felt like she'd entered a time warp when he hopped back in the car. Apparently Marcel did too.

"Wow. I haven't done that in a while," he told her as he buckled his safety belt.

Donna grinned and blushed coyly.

When they entered her house, she left him in the front room, while she went to get them a bottle of wine. Marcel was too anxious to sit down. Donna didn't know that he followed her to the kitchen, until she felt him approach from behind while she fiddled with a corkscrew. Marcel put both arms around her and held her close to his body. Donna felt weightless as she leaned back into him.

She placed her hands over his; all four of them resting on her stomach. He spoke directly next to her ear.

"Do you need help?"

Donna's heart was racing. She managed a shaky, "Yes."

He released her, and she stepped aside so he could get to the bottle. Marcel popped the cork with ease and poured the Moscato into two glasses she had on the counter. He offered one to Donna and watched her while she slowly sipped it.

He asked, "Are you nervous?"

She nodded.

Marcel brought his glass to his lips and sipped the sweet liquor sparingly. Wine was not his preference, but it was acceptable. Actually it was perfect, considering he was trying to cut back. Donna finished her drink and placed it on the counter. Marcel placed his beside it and approached her slowly. His eyes were dark with desire. Donna was so apprehensive, she felt her legs trembling.

191

Marcel put his hands on her waist and kissed her softly. Her lips were full and slightly cold from the wine she consumed. He slipped his tongue into her mouth and pulled her hips closer, until there was only heat and a few layers of clothing between them.

Donna closed her eyes and sighed pleasantly as she gave in to the passion that had been building up inside her for so long. Marcel was an excellent kisser. His lips and tongue worked in tandem; sucking and licking. He nibbled her bottom lip and tugged it slightly with his teeth. Every move he made set the embers in Donna's chest aflame. Gradually the fire rolled down her stomach and found a home between her legs.

Marcel pulled her hips closer still. His hands moved smoothly until he had full control of her ass. He squeezed her, gently at first, but gradually his confidence grew. Donna felt his hands caressing her ass from top to bottom. He fondled both cheeks, hard enough to make her moan softly as he drew them even closer. Donna felt juices moistening her panties.

She began to squirm in her pumps, and then she felt the floor disappear from beneath her feet.

"Oh!"

She cried out in shock and reflexively wrapped her legs around his waist. Marcel backed her against the counter and set her on top of it. Now they were the same height. He looked into her eyes and smiled when he saw Donna's expression of shock and wonderment. Her legs were spread wide to accommodate him. With the counter supporting her, he was able to release her ass and undo the buttons on his shirt. Donna watched, still somewhat in a daze. She barely felt him lift her off the tiles. And she wasn't a small woman. She knew he was strong, but...

Marcel got his shirt off, and everything became crystal clear. Of course he didn't have any trouble lifting her. Under the bright lights in the kitchen, Donna saw that every muscle he'd been hiding under his tee-shirts was as beautifully sculpted as she imagined. His massive pectorals were the most impressive, but his arms and shoulders were equally enticing. Every bulge fought for her attention. Donna wasn't aware that her mouth hung open. Marcel stepped closer, and she held both hands up – not to stop him, but to feel the goose bumps that were scattered across his chest.

She sucked air between her teeth the moment her hands came in contact with his dark flesh. He was so hot. And hard! She felt his powerful muscles ripple beneath her fingertips. She felt his heart thumping strong against his sternum. Her bottom lip slipped into her own mouth as she fondled him at will. His nipples were big and dark. She couldn't resist tasting them. Marcel's hand moved to the back of her neck as she ducked down and suckled his nipple unexpectedly. He looked up to the ceiling and took a deep, slow breath.

Donna licked one nipple, and then the other. She sucked them both and nibbled them softly. She stopped when the heaving of his chest became more pronounced. She looked up at him, her lips wet, her face flushed with heat.

"I want you," he said. "I need you. Now."

His eyes were low and drunk with passion.

The yearning between Donna's legs was white hot.

She nodded and grabbed hold of his shoulders, so he could help her off the counter.

●●●●●●●

In the bedroom, he helped her out of her dress and marveled at her physique for a few moments. Donna wasn't fully comfortable with her figure, but the hunger in Marcel's eyes quickly vanquished any traces of shame. He kissed her again, slowly this time, as he reached around and undid her bra.

When her breasts were free, his kisses snaked down her chest, leaving a trail of quivering flesh in their wake. Her nipples hardened before he took them into his mouth. He caressed her breasts expertly as he feasted. He licked around her areola and tweaked her nipples between his teeth until she cried out in pleasure. She cried out again when she felt his hand between her legs.

"*Ah! Oh!*"

She threw a hand over her mouth to muffle her sounds.

Marcel watched her, a mischievous grin parting his lips. He pulled her hand from her mouth and told her, "It's okay. I want to hear you. I want to know what makes you happy."

Donna didn't know how to respond to that. She continued to pant as his large, gentle hand returned to the treasure he discovered between her thighs. He rubbed the outside of her panties. She was so wet, she was beginning to leak through. He helped her onto the bed and laid her back, so that he could pull the panties down the length of her long, beautiful legs. He then placed his hands on her knees and stared down at a sight so naturally beautiful, men had risked their lives for it since the beginning of time. A roomful of scientists could never duplicate it.

He blinked quickly, each time rewarded with an exquisite vision that was no mirage. He saw that her labia glistened with her essence. Her exotic scent made his mouth water. He longed to devour her, to bury his face within her folds and suck and swallow every drop. The only thing that stayed him was the yearning between his own legs, which had reached critical mass and could be neglected no longer.

As he removed his shoes and pants and sheathed his sword with the prophylactic, Marcel made mental notes of what he wanted to do to her. Later. How he planned to please her, how hard and often he wanted to suck, how long it would take before her thighs slammed closed against his ears, how she would look down at him as he patiently pried them apart again.

Donna wasn't aware that Marcel was sizing her up, making plans to please her beyond this encounter. From her perspective he was a slow, methodical lover. Agonizingly patient. She watched as his pants fell around his ankles, and then the boxers. The sight of his huge erection made her whole body convulse in anticipation. She was already wet, but she felt her kitty produce another coat of lubrication, just for him. The way Marcel stared between her legs, she felt like he could see that she was leaking. She didn't care.

She didn't care that she licked her lips uncontrollably as he applied his condom. She didn't care if he saw how badly she wanted him to put it in her mouth. All of it, or at least as much as he could slide past her lips. If she could speak, she would have told him, demanded it. But breathing was a hard enough task at that moment. She still hadn't gotten her breaths under control when Marcel finally climbed onto the bed and hovered over her.

He was so big. She could see nothing but him. She feared that she wouldn't be able to take all of him. It had been so long. But Marcel was gentle with her. At first. When his face reached the same level as hers, he kissed her softly. So softly.

He said, "Baby, are you alright?"

She nodded, but her eyes said otherwise.

Marcel settled his hips between her legs. He reached down and rubbed the head slowly against her clitoris.

"*Ah. Oh God.*"

"*Relax,*" he told her. He continued to work the head up and down. He found her opening and invaded her as slowly as possible.

Donna wasn't aware that she was holding her breath. He brought his hand up and planted his forearms on the mattress. She felt every inch of him as he slid farther and farther, deeper inside her.

He paused and told her, "*Donna, baby you so wet.*"

She took slow, shallow breaths, watching his eyes.

"*Almost,*" he whispered and began to push deeper still.

Almost?? Donna would've sworn that was all of him, but there was still two more inches of rock hard chocolate that yearned for her tight wetness. She had her first orgasm the moment their pubic hairs meshed. It was so unexpected, she didn't have time to brace herself or stop herself from moaning loudly in his hear.

"*Oh! Oh! Oh my God. Oh God! Ooh, Marcel!*"

He felt her walls contracting, squeezing him rhythmically as her kitty purred. Donna's cries magnified his pleasure immensely. He began to pump his hips, hitting the back end with each long stroke. The deeper he went, the tighter she was. It was hard for him to concentrate on bringing her pleasure while her body effortlessly provided so much pleasure to him.

Donna's orgasm felt like a volcano in her womb that erupted ever so sweetly and sent prickly streams of lava flowing down her legs. She felt lightheaded. She closed her eyes and rode a wave of ecstasy that seemed to never end as the speed of Marcel's hips increased. She felt him hitting walls that had been neglected for too long. He stroked her long ways, making sure to brush her throbbing clitoris with each thrust. And he stroked her deeply, pushing the head further and further.

He told her, "*Baby, you feel so good.*"

He cried out as her nails dug into his powerful back, which fanned out like a deck of cards. As her second eruption gathered momentum, Donna began to push her hips into him, matching his movements precisely, ensuring that he went harder and faster with each stroke.

Marcel couldn't take much more, but his desire to please her was stronger than his own need for release. Donna's movements and shudders and touches took his pleasure to new heights. He felt her pushing off the bed as her body squeezed and coaxed his dick, demanding more. But it was hard for him to hold back.

"*I can't,*" he panted. "*Baby, I can't...*"

"*Cum,*" she beckoned him. "*I want, I want you to.*"

But Marcel refused – not until he felt her walls convulsing again, and her screams began to reverberate off every wall in the room.

"*Ah! Oh! Yes, baby! Do it! Yesss!*"

Her eyes rolled back as a second eruption, this one rivalling Mt. Vesuvius, exploded deep within her, sending tremors rolling down every limb. She dug her nails into his flesh deeply enough to break the skin. And then, only then did Marcel release his grip on a tidal wave he'd been holding back with only his willpower.

He slammed in deep, one last time. His grunts were animalistic. He pushed harder and harder, taking them to a place of celestial beauty. Cosmos shifted, and the stars aligned perfectly for their love. Donna's screams were music to his ears as his manhood pulsated, pumping hot semen with each one of his heartbeats.

They rode the wave of ecstasy together, for what felt like five glorious minutes. When Marcel finally rolled over and lay next to her, spent and exhausted, Donna knew that she was in love with him. Even better was the fact that she wasn't afraid of her feelings.

He went to dispose of his condom. He returned and spooned with her as she drifted off to sleep. Donna wasn't aware that she smiled as she slumbered. In her dreams, she was on a beach. Walking along the coastline. She loved the feel of warm, wet sand between her toes, even as the incoming tide washed it away with each step.

Marcel was there. He emerged from the ocean wearing black trunks. The water dripping off his body glistened beneath the fading sunlight. He walked to her with a look of hunger and longing in his eyes. Without saying a word, he made it clear that she was the only woman he'd ever have eyes for.

●●●●●●●

Marcel's feelings for Donna were equally intense, but as the minutes turned into an hour, sleep for him was elusive. He fought his cravings for as long as he could, but there was no peace in his mind. He felt conflicted because Donna gave him her all, and he tried to do the same, but his secret was eating at him; tearing his soul apart, telling him that their union was a lie.

He hated himself for not telling her in the beginning, and he hated himself for not being strong enough to conquer his demons on his own. He felt like a coward as he crept out of her bed. But the peace he sought could not be found in her bedroom. There was nothing Donna could do to make him better.

Marcel found his salvation in the kitchen. His body craved something stronger, and he didn't care much for the taste of Moscato, but he was far from home, and there was nothing else. He finished the glass he left on the counter earlier, but it wasn't enough. Of course it wasn't.

His eyes filled with tears as he picked up the bottle and brought it to his lips. With each swallow, he knew that he'd leave evidence of his addiction, evidence that he was not who he said he was. But that knowledge did not suppress the monsters that raged within him. Only alcohol did.

When he set the bottle down, it was completely drained. Marcel felt lower than dirt, but once he concealed the empty bottle in Donna's trash bin, he started to feel a little better. By the time he crept back to his woman's bed, the alcohol was starting to work its magic, and he was back to his old self.

He was able to sleep then, but his dreams were not pleasant. There was no beach or fading sunset or smiling Donna waiting for him with open arms. In his dreams, Marcel saw destruction. He knew that was all that would remain of the union he and Donna built when she finally saw him for who he truly was.

But there was still time. He could still fix everything.
All he had to do was
Stop.
Drinking.

LIFE AFTER

It was that simple.
There was still time.

CHAPTER EIGHTEEN
ADDICTION

The following morning Marcel woke up bright and early in an unfamiliar bedroom. It was the mouthwatering aroma of bacon and eggs that roused him. When he cleared the fog from his head and remembered where he was, his heart sank. Donna was not in the bed with him. If his sense of smell was correct, she was in the kitchen preparing a meal. Marcel knew he'd have to explain what happened to the rest of the wine, so he was slow in putting on his pants and shirt.

He racked his brain for a good explanation, but he couldn't come up with anything. He knew it was time to come clean. But when he got to the kitchen, Donna smiled and presented him with an awesome breakfast plate.

She stood on her toes so she could kiss him on the corner of the mouth. "Good morning, sleepy head."

Confused, Marcel took his plate and said, "Thank you."

Donna wore a blue camisole with boxer shorts. The camisole could barely contain her boobs. Her legs were long and enticing. She looked sexy as hell, even with a pair of furry slippers.

Marcel felt disgusting by comparison, not because he hadn't bathed, but because his secret stained him like mud. The fact that Donna continued to smile at him like she didn't see it made him feel even worse.

He took his plate to the kitchen table. There was so much food.

"I didn't know what you liked, so I made a little of everything," Donna said. She followed him to the table and watched as he looked over her meal.

199

Marcel saw that in addition to the bacon and eggs, he had a slice of toast, a few sausage links, half a grapefruit and a small bushel of grapes.

"This is awesome," he said.

"Are you sure? It's not too much?"

Marcel shook his head. There was a large variety of food, but each portion was small. "No. It, it's perfect. It looks delicious."

Donna smiled like a happy homemaker. "Good." She went back to the sink to finish up a few dishes she was washing.

Marcel watched her. Donna's ass looked perfect. Her hips were spread just right. Miss Hodge was a fine woman, from head to toe. Unfortunately Marcel didn't have an appetite for the breakfast she made him. His heart began to thud when he saw that she was washing their wine glasses from last night.

"Do you know what happened to the rest of that Moscato?" she asked over her shoulder.

Marcel's mouth went completely dry. His fork began to shake in his hand, so he sat it down on the table. "I, I'm sorry, but... I spilled it," he said. "I came in here last night, wanted some water. I couldn't see well, and I knocked it over. I'm sorry."

He had no idea where the lie came from, but it was plausible. Donna didn't question it at all.

"Sorry," she said. "I should've left a night light on." She still didn't look back at him.

"No, it's my fault," Marcel said. "I feel so bad about it."

She did look at him then. "It's no big deal. Just a bottle of wine. I think it was ten dollars." She frowned when she saw that he hadn't touched his food. "Are you sure you're hungry? You don't like it? I'm sorry. Tell me what you want, and I'll make it for you. Or we can go get something."

Marcel was relieved that she accepted his lie so easily. But it was a weak victory, and he knew that it came with a huge price.

"No, I do like it," he said and picked up his fork.

"Are you sure? Don't eat it just to make me happy."

"Look at me," he said with a smile. "Do I look like the kind of guy who would eat just to make someone happy? Me and food get along very well."

Donna grinned. No, he certainly did not look like a picky eater. Marcel looked like the kind of guy who required a lot of protein and carbohydrates to keep those muscles primed. And Donna loved to cook. She never complained, but her ex-husband's health food kick drove her nuts sometimes. She didn't feel like a provider when all she had to do was hand him a banana and a granola bar and a carton of orange juice.

She finished the dishes and then sat with Marcel while he wolfed down his breakfast. His plate was completely clean when he finished. Before he left, he said he had something he needed to talk to her about. Donna was all ears.

"I still have some issues I'm working on," he told her. "I'm learning a lot from my counselor, and we're working it out. But I'm not where I want to be yet. I'm still going through some stuff, because of what happened to my son."

"I know," Donna said. "I can only imagine how hard that must be."

"I'm afraid that some of my mess might affect you, at some point," he said.

Donna held his hand and looked deeply into his eyes, as if she was searching for the truth his mouth wouldn't provide. "Marcel, I care a lot about you. I know things aren't perfect. No one's perfect. I'm here for you. Whatever you need."

Marcel's heart swelled. He suddenly felt like there was hope for him after all. Donna was understanding. She wouldn't condemn him. But she would think of him differently, if he told her about his drinking. She would realize that depending on him was a risk. No. Marcel didn't want that. It would be much better if he could get over his addiction without involving her.

They embraced in the living room. They held each other for nearly a minute, neither of them saying a word. Donna's love made Marcel feel confident and powerful. He felt like he could tackle anything the world threw at him. His love made Donna feel complete. It was an all-encompassing emotion that she hadn't felt since her husband died. Everything felt *right*. She knew that she deserved to find true happiness, and she was optimistic. Only a small part of her still wanted to be wary.

●●●●●●●

The next morning at work, Marcel was surprised when his boss stopped by his desk and said, "Hey, could you step into my office?"

That was usually a bad sign, but Lieutenant Freddie Mueller didn't look upset today. Plus Marcel hadn't done anything wrong, that he could think of. He followed him to a corner office, and Lieutenant Freddie told him to, "Close the door."

That was another bad sign. Marcel did as he was told and then took a seat warily. He brought his hands together in his lap and twiddled his thumbs.

"How you doing?" Lieutenant Freddie asked him.

"I'm good," Marcel said. "What's going on?"

The lieutenant leaned back in his executive chair and watched him for a few seconds. Marcel admired his boss – not only because Lieutenant Freddie had reached heights that not too many black policeman achieved in Overbrook Meadows, but also because he was a *good cop*. There was as much corruption in their department as there was anywhere else in the state. But Lieutenant Freddie was not part of the problem.

"Got the results back from your exam," he said at length.

Marcel had no idea what he was talking about.

"The sergeant's exam," Lt. Freddie said. "You took it back in August."

Marcel did remember then. "Oh. I didn't hear anything back, so I thought I failed it."

Freddie shook his head. "No. Not at all. Over a hundred people took that test, and you got the third highest score."

Marcel's eyes widened. "Oh. That's, uh, that's great."

"I talked to the commissioner," Freddie went on. "Folks downtown wanna do something different next year, and your name came up."

Marcel was even more surprised. "Something different, like what?"

"A new task force," his boss said. "The mayor finally gave us the green light to start working on some of the major players. Mr. Brown is at the top of the list, but we're also looking at the Morales brothers and The Moose. You know, the big guys."

Marcel was already stunned, but every detail pulled him closer to the edge of his seat. "Really?"

Lt. Freddie nodded. "I know you've been talking about those men for years. I knew you'd be happy to hear that."

"Hell yeah," Marcel said. His heart thumped at the possibility of finally going after Mr. Brown. He was responsible for nearly a third of the crack cocaine in the city. The Morales brothers were big time heroin distributors with ties to the Mexican Mafia. The Moose was the leader of an outlaw biker gang that chose meth as their money maker. There were hundreds of dealers and enforcers associated with the kingpins Lt. Freddie mentioned. It would take years to get them all, but Marcel always felt like it was something that needed to be done.

"But what do I have to do with it?" he asked.

"I know you thought no one was listening to your complaints," Lt. Freddie said, "but you're wrong about that. And you have an exemplary record with the department. You're good police, Marcel. Everybody knows it. The commish wants to put you in charge of the new unit."

Marcel was floored. He couldn't stop his jaw from dropping. "But, but I'm not–"

"Your test score puts you in line for a promotion to sergeant," Lt. Freddie said. "You'd work under Lieutenant Shelton for the first year, but he'd only be acting as a figurehead. You'll be running the unit. You can choose your crew and everything. We got judges and the D.A. ready to get you whatever you need; wiretaps, twenty-four hour surveillance, the works. After the first year, the commish wants to promote you again to lieutenant, and the department will officially be all yours."

Marcel couldn't take any more excitement. This was too good to be true. But if it was real, why wasn't Lt. Freddie smiling? Why'd he appear to be in a somber mood when he called Marcel to his office? Unfortunately, the answer to that was forthcoming.

"The only problem is," Freddie said, "I can't sign off on this, and I think you know why."

Marcel did, but at the same time he didn't. The smile fell from his face.

"Your shit ain't right," Lt. Freddie explained. "You know I love you like a son, Marcel. I understand what you've been going through, with the death of your son and all. I know you're back in counseling, and I know you're doing your best not to let it affect your work. But your drinking is a problem, and I can't put a drunk in charge of this new unit. I won't do it. I'm sorry to speak so bluntly, but I think we've been pussy-footing around this issue for too long."

Marcel felt like the whole world suddenly turned upside down. What was this? Why would Lt. Freddie dangle a carrot in his face, only to snatch it away at the last minute?

"I'm, I'm working on it," Marcel managed. "I got it under control."

Lt. Freddie shook his head woefully. "No, son, you don't. I know you don't. You know you don't. And even worse, the whole department knows you don't. This is not something you can fix on your own."

"Yes I can," Marcel said. "I can take care of this, Lieutenant. I just need a little time."

His boss was still shaking his head. "No, Marcel. If you want this promotion, you're gonna have to get clean *publicly*. You have to get in some kind of treatment center, so everyone will know you're serious. It would be bad for morale, if we put you in charge of the new unit in your current state."

Marcel knew that what he was saying was true, just as he knew that he probably couldn't fix himself alone. But with the promise of a new position that would make him feel good about his job, make him feel like his work actually had meaning, maybe he *could* stop drinking, if he gave it one more shot.

"Whenever you're ready to check yourself in somewhere," Lt. Freddie said, "I can give you a couple of weeks off. Just say the word."

That was too much of a commitment for Marcel. A treatment center was a sign of weakness and failure. He'd have to tell everyone he was in *rehab*, like a junkie. He would have to tell Donna. His mother. He shook his head.

"Lieutenant, please give me a chance. I'm telling you, I can beat this. You have to trust me."

Lt. Freddie had seen many addicts in his time. Some screwed up their lives so badly, they'd jump on a legitimate offer to get clean. Others wouldn't take hold of a helping hand until they hit rock bottom and lost everything and everyone in their life who cared about them. He hated to think Marcel might take that route, but he knew that ultimately it was Marcel's decision.

He sighed. "Alright, officer. Go ahead and try to get yourself straight. But if you can't do it, you need to come and talk to me. Because if things keep going like they are, you're gonna end up with a *mandatory order* to go to rehab. If that happens, there won't be a promotion to sergeant, and you definitely won't be in charge of this new unit. Trust me; you do not want us to have to force you. I'll keep this conversation between us for a few weeks. But you'd better show me something."

"Okay," Marcel said, his heart filled with hope again. He was stronger than his alcohol dependence. He could prove it. And when he did, Mr. Brown was finally going down. That was reason enough to get sober.

He stood and reached over the desk to shake his boss' hand. "Thank you, sir. I won't let you down."

● ● ● ● ● ● ●

Marcel's drinking problem was the only thing on his mind for the rest of the day. When he got off work, he went through his house, collecting all of the bottles of alcohol he could find. Most were empty, but a couple of them were still full of the delightful brown stuff. It hurt his heart to pour it down the sink, but he thought of Donna and his promotion, and that made it easier.

He tossed the bottles in the trash and then took the trash to the curb, so he wouldn't be tempted to sort through them again later in the night. That's when his cravings were always at their worst.

The moment his house was free of alcohol, Marcel realized he needed a drink. Badly. It was 7:29 pm. The liquor stores closed at nine, so if he could hold out until then, there was no way he could get more Crown Royal that day.

To pass the time, he went to his computer and researched *alcoholism* and *addiction*. He found a site that gave some of the warning signs of an alcoholic. Marcel had been avoiding the label for so long, he was starting to believe he really wasn't an addict. But the list said otherwise:

Feel guilty or ashamed about your drinking
Check.
Lie to others or hide your drinking habits
Check.

Have friends or family members who are worried about your drinking

Marcel thought of his brother Terrance and his boss, and he had to check that one, too.

Need to drink in order to relax or feel better

Marcel didn't think he drank to relax, but it certainly helped him feel better about Jaylen. Check.

Regularly drink more than you intend to

Check.

Black out or forget what you did while drinking

Marcel was glad to finally reach a symptom that didn't apply to him. But that was the last one on the list. Out of the six warning signs they offered, he had checked five.

Oh, God.

He caught himself before he slipped into a fit of despair. Okay. So he was an alcoholic. That was fine – not fine, but it was okay because accepting that he had a problem was the first step in finding a solution.

Next he typed, "How to stop drinking alcohol." That search provided good information, but mostly it was things Marcel already knew. He learned that he should avoid people and places where he was likely to drink. Done. He wouldn't go to the bar, and he didn't generally drink with people to begin with.

The website said he should get rid of all of the alcohol in the house. Done. He should pick a specific day to stop drinking. Got it. Today was the day. He should drink a lot of water. Marcel thought that was an excellent idea. He wanted a drink that very moment, but he went to the fridge and got a bottled water instead.

But not all of the information he found on the internet was helpful. One website said alcoholics should initially try to cut down on the amount of liquor they consumed each day. Marcel knew that wasn't good advice for him. But out of all of the things he read that night, that one sentence stayed with him the most.

Initially, try to cut down...

His sensible side told him, *No, don't go back! You already decided to quit cold-turkey, and you need to stick to that. Don't try to bargain with the devil. You can't win!*

But the addicted part of his brain told him, *The website says you should cut back **first**. It says you shouldn't go cold-*

turkey without consulting your doctor. You never tried to cut back, so how do you know it won't work? You have no idea what you're doing. Is it wise to argue with the expert who wrote this article?

Marcel didn't know what to do, but he knew that he'd been biting his nails furiously for the past half hour. And the bottled water did nothing to stop his cravings. He checked his watch. It was 8:45. He still had time to make it to the liquor store, if he hurried.

He got up and grabbed his keys, but his cellphone rang before he made it out of the house. It was Donna. Marcel knew she was a Godsend. He took a seat on the couch, and they talked for an hour. Nine o'clock came and went without him noticing. Marcel didn't crave alcohol at all when he was on the phone with her.

But by eleven-thirty things were different. Marcel tossed and turned in his big, lonely bed. The house was hot, even with the AC blowing. His pillow was moist with sweat. He couldn't get Crown Royal at that hour, but he got dressed and made it to the corner store in time to buy a six pack of Colt 45. The tall cans. He didn't like the taste of malt liquor, but that's what his dad used to drink, and it did the trick.

An hour later Marcel sat on his couch grinning at old Martin reruns. He popped the tab on his fourth beer and decided that cutting down was a better alternative to quitting cold-turkey. And drinking *beer* was a step down from hard liquor. He did drink more than he intended to that night, and he was drinking to relax and feel better, and he did feel ashamed of his drinking when he finally went to bed at two am.

But that didn't mean he had to go to rehab. Today was the first day he seriously confronted his problem, and he believed he accomplished a lot. He learned about his addiction, he disposed of all of the liquor in the house, and (between his job and Donna) he had two big incentives to get his life together.

He did give in to temptation in the end, but that was only a few beers. Well, he drank all six beers, if you wanna get technical about it. But Marcel still considered his first day of sobriety a success.

Inside I knew
I compromised
My life, my mind
My peace, my pride
Doors locked – I hide
But I can't hide
The pain that ripped
My soul, the price
Too high – Oh Christ
Dear God. Damn. Why?
Can't catch this bitch
This fix – this itch
This devil's dish
This mix. This shit

CHAPTER NINETEEN
CURSED

The next thirty days were filled with highs and lows for Marcel. Initially things looked bright for him, with the new job offer and the budding love he shared with Donna. But after a while Marcel started to feel like he took one step back for every two steps forward. He began to believe what his mother told him about a generational curse.

That talk started on Tuesday, October 5th. His mother Gaynell called while he was at work and asked if he wanted to go to the cemetery. Marcel told her he did not, but he called her back when he left the precinct and told her he would pick her up at six.

By the time they got to the Meadow Lawn Cemetery on Rosemont, the sun was starting to set, and the place was deserted. The cemetery was beautiful, but it always seemed like a dying place when they went. Marcel knew that was because the trees were all losing their leaves in October. They shed their beauty faster than the groundskeepers could keep up with.

Dead and dying leaves crackled under Marcel and his mother's shoes when they exited his car. The wind was fierce that day, rattling the bone-colored branches of the mighty oak trees that stretched towards the heavens. Marcel Sr.'s gravesite didn't have a tombstone, just a placard that had sank a little lower than the grass that was growing around it.

Marcel knelt to clear the debris. He plucked a few graveyard weeds and tossed them aside before rising to stand next to his mother. They looked down at the grave for a long time, neither of them speaking.

Marcel broke the silence by telling her, "I been drinking a lot."

Gaynell wasn't surprised by that. Her eyes were still focused on the grave when she asked, "How bad is it?"

"I haven't missed any work," he said. "I don't black-out, and I don't have a bad temper. But I can't stop." That was the first time Marcel revealed so much to anyone. He knew his mother would understand.

But he was surprised when she said, "The Bible speaks of generational curses. Sins of the father. Have you read that?"

Marcel shook his head.

"It's true," his mother said. "Scientists say they can even find it in people's *genes*; how they're predisposed to certain things, addictions. They can get it from their parents."

Marcel considered that. His father was a drunk, true indeed. Marcel Senior was actually the reason his son kept so much to himself. As a child, Marcel never wanted to be like his father. As an adult he continued to distance himself from his bloodline by omitting the "Junior" from his name. Before he died, Marcel Senior was a monster in his own home. He was never sober. He beat his children for the smallest infractions. He beat his wife, too.

The first time his body shut down, and he slipped into a coma, Marcel secretly hoped his father would die. He was only eight at the time. He knew his father didn't work, so they wouldn't miss him financially. And the house was very peaceful while he was in the hospital.

But Marcel Sr. didn't die. Gaynell said he was too *mean* to die. He limped out of Jackson Memorial with less than ten percent of his liver functioning properly. The doctors told him he'd be dead in a year, if he continued to drink. A year later he was back to his old self; chugging Colt 45 at six am, the tall cans.

It took another three years for him to die. The doctors said he had *ischemic bowel*. Marcel was young, but he looked it up, and he understood what killed his father: His liver couldn't filter the toxins he was forcing down his throat, and over time the poisons leaked into his body. Marcel Sr. literally drank himself to death.

As he stood over his father's grave that day, Marcel Jr. had a revelation. He realized why he couldn't tell anyone what was wrong with him. He felt like if he acknowledged that he was an alcoholic, then he also had to acknowledge that he had become his father. And that was not something he could not do.

"I didn't start drinking until Jaylen got killed," he told his mother.

She reached and held his hand. Marcel towered over his mother by a full two feet. She looked up into his cold, dark eyes.

"You're nothing like him," she said.

Marcel hated that that was actually a compliment.

"What are you gonna do?" his mother asked.

"I got a buyer for my house," he said. "I think I'll be better then, once I live somewhere else."

She squeezed his hand tighter. "That's good, baby. Have you talked to Terrence about this?"

He shook his head.

"You know you are not your father, don't you baby? Even if he passed it down to you, that don't mean you have to accept it."

"I know. I'ma get right, Mama. I promise."

Gaynell didn't know if she believed him or not. Marcel Sr. made similar promises many times. But Marcel Jr. had a good head on his shoulders. She decided to give him a little time before she did anything drastic, like stage an intervention. Stubbornness was another thing Marcel got from his father, but there weren't too many similarities past that. Marcel was too strong to fall into the same pattern of self-destruction. And Gaynell would die before she allowed it to happen.

●●●●●●●

On Friday, October 16th the deal closed on Marcel's home. It was sold to a family of three who recently moved to the city from Oklahoma. Marcel's real-estate agent did not tell them that a young boy had been killed in the house.

The same agent helped Marcel secure a three bedroom home on the west side, and he moved in the following weekend. He had his official house warming party on Sunday, October 25th. Terrence came, with his whole family, as well as a handful of people from the police department and a few other friends Marcel had known for years. Donna came, too. She brought him a painting to hang in the front room.

Marcel barbecued hot links and ribs and burgers. There was plenty of music and food and Corona's for everyone. But when the crowd left at sunset, and he was alone in his new home, Marcel realized that moving did not solve his problem. He was still buying three to four bottles of Crown Royal a week. He didn't even drink out of a glass most of the time. The bottle felt good in his hand.

As he drank that Sunday night, Marcel came to understand that his drinking had reached a point where he could no longer blame it on anything. He was still depressed because of Jaylen, but thinking about Jaylen was no longer the catalyst. *Everything* was now a catalyst. Marcel felt like drinking when he was happy. He wanted to drink when he was not. He had to drink when he got off work, and going to bed sober was never an option.

Stress was a major component, which was ironic because he couldn't have any serious thoughts about quitting without stressing himself out. Each time he considered going to rehab or confiding in Donna, there was stress. He would inevitably pick up the bottle, rather than take the necessary steps to fix his life. Everything was so *hard*. But drinking was easy. Marcel now understood why his father chose to escape reality on an hourly basis.

●●●●●●●

On Friday, November 6th Marcel's boss called him into his office again. Marcel had been avoiding Lt. Freddie since their last

211

talk. He reluctantly took a seat across from his desk and girded himself for what was sure to be an unpleasant meeting.

"How are things going?"

"Good," Marcel said, nodding. "I'm good."

"I, uh, I notice you haven't taken those two weeks off yet," Lt. Freddie said. "It's been over a month. Do you still plan on going to rehab?"

"I thought about it," Marcel said. "But I don't think that's for me. I've been cutting down on my own."

Lt. Freddie nodded and smiled. It was a strange smile that didn't convey much amusement. "Okay, so you're saying you're ready for the promotion? You're ready to move ahead with the new unit?"

"I, uh…"

"I need you to be sure," Lt. Freddie said. "Because being in charge of a group of men is a huge responsibility. There will be a lot of hard work. Long hours. A lot of sleepless nights. You have to be a leader; someone they can respect and look up to. You ready for that?"

Marcel had never turned down a leadership role in his life. He was shocked to hear the next words that came out of his mouth. "I, um, I think I need a little more time…"

Lt. Freddie suspected as much. His smile went away as he studied his fallen star. "Is this where you want it to end?" he asked bluntly. "You've reached your peak in the police force? You want to wallow in this department for the rest of your career, do just enough to get by?"

Marcel shook his head. "No, sir. I want the promotion, I just…" He scratched his head, unable to finish the sentence.

"You can't stop drinking," his boss said. "I know you can't."

Marcel's lack of a denial took away a good deal of the compassion the lieutenant had for his situation.

"Okay, I already told you how this was gonna go," Lt. Freddie said. "I told you that if you didn't check yourself in somewhere, we were gonna make it mandatory, and your promotion would be dead in the water at that point. Is that what you want?"

Marcel shook his head. "No, sir."

"Well your time is up," Lt. Freddie said. "You've got exactly one week to either get your affairs in order and admit yourself to a rehab facility *voluntarily*, or you'll be forced to do so by the department. If you refuse to go then, you'll be fired. Do you understand what I'm telling you?"

Marcel took a deep breath and nodded. His heart was in the pit of his stomach. He needed a drink very badly. He couldn't wait for his boss to get this over with, so he could get to the bottle in his car.

Lt. Freddie softened his voice and his demeanor. "Son, I think you're a good cop, probably the best in this department. Everything I offered you is still on the table. You can still be a lieutenant in a couple of years. All you have to do is make the right decision."

Was that all? Marcel chuckled to himself. *Wow, I didn't know that was all I had to do. Really? It's that easy? Just make the right decision? I'm surprised I didn't think of that.*

He stood to leave, but his boss told him, "Wait, there's something else."

Marcel lowered himself back into the chair.

Lt. Freddie sighed and frowned for a few seconds. He knew there was no easy way to broach the next part of the conversation. "I, uh, I talked to an old friend the other day," he said. "I've known her for years. I was once really good friends with her husband, Nolan Hodge."

Marcel's eyes widened. He stared at the man like his nose just fell off.

"I called her, to see how things have been going," Lt. Freddie said. "I hadn't talked to her very much since Nolan's funeral. I was glad to hear that she's doing better; much better than she was the last time I saw her. But she gave me some troubling news. She told me she was dating a cop. You can, um... You can imagine my surprise when she mentioned your name."

Marcel's mouth went completely dry. Not only were his two worlds spinning out of control, but they were colliding. He knew he'd be destroyed by the impact.

"I told her I knew you, but I didn't tell her about your drinking," Lt. Freddie said. "She sounded very happy, when she talked about you. I felt like an ass because I know you're not the person she thinks you are. And I know what she went through with Nolan. Donna has had more pain in her life than she deserves. I'm afraid that I cannot, in good conscience, allow you to deceive her.

"If you care about your job and you care about Donna, then do the right thing. Tell her what's going on and check yourself into a facility. I can't say that she'll stay with you or even forgive you. All I know is she deserves better.

"I won't say anything unless another week passes, and we have to suspend you and force you to go to rehab. And I apologize for bringing your personal life into this. That's all, detective. You're dismissed."

●●●●●●●

Marcel knew that his boss was right, and he didn't harbor any ill will for the intrusion into his personal life. Shit was about to hit the fan, but it didn't have to. Nothing was set in stone yet.

When he got home that evening, Marcel hurried to his computer to do more research. This time rather than look for an understanding, he sought a treatment center that could help him find a solution to his problem. It was unnerving, knowing that he'd have to put his life on hold for two whole weeks. He'd have to tell everyone what was going on. His problems would be exposed for all to see and speculate and judge and condemn him.

He wasn't willing to pay that price for a promotion, but for Donna he would. He would do anything to keep her in his life. He thought about how close they had gotten since she let her guard down and invited him into her world.

In the past few weeks she called him to her home several times. He had dinner with her and Colton. He took them to Six Flags last Saturday, and they all had a good time. Donna was too afraid to ride most of the scary stuff, so Marcel stood in line with just her son for hours. Colton still had a few reservations, but he was opening up to his mother's boyfriend, little by little.

As he perused the internet, Marcel thought of what Colton would think when he found out he was going to rehab. Would it change his opinion of him? Would he still think his mom picked a winner? Would Donna stand by him?

Marcel felt like she would, but there was no way to know for sure. They had only been dating for a little more than two months. Marcel never experienced a relationship that developed so quickly in such little time. He knew that he had totally given in to their love. He truly believed they were meant to be. But maybe Donna's commitment wasn't that strong.

Marcel also wondered what would happen if he didn't make it through rehab. What if he turned out to be like some of the other addicts who tried again and again but simply couldn't get right? Donna would have to leave him then. She couldn't allow Colton to be around someone like that.

Marcel drank half a bottle between the time he got home from work and the time he went to bed, but he also made a little progress. He found the clinic he wanted to admit himself to. It was called Pinewood. According to their website, they accepted his insurance and had been restoring broken people for more than twenty years. He bookmarked the page so that he could complete the application on Monday.

He didn't feel bad about drinking that night, because he wasn't some stupid, old drunk anymore. He was now a man with a plan. He'd been tricked into thinking he was weak, but the devil is a liar. Marcel was as strong as he'd ever been. On Monday he would prove it.

●●●●●●●

The next day he showed up at Donna's house at ten am sharp, so he could take Colton to his football game that started at noon. Marcel's involvement in the activity was not required, because Donna didn't have anything to do that day other than get her toes and nails done. But she asked Marcel to take him.

The two men in her life were not as close as she wanted them to be. She didn't want to push the issue, especially with Colton. But when she asked her son how he felt about Marcel going to today's game in her place, he said it was fine with him. He knew that his mother had taken a strong liking to the big cop, and Marcel was winning him over as well.

The youngster answered the door and said, "Hey, Mr. Webber. Hold on a sec'. Let me go get my bag."

"Call me Marcel," Marcel said (for what had to be the twentieth time).

Colton grinned. "I don't think I can, sir. Mama wouldn't like that."

Donna appeared in the hallway at that moment, looking heavenly, as usual. She wore a loose skirt with a tank top. Marcel's heart leapt at the sight of her. Every time he laid eyes on her, he had the same reaction. He hoped that would never change.

"Morning, handsome," she said as she approached and planted a soft kiss on his lips.

Marcel was surprised by the open affection. He looked over her shoulder, hoping Colton didn't see anything. Thankfully the boy had already ducked into his room.

"What's wrong?" Donna asked him.

"I thought Colton was still around," he said in a hushed tone.

Donna looked back and then laughed at him. "He's seen us kiss before."

"No he hasn't," Marcel said matter-of-factly. He went through great lengths to make sure of it.

"Oh, well I'm sure he's aware that the phenomenon occurs," Donna said with a smile.

She looked so good, Marcel wanted to skip the game with Colton and tag along when she went to the beauty salon.

"What are you doing later, after the game?" he asked.

"I don't know," she said. Her grin was flirtatious. "What do *you* wanna do?"

Marcel had so many things in mind, he couldn't get a response out before Colton reappeared toting a huge duffle bag.

"I'm ready."

Donna grabbed his arm and pulled him to her before he made it to the door.

"Boy, don't try to run out of here without giving me some sugar!"

She planted a kiss on his cheek as he tried to squirm away.

"Come on, Mama."

Marcel laughed at them. He loved watching the two of them interact. It reminded him of Coleen and Jaylen.

His smile slipped as that thought entered his mind and decided to hunker down for a long stay, despite his best attempts to forget about it.

●●●●●●●

Colton's football game started with a bang. The kickoff returner for the opposing team caught the ball on the twelve yard line and proceeded to shake and bake, juke and jive his way all the way back to the opposite end zone. Nearly every member of Colton's team had a chance to tackle him, but the boy squirted past them like a greased pig. Marcel watched from the stands in awe and admiration.

The kid who scored the first touchdown wore jersey #12. In addition to returning kickoffs, he was the starting running back. Marcel sat near the fifty yard line in the packed stadium. He was there to support and root for Colton, but he kept his eyes on #12 from the opposing team throughout the game. That boy was something special. Even more impressive was the fact that he was the smallest player on the field.

Marcel laughed at times as he watched the phenom make fools of the burly linebackers that tried to tackle him. He rose from his seat and had to stop himself from cheering when #12 converted key first downs. Everyone around him wore blue and white and rooted for Finley High. Marcel did too, but he was a sports fan first and foremost, and #12 was the best player on the field. Hands down.

He made it all the way to the third quarter before he realized that it wasn't only the player's skills that had him riveted. Marcel remembered that his son wore #12 when he played football in middle school. Marcel used to sit on metal stadium benches similar to the one he was sitting on now with his eyes glued to Jaylen's jersey. Jaylen played running back, too. He wasn't as good as the #12 Marcel was watching now, but he had some pretty smooth moves. If he had lived, who knows? Maybe Jaylen would've been this good, by the time he made it to high school.

Marcel realized he had a problem when he sniffled, and his nasal passage quickly filled with moisture. The whole field began to drift out of focus. Marcel wiped the tears from his eyes, and he could see the players again. He tried to talk himself down. He could get through this. It was only a football game. And that kid was *definitely not Jaylen.*

But despite his reasoning, Marcel's brain kept making connections between Jaylen and the other player. He remembered how Jaylen was always the smallest player on the field, but he never let it stop him from giving his all. Jaylen would run full speed at a defensive back and do a spin move at the last moment – just when a tackle appeared to be a sure thing.

One of Marcel's proudest moments was a game against Castleberry twelve months ago. All of the players on their squad looked like high school students, and Jaylen's team was down by six points with fifteen seconds left in the game. It was late November. Mother Nature offered as much competition as the opposing team. It was bitterly cold and raining. The field was so muddy, it was hard to tell the players' uniforms apart at times.

Not many parents attended that game, but Marcel was there. He cheered his heart out, even though the outlook was bleak from the start. But then the impossible happened. The quarterback handed the ball off to Jaylen on the twenty yard line, and the pint-sized powerhouse took off like Barry Sanders.

Initially Marcel thought it was a horrible play. Jaylen's team needed a touchdown to win, and they only had one time out remaining. He couldn't believe their coach called a run play. And as Marcel watched wide-eyed and freezing, three huge linebackers converged on his little boy at the same time.

Marcel cringed, afraid to look. But he didn't hear the referee blow the whistle. He dared to open his eyes, and what he saw warmed his whole body like a bowl of Campbell's Thick and Hearty. Jaylen had somehow maneuvered past the three defenders. He did a smooth spin move that left a fourth grasping at air. There were only ten yards between Jaylen and the goal line. He lowered his shoulders and sprinted all out. Marcel was on his feet by then. He left his seat and ran along the sidelines like a mad man, screaming at his boy to, "*Go! Go!*"

But there was one more defender. He waited a few yards out of the end zone. Despite the commotion around him, he was keenly focused on #12. Marcel screamed for his son to go around him, but Jaylen kept plowing full speed ahead. Marcel flinched when the two bodies collided. The defender was taller and bigger. Marcel knew that Jaylen would get close, but not close enough. But at the last moment his son stuck out a mean stiff-arm that sent the defender reeling.

Marcel finally heard the whistle. The referee threw up both hands, indicating it was a touchdown!

Marcel lost all of his composure on that muddy November afternoon, and as he watched this new #12 pull off similar feats of grace and athleticism, he felt his grip on reality slipping again. He knew it wasn't Jaylen on the field. But that knowledge only deepened his agony because he knew that it would *never* be Jaylen. Never again. Jaylen was dead, and it wasn't fair. It wasn't fucking fair!

Marcel buried his face in his hands. He tried to keep it together, but his fingers were trembling, and tears squirted from his eyes.

How long? Dear God, how long?! How long will his memory haunt me? How long before I stop seeing him in every kid's face? Why, God? Why did you take him from me? Why did he have to die?!

"Oh, God. Oh, Jesus..."

When he realized he was speaking aloud, Marcel wiped the tears from his face and looked around. The woman next to him appeared very distressed and uncomfortable. She stared at him like he was crazy, which made perfect sense because Marcel understood that he was indeed losing his mind.

Oh, God, help me. Get it together. Please.

He stood and hurried past the woman who was staring at him. He had to get out of there. He kept going when he reached the stairs, and he kept walking when he reached the stadium's parking lot. When he made it to his car, he popped the trunk and dug for his stash under the spare tire. The bottle of Crown Royal was nearly full. Marcel twisted off the top and brought it to his lips before he realized he should've sat in his car first.

He took a few swigs and then looked around anxiously. There was no one there. Everyone was inside the stadium watching the game. Wait, there was one woman, about twenty feet away. She stared at him like he was drowning a bag of kittens before hurrying on her way.

"Goddammit. I'm a fool," Marcel told himself.

This was his rock bottom. It had to be. He had become his father. But no, not yet. He was going to rehab on Monday. He could fix this. He could fix everything. He only had to tell one more lie. Just one more, and he could start his journey to recovery.

When he got in his car, he was sweating, despite the brisk November weather. He was crying, too. He took a few moments to compose himself before he called Donna. His heartbeats drummed in his ears while he waited for her to pick up.

"Hello? Marcel?"

"Hey, baby. I, uh, I'm sorry, but I have to leave. I got called-in to work."

"Leave where? Aren't you at the game?"

"I am, baby. But I can't stay 'till it's over. I gotta go now. Can you come get Colton?"

Donna couldn't hide her disappointment. "But you were supposed to take him out for lunch afterwards. This was your chance to get to know each other. You didn't tell me you were on-call. What are they calling you in for?"

Marcel's lie was crumbling as badly as his life, but he wasn't messed up enough to drag an innocent kid into his shit. There was no way he could be around Colton in this condition.

"I'm sorry," he said. "I gotta go. You gotta come get him."

Donna sighed. "What quarter is the game in?"

"The third. The end of it. Maybe the fourth by now."

"Alright. I'll pick him up."

"I'm sorry," Marcel said. "I love you."

He hung up before he realized that was the first time he ever told her that.

CHAPTER TWENTY
ON BENDED KNEE

Donna made it to the stadium in time to greet her son when he exited the locker room. Finley High lost by ten points. Donna was not upset anymore. Colton was confused to see her.

"Where's Mr. Webber?"

"He had to go to work," she told him. "It was an emergency. He says he's sorry."

"When did he leave?" Colton asked. "I hope he didn't see the fourth quarter, when I fumbled."

Donna was shocked. "*You* fumbled?"

"I got stripped," Colton said. "But they call it a fumble. Those guys were playing real dirty. They injured Jabari. I know they did it on purpose."

"Did you–"

"Donna. *Donna!*"

She looked back to see one of the booster moms walking towards her.

"Hey, Cheryl. How's it going?"

"I didn't expect to see you here," she said. She shot Colton a glance. "Can I, uh, can I talk to you in private?" She looked upset.

Donna gave her son a mean look.

"I didn't do nothing," Colton said.

"Wait here," she ordered.

She and Cheryl stepped away from him and turned their backs.

"What's up?"

"Your boyfriend," she said. "The guy in the black Charger..."

Donna had never officially announced Marcel as her boyfriend, but with his size and dashing good looks, he was hard not to notice.

"What about him?"

"He was *drinking*," Cheryl informed her. Her cheeks were red with embarrassment. Her beady eyes were wide. "I saw him! He got some liquor out of his trunk and drank it in the parking lot. I saw him. He gave me a *look*. It scared me. He's a scary man."

Donna almost told her that Marcel was big and strong, but he was a sweetie pie, and she shouldn't be afraid of him. But then her brain caught up with the first part of the conversation.

"He, what? *When?*"

"During the game," Cheryl said. "In *broad daylight*. I couldn't believe it."

Donna felt like someone reached inside her chest and grabbed hold of her heart and started squeezing, as hard as they could. She stared in confusion, trying to visualize what this woman was telling her. But she could not. Marcel? Drinking? No way.

But just as quickly, everything started to make sense. And her heart started to beat again, hard and painfully.

"I'm sorry," Cheryl said. "You didn't know..."

Donna shook her head. She was angry and embarrassed and heartbroken. He told her he loved her. Did he say it because he was drunk? He got drunk around her child? How could he?

"Thank you," she told her friend.

"I'm sorry," Cheryl said, shaking her head woefully. "But I knew I had to tell you."

"I know," Donna said numbly. "Thank you."

She turned and rejoined her son. She could barely look him in the eyes. What had she done? Lord only knew what could've happened. How could she be so stupid? Tricia warned her, but she didn't listen.

"Mom?"

"It's okay," she said, fighting back tears. "Let's go."

Colton followed nervously. "Mama, what happened? What'd she say?"

"Nothing, baby." She kept moving, still avoiding eye contact. "It's not about you. We'll talk about it later."

With each step, she moved closer to a realm of uncertainty and pain. Anger and agony battled for possession of her soul.

• • • • • • •

Donna dropped her son off at home. She didn't get out of the car. Colton had been in a state of high anxiety since they left the stadium, and he was eager to flee the vehicle. His mother wouldn't say what the problem was, and he still thought it had something to do with him, despite her assurance that it didn't.

Donna didn't call Marcel back. She knew where he lived. And she didn't want him to know she was coming. She didn't worry that he might have actually gone to work. Marcel had never been called-in unexpectedly, the whole time she'd been with him. The only reason she swallowed the lie was because he never lied to her – that she knew of.

Knowing that he might be an alcoholic made Donna wonder what other stories he fed her over the past couple of months. She knew he was a cop, only because Lt. Freddie backed that up. But everything else was questionable now.

Donna fought back tears as her SUV ate up the interstate. She wondered if she was cursed. The last two men she gave her heart to were deceivers. Everything she believed in was all smoke and mirrors. She knew that confronting Marcel was a waste of time, but she kept the pedal to the metal, because she couldn't sit back and take whatever shit life dumped on her anymore.

Nolan died before she had a chance to look him in the eyes and tell him how badly he hurt her, how he destroyed their family. But Marcel was still alive, and he needed to know what he did to her. He needed to see it with his own eyes.

His car was in the driveway of his new home when she rounded the corner. Donna pulled in behind it so recklessly, she had to stomp the brakes as hard as she could to avoid plowing into it. She exited her vehicle quickly and bounded up the porch with her little fists balled. She ignored the doorbell and pounded hard with both hands. If Marcel had any sense, he'd do his best lying now and pretend he didn't know there was a hellcat on his porch. But after a few seconds he opened the door.

He wore the same outfit he had on earlier that day, but he looked totally different to Donna. His expression was anxious and regretful. His eyes were almost completely bloodshot. Initially she thought he'd been crying, but Donna smelled the alcohol on him, and she knew that he was drunk. Her nostrils flared as she sneered at him. It took all of her willpower to keep her arms by her sides, rather than attack him, scratching and clawing until his lying face didn't hurt her anymore.

"So you, you had to go to work, huh?" she panted.

Marcel's massive chest rose and fell slowly. "Donna, I, I'm sorry. I gotta talk to you."

"Yeah you gotta talk to me," she spat. Her fists were still itching to attack, so she folded her arms roughly, and tucked her hands next to her rib cage.

"I got a problem," Marcel said solemnly. "I been meaning to tell you. I got a problem."

"Yeah, you got a fucking problem!" she screamed and could hold herself back no longer. She breached the doorway and pounded on his chest with both fists, much like she had done to the door a moment ago.

Marcel took a step back but made no further moves to stop her. He turned his face away from some of the higher blows that almost came in contact with his chin. Other than that, he allowed her to vent. He knew he deserved it. Donna looked like a child wailing away uselessly at her father, but when she was spent, she felt a little better.

She lowered her hands and stared at him, breathing roughly. Tears streamed down her face. She looked a mess, but she was still the most beautiful creature Marcel had ever laid eyes on. Seeing her in this condition ripped his heart in two.

"I got a problem," he said. "I'm going to rehab. I was gonna tell you."

"*When?*" Donna spat. "When were you gonna tell me, Marcel?"

"I don't know. Today. Tomorrow."

Fresh tears rolled down his cheeks as well. He looked as forlorn as Donna, but she didn't have any room in her heart to offer sympathy – not where her child was concerned.

"You drank around Colton!"

"I didn't!" he said. "I didn't, Donna. Never."

"Somebody saw you, you liar! You were drinking at the stadium!"

"But not around Colton!" he said. "That's why I left. That's why I called you. I couldn't be around him like that. I knew I was wrong, Donna. That's why I left. I'm sorry."

That one good deed didn't quell her anger. It wasn't nearly enough.

"You been lying to me this whole time," she howled.

"I know. I'm sorry."

"You drank that Moscato, didn't you?"

He nodded. "Donna, listen to me. Please."

"*What, Marcel*?!" she screamed. "*What the hell do you want to tell me*?"

"*I need help*," he cried. "It's just, Jaylen..."

"We talked about that. You had plenty of chances to tell me!"

"I know. I didn't want to. I thought I could... I thought I could stop."

"*I trusted you!*" Donna cried. She was sniveling so badly, her words were nearly indecipherable.

"I'm going to rehab. I was gonna tell you."

"*No you weren't!*"

"I swear, Donna. I was."

"You could've told me when you got drunk in my house!"

"I'm sorry."

"You could've told me *today*, Marcel! You could've told me when you were in the parking lot drinking! But no, I had to hear about it from somebody else!"

"You don't understand..."

"I *do* understand! I understand that you're a *liar*! I can't believe I let you around my son!"

"Donna, please..."

He reached for her. She recoiled like he was a poisonous snake.

"*Don't touch me!*"

Marcel's thinking was badly delusional at that point, drenched in a sea of honey-colored whisky. But he had enough sense to understand that losing Donna was the worst thing that could happen to him right now. He never begged a woman for anything – *not once* – but he dropped to his knees in the middle of his living room. He was at the lowest point of his life. Lower than dirt. From this humbled position, he reached for her like a sinner groveling at the feet of the Messiah.

"*I need you,*" he cried. "*Please don't leave me.*"

But Donna continued to back away. She kept going until she was completely out of his home and out of his life.

"You don't need me, Marcel," she said from the porch. "You need *help*. And I can't give it to you." She turned and left him in that wretched state.

Marcel wallowed in grief for nearly five minutes before he mustered the strength to get up and close the front door.

CHAPTER TWENTY-ONE
QUOTH THE RAVEN,
"NEVERMORE"

On Friday, December 11th, Donna met with her girlfriends at the Red Lobster in Arlington for happy hour. They generally avoided pricey locales for their weekly gatherings, but Kendra got a gift card for her birthday, and she didn't mind splurging on her two best friends. Plus Donna had been in a funk for the past few weeks. Kendra hoped Red Lobster's world famous cheddar biscuits would bring her back to the world of the living.

In addition to the gift certificate, Kendra also got a new Gucci bag that Tricia thought was absolutely to die for. They passed it around the table while sipping Appletini's and Long Island iced teas.

"Patrick got you this, too?" Tricia asked as she ran her fingers across the scaly design.

"Yep," Kendra said, smiling broadly.

"What is it?" Tricia asked. "Snakeskin?"

"Python," Kendra confirmed.

"They had to kill a whole snake, just so you'd have something to put your lipstick in?" Donna grumbled.

"No, it died of old age," Kendra countered. "And they didn't let the skin go to waste."

"You're full of shit," Donna said. "How do you know it died of old age?"

"It was in the pamphlet," Kendra said with a straight face. "They gave me a link to the snake's Facebook page. His name was

Gary, and he lived a long, full life. He always dreamed of being my purse one day." She cradled the bag like it was a baby.

Tricia cracked up, but Donna didn't find the humor in that.

"What does a purse like that cost anyway?" she asked. "Two thousand?"

"Three," Kendra said. "But it's not like I went online and researched it or nothing..."

"Yeah, I'm sure you didn't," Donna said. She downed the rest of her glass and looked around the restaurant. "Where's our damned waitress?"

Tricia and Kendra watched her knowingly, and then they looked at each other. Today Donna had her hair pulled back in a ponytail. She didn't have on any makeup, and it was easy to see the stress eating away at her. It had been over a month since the big blow-up with Marcel. Her friends were surprised that she was still upset after so long.

"Hey," Donna called when she spotted their waitress. "Over here, please! *Jeez,*" she told her friends. "I hope she's not expecting a big tip for this."

"I like our waitress," Tricia said.

"Me, too," Kendra said. "She didn't do anything wrong."

"Hi!" The waitress' smile was as bubbly as ever when she approached their table. "You ready for another?"

"Yes," Donna said with a little attitude. "Thank you very much."

"Okay, be right back," the girl said and went on about her merry way.

"How is she a good waitress?" Donna asked her friends. "She's supposed to *ask me* if I want something else to drink, not the other way around."

"Maybe she's not expecting you to be done so fast," Tricia offered.

"Yeah, you're about to get *number three,* and we just got our second one," Kendra agreed.

"She probably doesn't look forward to coming to our table," Tricia added.

"I know I wouldn't," Kendra said and looked away innocently.

Donna frowned at her. "If there's something you wanna say, why don't you just say it?"

"I didn't say nothing," Kendra said, but she wouldn't meet her eyes.

"I'll say it," Tricia said. "Your stinky attitude is killing the mood, Donna. You're really being a killjoy right about now."

"Oh, is that so?" Donna snarled.

"Yes, it is so," Tricia said.

"I wasn't gon' say nothing," Kendra chipped in, "since I know you're still mad about Marcel. But it's been so long..."

"It's been a month," Tricia agreed. "And you were only with him for two months. So what are you so pissed off for?"

"And the way you're knocking back those martinis," Kendra said, "kinda makes me wonder how you can break up with somebody for drinking too much..."

"I also find that hypocritical," Tricia said, and she laughed. Kendra did too.

Again Donna failed to find the humor in her friends' banter. "I know I'm not hearing that from *you*," she told Tricia. "You were the one saying *I told you so*, when I told you what happened with Marcel."

"I did not say I told you so."

"Yes, you did," Donna countered. "You said, '*I told you when I first met him that he was a lonely drunk.*'"

"Well, I did tell you that."

"And while we're pointing out our imperfections," Donna went on, "I think it's straight *wrong* for you to throw that in my face like that. Sometimes people don't want to hear, *I told you so.*"

Tricia laughed. "I already said I was sorry for that. And that was also a month ago, Donna. You're telling me you're still pissed at me, too?"

"She's not mad at you," Kendra said knowingly. "She's mad at herself, and she's mad at that man. But instead of calling him, she wants to take it out on us."

"I'm not taking anything out on y'all," Donna said.

"Yes you are," Kendra countered.

"I second that," Tricia said. "*And* you're being mean to our waitress."

The girl appeared at that moment and placed a fresh drink in front of Donna. "Here you go."

"Thank you. And I'm sorry if I've been rude tonight," Donna told her.

"Oh, no problem," the waitress said. "I haven't noticed anything. Let me know if you need anything else."

"She's lying," Tricia said when she walked away. "She can't stand you. I can tell. She probably spit in your drink."

Donna's jaw dropped. "*Ewww.*" She stared into her glass but didn't see anything suspicious.

"I'm just kidding," Tricia said.

"I can't drink this," Donna said and pushed the glass away.

"So why haven't you called Marcel?" Kendra asked her. "What are you waiting on?"

"Who said I was gonna call him?"

"It's pretty obvious," Tricia said. "Y'all broke up back in November, and you're not over him yet."

"Y'all broke up?" Kendra asked. "I thought you were just giving him some time to get his shit straight."

"Yes, they broke up," Tricia said. "Donna doesn't have time to sit around and wait for some *alcoholic* to get right."

"That's cold," Kendra said. "Did you tell him that? You didn't tell him that, did you?"

Donna shook her head. "I don't know what we're doing. I guess I didn't officially break up with him. But I haven't talked to him since that day."

"That's part of the problem," Tricia said. "You're upset because you didn't get any closure. You need to call him and tell him it's over."

"He hasn't called you?" Kendra asked.

"Not anymore," Donna reported. "He did call a lot at first. I didn't answer. I listened to his messages, though. Now he just sends me text messages."

"What do they say?" Kendra asked.

Donna fished her cellphone from her purse and found the conversations with Marcel. Technically they weren't *conversations*, since she didn't reply to any of them.

"Checking myself into Pinewood," she read. "Got two weeks off work. You can visit, if you want. And he gave me the address," Donna said. "That was right after our fight.

"And then I got this one: I made it. Finished two weeks inpatient. Feeling great. Going back to work on Monday. Miss you. And then I got this one on Wednesday: Going to AA

230

meeting. It's from 6-8pm. You can stop by, if you want. And he gave me the address to that place, too."

"You didn't respond to any of it?" Kendra asked.

Donna shook her head.

"Why not?"

"Because I don't know what to say," Donna said. "I don't know what to tell him."

"It sounds like you're not going to break up with him," Tricia said with a sigh.

"I don't think you should," Kendra said. "He's going through a lot right now. It might make it worse."

Donna nodded. "That's what I was thinking. I don't want to add any extra stress to his life."

"But you can't keep your life on hold, just because you don't want him to start drinking again," Tricia said. "If you're going to leave him, you need to do it now. If he can't handle it, that's on him."

"Are you going to break up with him?" Kendra asked.

Donna couldn't come up with a response. She'd been asking herself that same question since their fallout. "I kinda wanna see if he'll make it," she revealed.

"So if he tells you he's sober, you'll stay with him?" Tricia asked.

"I don't like the way you're asking me that," Donna said honestly. "You make me feel like I'm stupid if I say yes."

"I'm sorry," Tricia said. "I didn't mean it like that."

"Well, you're one of the main reasons I haven't called him," Donna told her. "I keep thinking about what you said about him. I don't want to feel like he's making a fool out of me."

Kendra smacked her lips. "Girl, don't listen to this heifer. She hates for people to be happy."

Tricia's jaw dropped. "I do not."

"Yes you do," Kendra said. "That's why you're always talking bad about me and Patrick."

"All I said was it's wrong for you to use him," Tricia argued. "And I think he's gonna leave you before you realize what a good catch he is."

"Yeah, and I told you I'm happy, and Patrick is happy," Kendra said. "So what's the big deal? Why can't you be happy for us?"

"I didn't mean it like that," Tricia said. "I am happy for y'all. And Donna, I didn't mean for you not to call Marcel back, either. I was worried, because I didn't want him to hurt you. He lied about something pretty damned major. And if he can't get clean, you're probably in for *years* of heartache. I don't want that for you."

"Maybe he can stay sober, if Donna is there for him," Kendra countered.

"It sounds like he's getting clean on his own," Donna added. "He doesn't need me."

"So are you going to call him back or not?" Tricia asked. "The last thing I want you to do is blame me if you decide to break up with him. That should be your decision, Donna, all by yourself."

"I know," she said. "But I am worried. I'm glad he admitted himself somewhere, and I'm glad he's doing the AA thing now. But I'm scared that if I trust him again, he'll do the same thing. All he had to do was tell me he had a problem. I gave him plenty of chances. I'm hurt that he lied to me. I'm hurt that he didn't trust me enough to tell the truth."

"Men have been doing shit like that for years," Kendra said. "I was with this one guy who smoked weed all the time. When I met him, he said he only smoked on the weekends, if he was kicking it with his cousins. Come to find out, he smoked weed every goddamned day. All day. He smoked before work, during his lunch break and as soon as he got off. That nigga was growing plants in his closet and everything."

Her friends laughed.

"You broke up with him?" Donna asked.

Kendra shook her head. "Nope. By the time I found out, we had been together for three months, and I was all sprung by then. They do that mess on purpose. They won't tell you their *real shit* until they know for sure that you're too sprung to leave them."

Donna knew there was some truth to that, and she hated it.

"So, what do y'all think I should do?" she asked her friends.

"I'm not saying *anything*," Tricia replied. "You just said you haven't called him back because of me. Uh-uhn." She shook her head. "I'm out. I told you; I don't want you to look back on this in ten years and blame me for what could've been."

"I already told you what I think," Kendra said. "But you do need to make your own decision, Donna. I know you heard this a million times already: You have to follow your heart."

"And I notice you didn't let a little spit ruin your Appletini," Tricia said with a grin.

Donna looked down and realized she was halfway through the drink she pushed away a few minutes ago. She laughed at herself and re-read Marcel's latest text message. Did he honestly think she would attend one of his AA meetings? Even if she decided to stay with him, Donna didn't think she would ever want to see him stand before a room full of people and say, "*Hi, My name is Marcel, and I'm an alcoholic.*"

Ugh! She cringed at the thought.

●●●●●●●

On Saturday Colton had another football game, this time against the Northside Raiders. Donna remembered that the *Raiders* were once the *Rebels*, back when she was in high school. Northside made the local news when a pep rally ended in a riot in 2001. One of the football players started waving a confederate flag, which was traditional "rebel" imagery, and the black students flipped out. An all-out rumble ensued. Over the summer, the school took a vote and agreed to become the Raiders from that point on.

Their mascot certainly did a lot of cheering on December 12th. Northside had a freshman quarterback who would surely play for a top university one day. He shredded Finley High's defense on nearly every possession. Colton emerged from the locker room with his head down after a 38-12 blowout.

"It's okay," Donna told him. She put her arm around him and kissed him on the side of the head. "You'll get 'em next time."

They went to Chili's afterwards. Colton's mood was brighter by the time he finished his meal. Donna was still unsure of herself and her future with Marcel. Eating at Chili's didn't help any. She remembered how she met Marcel there and got the first glimpse of his alcoholic tendencies. She could've saved herself a lot of anguish if she'd listened to Tricia that day. Instead she gave Marcel the benefit of the doubt and ended up paying the price.

"What happened to Mr. Webber?" Colton asked out of the blue.

Donna was stunned, thinking the boy was reading her thoughts. "Huh? What do you mean?"

"How come he doesn't come to my games?" Colton asked. "You're not going out with him anymore?"

Donna half-smiled. "I'm surprised you noticed. I thought you didn't like the idea of him being around."

Colton looked confused. "I never said that."

"You never told me you liked him, either."

"Why would I tell you I like him, Mama? That's gay."

She laughed. "You know I don't mean like that."

"But I still can't run around talking about I *like* some guy," Colton said.

"Oh, well *excuse me*," Donna said. "I forget how homophobic you youngsters are nowadays."

"But what happened to him?" Colton asked. "It had something to do with that game he took me to, didn't it?"

Donna nodded, her smile fading. "How'd you know that?"

"Because you got real mad that day," Colton recalled. "But you never would tell me what happened. At first I thought you were mad at me, but you weren't, so I knew you were mad at Mr. Webber. Are you mad because he had to leave, and he couldn't take me home?"

Donna nodded. "Something like that."

"What did that lady tell you?" he asked. "Why won't you tell me?"

Donna noticed how deep his voice was becoming. The hair above his lip was getting a little thick as well. It seemed like every day she noticed more of his manly attributes. She hated to see him growing up so quickly. But it also made her proud, to watch his march to maturity. Nolan would've been proud as well.

"Do you think you're old enough to know about stuff like this?" she asked.

Colton nodded, but he didn't look so confident. "What is it? What'd he do?"

Donna sighed. She never told him about Nolan's foolishness, but if there was a chance that Marcel might return to their lives, then Colton deserved to know about his faults.

"Marcel has a drinking problem," she said. "He's an alcoholic. He was drinking at your game that day. That's what Cheryl told me. She saw him drinking in the parking lot. Marcel told me he had to leave because they called him in to work, but that wasn't true. The real reason he had to leave is because he got drunk, and he didn't want us to know."

Colton's eyes grew large. He stared at her for so long, Donna wondered if this may be too much for him.

When he finally got his thoughts together, he said, "I never saw him drinking."

"I didn't either," Donna said. "He was good at hiding it from us."

"Why don't he go to rehab?"

"You mean *why doesn't he*. And he has gone to rehab. He got out two weeks ago."

"So, why hasn't he come to my games?" Colton asked.

Donna was surprised that he was willing to forgive so easily. "Because he lied to us," she said. "I'm not sure if I forgive him, and I definitely don't trust him around you."

"Why not?" Colton asked. "You said he went to rehab."

"That doesn't mean he's better," she argued. "Some people go to rehab and keep drinking when they get out."

"Mrs. Freeman's husband went to rehab, and she said he was a lot better when he got out," Colton said.

Donna frowned. "Who's Mrs. Freeman?"

"My English teacher."

"She told you her husband went to rehab?"

He nodded. "It was her ex-husband. They're not together anymore. But they didn't break up because of his drinking. It was something else."

"Wha, why would your teacher tell you that?"

"She was just talking," Colton said. His face lit up. "Oh, I remember. We were reading *The Raven*, by Edgar Allan Poe. And the book said he was an alcoholic, and he died in the gutter, or something like that. Mrs. Freeman said he probably would've been okay, if he had someone there for him. But no one cared, so he didn't go to rehab."

Donna still didn't understand why his teacher would share something so private, but she understood why Colton thought things were so black and white.

"It's not that simple," she told him.

"Why not?"

"Well, first of all, I must say I'm surprised that you're in Marcel's corner all of a sudden. You're the *last* person I expected to tell me I should have a boyfriend. If I remember correctly, you told me to wait until I was *fifty*, before I go out with another man."

"I was immature back then," Colton said.

Donna laughed. "You mean three months ago?"

"Yeah," Colton said. "*Waaay* back then."

"You are so full of it."

"You were happy when you were with Mr. Webber," Colton recalled. "Now you're always mean."

"I'm not mean."

"You're not happy, either."

"Well, I'm sorry if my broken heart is getting on your nerves."

The boy's smile went away. "He broke your heart?"

"Yes," Donna said. "That's what happens when you trust someone and find out they're lying to you."

"I didn't know he broke your heart."

Donna thought that would be the moment when his defense of Marcel waned, but Colton was full of surprises that day.

"Maybe he only lied because he didn't want you to break up with him."

"I'm sure that's exactly why he lied," she said.

"But if he went to rehab, then he probably won't lie anymore."

"I'm sure that's what he'll tell me, if I call him back."

"Are you gonna call him?"

"I'm still trying to decide."

"If you do call him, you should tell him that you'll give him *one more chance*, and if he breaks your heart again, you'll break up with him forever," Colton suggested. "And I'll beat him up."

Donna got a good laugh out of that. She knew Colton was doing his best to lift her spirits. When she stopped giggling, she told him, "You do realize that I can forgive him, and six months could go by before I find out he's still drinking..."

Colton processed that and said, "So you think he's not worth taking a chance on?"

236

"The main thing I'm thinking right now is how weird it is to have this conversation with you," Donna said. "But yeah, I don't know if he's worth taking a chance on. I already did that, and he let me down. *Big time.*"

"Do you want *me* to call him?" Colton offered. "I could talk to him for you."

Donna grinned. "No, I don't want that. But the fact that you would even suggest it says a lot about how much you care for him."

"That's gay, Mama."

She rolled her eyes. "Boy, it's not gay to say you care about someone. Do you think I'm gay because I care about Kendra and Tricia? I love both of those women, and we're not even related."

"Ewww! Mama, you gay!" Colton joked and burst into laughter.

"And *that* would be the comment that ended our *adult conversation.* Thanks a lot, son. You really make me proud," she said sarcastically.

My God, this galactic wonder
Supreme physique. I long to plunder
To ravage – Ah, I've gone too far
Yet, light is ebbing. In this dark
The shadows make me bold. Your toes
Are cold. I kiss each one. Behold
Each kiss is higher than the one
Before. Each kiss gets to the point
Your scent – exotic taste, it's just
Too much, to touch, it's such a rush
So plush, your intersection is
This lust – this pleasure that you give
My will is yours. I yield. Just come
Here, let me show you, love. Just cum

CHAPTER TWENTY-TWO
THE FINAL CHAPTER
UNDER THE MISTLETOE

On Wednesday, December 16th Marcel attended his weekly
AA meeting from six to eight p.m. at the YMCA on Altamesa. This
was his third time. He was usually apprehensive about going, but
today wasn't so bad. Marcel was getting into the groove of his
recovery, and he understood that AA wasn't some terrible place
where hopeless people went to tell their hard luck stories. The
people at the meetings were survivors. They banded together
because they all battled the same demons, and there was
camaraderie in that. They were all warriors on a spiritual
battlefield, and they knew better than to go to war alone.

That Wednesday Marcel sat close to the front of the room,
as he always did. When he was in middle school, his favorite
teacher told him something that always stuck with him: Mr.

Griffin said there was a clear pattern in his classroom. The kids on the front two rows generally made A's. The kids in the middle of the room made B's. The further back a student sat, the worse their grade tended to be.

The Alcoholics Anonymous meeting wasn't a classroom, but Marcel never forgot what his teacher told him, and he wanted to do his very best at recovery. He knew that there was some truth to the seating pattern, because whenever there was unwelcomed talking during the meetings, it usually came from somewhere towards the back of the room.

In the two meetings he had attended thus far, Marcel learned some things about himself, a lot of which made him feel foolish and grateful to be there. The most poignant thing was he was not as bad off as most of the others. His sponsor didn't like him to think like that. Jesse warned that saying he was *not that bad* would surely lead him to take another drink.

Marcel knew that was good advice, but he couldn't help reflecting on how awful things could've gotten. The majority of the people at the meetings had been alcoholics their whole lives. They left many tattered souls in their wake. Marcel had only been an alcoholic since Jaylen died. He never lost a home or job or spouse because of his drinking. He never went to jail for public intoxication or a DUI. He was no doubt headed down those dark and shameful roads, but God's grace was upon him. Compared to the others, his losses were fairly minimal.

But that didn't stop Marcel from being an apt pupil. He worked hard at rehabilitation. He never looked at his drinking as spiritual warfare before, but he now knew that the devil was constantly plotting to end his life. Marcel thanked God (many times a day) for delivering him from his self-destructive tendencies.

Not everyone who stood behind the podium had a hard luck story to share. That night Michael B. proudly announced that today was his fourth year of sobriety. Michael, once known as *Two Forty Shorty* because of his propensity to buy two forty ounces of malt liquor after work each day, achieved his first year of sobriety in state jail. He was sentenced to fourteen months for assaulting his then-girlfriend for the third time in less than a year.

Michael started his AA journey while behind bars, and he surprised everyone by remaining sober after his release. In the past three years he repaired the relationship with his girlfriend, got a job, got married and purchased his first home ever (at the age of 53). Tonight his sponsor gave him an AA medallion with the number 4 on it. It didn't look like much, but it was a powerful token that brought Michael and a few more people to tears.

"I never thought I'd see one of these," Michael said as he gripped the bronze medallion in one hand and steadied himself with a firm grip on the podium with the other. "I thought I'd be dead by now," he said, his voice straining, his face and neck reddening. He let go of the podium so he could wipe the fresh tears from his eyes.

A woman, presumably his wife, stepped forward. She took hold of Michael's hand and held it tightly. She was in tears as well.

"This place works," Michael said adamantly. "I'm proof. We all are."

The crowd erupted in cheers. Marcel was awed and humbled by his emotions. He never thought he could care so much about complete strangers. But even still, even though his sponsor told him not to, Marcel couldn't help but thank God for sparing him some of the devastation people like Michael endured. Marcel considered his losses to be pretty bad, but each Wednesday night he saw that things could've been worse. Much worse.

When the meeting ended, Marcel was surprised to see a familiar face sitting on the back row. She stood as he approached. Marcel's eyes widened. He felt every one of his cells go completely numb. He blinked quickly, but the vision of Donna didn't disappear. He took a deep breath and swallowed roughly. The hairs were standing on his arms as he walked towards her.

Donna was similarly affected when she and Marcel locked eyes. She felt something shift in her inner being. She'd been watching him for thirty minutes. She listened to the speakers, but her attention never left Marcel. He sat on the front row, and he stood head and shoulders over the others. Marcel appeared very supportive and attentive. He didn't look like he was simply going through the motions. But then again, Donna knew she was being hopeful.

When she finally got a chance to speak to him, she couldn't find the words. His presence, and his dark eyes focused keenly on her, was overwhelming.

Marcel exhaled slowly when he was within touching distance. Some of his new friends bid him adieu, but he didn't notice. He told her, "Hi."

Donna half smiled. "Hi."

Marcel's heart was in his throat when he asked, "Do you wanna, go somewhere and talk?"

Donna nodded, and they exited the building together.

●●●●●●●

"My dad was an alcoholic."

The place they went to talk was his Charger sitting in the parking lot. He couldn't go any further than that with so much tension between them. The sun had set on the brisk winter night, but there were few stars in the sky. Marcel started his car and turned the heat on. Donna missed being in the Charger's bucket seat. She missed being this close to Marcel.

"Why didn't you tell me?"

"Embarrassed," he said. "Same reason I never use *junior* on my name."

Donna's eyes widened. "You're a junior?"

He nodded. "My dad died when I was eleven. By then, I pretty much hated him. I knew what was going on. I knew how disgusting his drinking was, how bad he treated my mom. When I got to high school, I told my mom I didn't want to be a junior anymore. I just wanted to be Marcel Webber. She said that was okay."

Donna's heart wept for him.

"I still go to his gravesite, almost every year," he said. "My mom never misses his birthday. She never did stop loving that man," he said thoughtfully. "My whole life I dreaded being like him. When it finally happened, I didn't want anybody to know. The only person I told was my mom."

Donna understood that. "You could've told me."

He looked at her. "I know that now. I should've told a lot of people, anyone who cared enough to help. Being a man, sometimes it's hard to admit when I'm wrong. It was even harder to admit that I have a dirty, disgusting addiction that I can't fix. I couldn't bring myself to look you in the eyes and say that."

241

"I understand," Donna said. "Well, I don't fully understand. But I'm trying to."

"What do you think of me?" he asked. "I feel like such a fool. I feel weak."

"I don't think that," Donna said. "I know you're not weak. I think you're a good person, Marcel. You got a good heart."

"You don't think any less of me?"

Donna couldn't lie to him. "You let me down. You did. You hurt me really bad. I feel like, I trusted you. I let you around my son..."

Marcel sighed and nodded. "I know. That's one of my biggest regrets. I can't believe I let you down like that. I'm afraid to ask what Colton thinks. I know I let him down, too."

"Actually," Donna said with a smile, "he said I should forgive you."

Marcel stared at her in disbelief. "Really?"

She nodded. "He cares about you – but you can't tell his friends that, because apparently they'll call him gay."

Marcel laughed. It was a hearty, manly laugh. "Wow. That's, that's crazy. All this time I've been worried sick about him."

"He asked why you haven't been to any of his games."

Marcel's smile made Donna's heart happy.

"I never would've expected that. Not in a million years." Gradually his smile faded. "I need you to know that I miss my son, Donna."

She nodded. "I know that."

"I miss him more than anything," Marcel said. "I don't go a day without missing him. Sometimes I get so upset, I break down and cry. I was ashamed to tell you that, but it's important for you to know. I can't be afraid to tell you that I'm hurting. Jaylen was my whole world. Losing him drove me crazy."

Donna's eyes glistened. "Thank you," she said, "for telling me."

Marcel sighed. He cleared his throat and asked, "So where does this leave us?"

Donna gave that some thought. "I like my life better with you in it, than without you," she said. "But..."

Marcel felt like his entire existence waited for her to finish that sentence.

242

"I don't trust you," she said. "It will be hard for me to learn how to do that again."

"I deserve that," he said. "But, are you willing to try?"

He didn't breathe again until she nodded.

"Yeah. I am."

The wave of euphoria that rushed over him was all-encompassing. He was bowled over, set adrift on a sea of hopeful bliss.

"Okay," he said. "That's great. That's all I could ask for. I won't let you down again."

Donna's smile set his heart on fire.

"I gotta go," she said.

"Okay. Where'd you park?"

"Right over there."

She pointed to a spot only twenty yards away, but Marcel still opened his door.

"I'll walk you over there."

He went around to the other side of the car in time to help Donna out. His strong hand wrapped around hers made her feel all kinds of wonderful.

"Hey, why didn't you tell me you knew Lieutenant Freddie," Marcel asked as they walked.

"Oh. I don't know," Donna said. "I talked to him a little while ago. He said he knew you."

"Yeah, he's my boss," Marcel said. "He was none too pleased that I was dating you, with my drinking problem and all."

"Oh no. Did I get you in trouble?"

"No, he actually gave me a promotion," Marcel said. "It was in the works before he found out about us. He could've taken it away, though. But he didn't."

"You got a promotion?"

"The ceremony's in a couple of weeks," Marcel said. "I'll be a sergeant. They want me to run a new major crimes unit. We're finally going after the big players. In a year I'm supposed to get another promotion to lieutenant, and the unit will be all mine."

"That's wonderful!" Donna said. "Congratulations!"

"Thank you very much."

When they reached her vehicle, Marcel pulled her into his arms, which was the true reason he wanted to escort her. Without warning he kissed her fully and deeply. Donna scarcely had time to close her eyes before she felt his hot, luscious lips on hers. His strong hand slid smoothly to the small of her back and helped steady her when she took a wobbling step to the left. Donna's body was suddenly on fire, despite the frigid temperature.

Just as quickly as it started, the kiss ended. Marcel continued to hold her close to his body. She felt his warm breath on her ear. It sent sensual fingers tiptoeing down her spine.

"You alright?" he asked.

"Yeah, uh..." She had to catch her breath. "Kinda caught me off guard," she managed.

"I know," he said. "That's because you said I had to build my trust back."

"So you kiss me out of nowhere?"

He chuckled. "No. What I meant was, I didn't know if you planned on taking us back to *square one.* And if so, I didn't know if that meant I could kiss you or not. So I figured I'd go for it and find out later."

"Oh," Donna said. "That makes perfect sense."

She said it sarcastically, but she appreciated Marcel's bold reasoning. There was something alluring about a man who took what he wanted and asked questions later. Another thing that made perfect sense was the feel of Marcel's arms around her. Donna didn't realize how much she missed his touch and his smell and his body very close to her body.

"So are we going back to square one?" he asked.

"No. I don't want to go back that far." Donna couldn't believe she was being so forward. She couldn't help but blush as she grinned under the moonlight.

"That's good," he said. "Because it would be weird for me to be in love with a woman I just met."

Donna chuckled.

Marcel cleared his throat. Loudly. *"Ahem."*

She laughed.

"That's the second time I told you that, and you haven't responded," he said.

"That's because the first time you said it, you hung up right afterwards because you had to go to work – which turned out to be an excuse you used after getting drunk at Colton's football game."

"Ouch," Marcel said. "Touché. But what about now?"

"Isn't it obvious by the fact that I came all the way over here to see you?"

"No. Not really. Maybe you only came to see if I was really here."

She backed away and looked into his eyes. "I love you, Marcel. Happy?"

He clearly was.

●●●●●●●

Trust is not something that's given. It has to be earned.

Marcel knew that ahead of time, so he wasn't upset when Donna kept a firm distance between him and Colton, like she did in the early days. She didn't even invite him to her home for Christmas.

Marcel didn't mind, because he had plans of his own. His brother Terrence always hosted the dinner for their family. This year he outdid himself with a fried turkey, more deserts than you could shake a stick at and a live appearance from Santa himself. Marcel didn't know the guy Terrence hired for the event, but he appreciated the fact that Santa was black, and his bag was filled with real gifts. He had something special for everyone in attendance.

Donna rang Marcel's doorbell at nine o'clock that night. She looked cute in her leather jacket, scarf and stocking cap. Marcel was already settled in for the evening. He wore sweat pants with a tee-shirt and pristine white socks. He smiled and invited her inside his warm home.

"Merry Christmas."

"Merry Christmas!" Donna said. Her smile was delightful, her cheeks rosy. "Sorry I couldn't make it earlier," she said. "But I brought your gift."

"Thank you." Marcel accepted the small box.

"Are you gonna open it?" Donna asked when he set it on the coffee table.

"You want me to open it now?"

"Yes. Of course."

"Well, you gotta open yours, too." Marcel went to his tree where one gift remained unwrapped. He presented it to her. "This is for you."

Donna took it from him, and they tore the wrapping paper off at the same pace. Marcel's gift was a luxury watch made by Gucci. His jaw dropped as he stared at the intricate design. Donna's box contained the new Apple iPad as well as two tickets for a full day of pampering at her favorite spa.

"I can't accept this," Marcel said.

Donna was thinking the same thing. She knew that the spa tickets alone were a hundred bucks apiece.

"I can't either," she said and tried to give it back to him.

"You're not rejecting my gift," Marcel said, refusing to take it.

"You just rejected mine."

"Yours costs too much."

"Not really. I got it on sale. But I know this iPad wasn't on sale."

"I lost the receipt," Marcel said. "And I forgot where I bought it. So you have to keep it."

"You're full of it," Donna said.

Her smile lit a fire in Marcel's belly. He set his watch aside and wrapped both arms around her. He kissed her softly. Donna returned the affection. Their tongues danced as Marcel's hands slid down her backside and found a home on her perfectly squeezable ass. He leaned back on the arm of his sofa and pulled her between his legs. He continued to fondle her ass until Donna felt tingles followed by moist heat between her legs. She also felt Marcel's erection there.

He told her, "I got something else for you."

She grinned against his lips. "I'll bet you do."

"You should open it," he said.

Donna backed away enough to look down at the huge bulge in his sweat pants. Her head shook slowly as her eyes returned to his. Her Christmas smile remained.

"I gotta go. I told Colton I would only be gone for a few minutes."

"Does he know where you are?"

She nodded, her gaze slipping to his bulge again. Her heart began to knock pleasantly in her chest.

"Then he's not worried about you. I know you got him a new game for Christmas..."

That was true. Colton had the new Call of Duty at the top of his list this year. He'd been stuck on his Xbox since he unwrapped it. Surely he wouldn't notice that his mother was gone a little longer than expected. She set her iPad on the coffee table and reached for her *other* gift with both hands. Even through the fabric of his sweat pants, she felt heat radiating from his swollen member. It jumped in her hands when she squeezed it.

Marcel was still standing, leaning back against the sofa. Donna licked her lips as she pulled the front of his sweat pants open. His dick popped up to greet her, hidden by only his boxer shorts now. She pealed the boxers down slowly and inhaled sharply when she saw the fat head winking at her. She never took a moment to fully admire his dick before. She did so now, running her fingers along the shaft. His veins were thick and engorged. Donna's mouth watered.

She knew she should make him wait longer, but in her mind's eye she saw a fresh sprig of mistletoe dangling above his big dick. *'Tis the season*, she thought as she dropped to her knees.

"Oh, you..."

Marcel's words were lost when she wrapped her warm lips around him and sucked him into her mouth.

"Oh, *ooh*..."

His dick jumped again, and she tasted the saltiness of his pre-cum. She swallowed it down, savoring the flavor of his essence. She began to work her head back and forth, her lips and tongue creating a wave of ecstasy with each stroke. Marcel stared down at her in awe. His mouth hung open. His chest rose and fell at uneven intervals. Donna held the base of his dick with one hand and ran the other one up and under his tee shirt as she sucked. His stomach was flat and tight with tension.

He gradually reached for her. Donna felt his large hand slip behind her neck. She smiled inwardly. She was such a bad girl, but being bad had its rewards. Marcel began to pant and grunt quietly as her mouth did things to him that he would never forget.

His head rolled back, and his toes dug into the carpet as her slurping sounds filled his ears. Donna was in a subordinate position, but she felt powerful. She concentrated her efforts on his fat head, her tongue and lips working in unison. After a few glorious minutes, he pushed her away. She looked up at him, his dick throbbing in front of her nose.

She kissed the tip and asked, "Why'd you stop me?"

"I'm, I'm about to cum," he said honestly.

Donna narrowed her eyes and kissed the tip again. "So?" She giggled at the expression that took over his features.

Marcel helped her to her feet and took off her coat. He left the room and returned with a condom. He sat Donna on the couch and lifted her legs one at a time, so he could remove her leather boots. He then pulled her sweater and tee shirt over her head and laid her back on the cushions while he worked on her belt buckle.

Donna felt moistness between her legs as he pulled her jeans and panties down and off completely. Every movement hit her like a convulsion that made her clitoris throb and her legs tremble. When she was down to nothing but a bra, Marcel removed that as well and feasted on her nipples, which were as dark and hard as ripe blueberries.

Donna cried out when he caught one of them between his teeth and tugged at it slightly. His tongue continued to caress her areolas expertly. Donna felt smooth tendrils of electricity shoot through her breasts, down her stomach and settle directly on her clitoris. Everything seemed to travel there; every touch, every flash of heat. And without warning, Marcel's face was there as well.

"Ooh, ooh!"

Donna yelped out of shock and also because of the instant gratification Marcel's tongue provided when it slid eagerly between her labia. He wrapped his warm lips around her clitoris, which was already firm and sensitive. Donna's hips squirmed on the couch cushion. Marcel grabbed hold of her thighs and eased them further apart. He pushed his tongue deeper into her wet center and lapped her juices pleasantly.

"Baby! Oh my God!"

Donna reached between her legs and grabbed hold of his nearly bald head as it worked up and down, in and out. His lips were magical. His tongue was an orchestra conductor. Together they made music in Donna's heart and mind. Cymbals banged hard in her chest. Harp strings strummed lazily between her labia.

The saxophonist hit a high note as the rivulet in her kitty became a mighty torrent.

Marcel felt her legs trembling, but he would not let them close him out. He ran his hands down her inner thighs and coaxed her eruption like a surgeon. He sighed pleasantly when she began to buck against his face. He continued sucking, flicking his tongue quickly, as the pressure in her clitoris reached its climax. Donna threw her head back and stared up at his huge Christmas tree, which was upside down from her vantage point.

The brightly colored lights twinkled and swam in and out of focus as her orgasm reached a crescendo, squirting her essence in his mouth, coating his tongue. Marcel sucked it down dutifully. He didn't stop until her screams became whimpers and eventually soft, sweet pants that told a story of liberation and fulfillment.

Donna was so content, so thoroughly satisfied, she nearly forgot that he had more to offer until she heard him tear the condom wrapper open. The sound came from somewhere far away, as if she was lost in a dream. Marcel spread her legs again and slid in smoothly, bringing her back to reality.

Donna's eyes fluttered open. She looked up at him longingly. Marcel had removed his shirt. There was nothing but black skin, dark chocolate and smooth muscles, as far as the eye could see. The muscles in his stomach flexed rhythmically as he pumped his hips slowly yet forcibly. The pleasure he provided with each stroke titillated Donna's clitoris, and her walls began to massage him, milk him.

The look on Marcel's face as he stared down at her nude body was inspiring. It was the look of an artist admiring his greatest masterpiece. From her vantage point, Donna couldn't tell where his body ended and hers began. Her eyes rolled back as he increased speed and began to pound her box in earnest.

Donna saw the tree again, the silver garland, the twinkling lights. She half-smiled and then sucked air between her teeth as another climax began to build deep inside her. Out of all the gifts she got this year, this had to be the best one. She was so glad she took the time to unwrap it.

Soft breezes
That smell like the ocean
Caress my face
This place is addictive
The sights
The smells
The moon-driven waves
That lick the shore
In this place
Where it never rains
And it never snows
I'm reckless in my pursuit
Of sandy shores
Stunning sights
Delectable aromas that
Flow in color like a rainbow in my mind

EPILOGUE

A month later their relationship had flourished past the point they reached before Marcel checked himself in to a rehab facility. He hadn't had a drink since then, not even a sip of egg nog at his department's Christmas party.

Marcel also achieved heights with Colton that Donna thought were unreachable. After Finley High lost a close game to Eastern Hills, Marcel told Colton he would be more effective as a wide receiver if he worked on the way he came off the line. Donna thought her son would blow him off, but Colton surprised her by saying, "Show me what you're talking about."

When they returned to Donna's house, Marcel took Colton to the back yard and told him to try to keep up as he exploded off an imaginary line of scrimmage. Donna watched from the kitchen window with a lump in her throat. She had never seen Colton practice with anyone but his coach after Nolan died.

And Marcel knew what he was talking about. He played football all the way through high school. He still had smooth moves that left Colton scrambling to catch up. After a while they switched positions, and Marcel tried to guard his young protégé. Donna's heart sighed when she heard him instructing Colton to, "Push off me! You can get physical in the first five yards! Make me get out your way!"

When they reentered the house thirty minutes later, Colton was sweating and excited about the lesson. Marcel's chest swelled with pride. It was a feeling he hadn't experienced since Jaylen died.

●●●●●●●

On Saturday, February 6th, Marcel's new major crimes unit made their first big bust. They didn't get the notorious Mr. Brown, but they got twenty-nine of his henchmen, including his right-hand-man, a fifty year old goon named Solomon Pitts. The arrest was a chink in Mr. Brown's armor and a huge blow to his operation, which had been considered untouchable for more than a decade.

During the bust, Marcel's task force uncovered six safe houses where they found nearly four million dollars in cash and enough weapons to supply a small army. Word on the street was Mr. Brown fled to Florida, in anticipation of one of his associates testifying against him for a lighter sentence.

Marcel's picture graced the front page of the Overbrook Meadows Telegram the following day. He stood before a mountain of drugs, money and weapons that had been retrieved from the safe houses. The best thing was the arrests weren't just for show. Marcel knew he made a real difference this time. He deserved the accolades he garnished from the commissioner, the mayor, and the rest of the city.

●●●●●●●

That year Valentine's Day fell on a Sunday. Donna had butterflies in her stomach from the moment she woke up. She knew Marcel had something big planned, but he still managed to surprise her. At five p.m. he called and asked, "Are you ready?"

"For what?" Donna asked coyly.

"For romance," he said in that sultry, bass-filled voice that still gave her goose bumps.

"Yes," she said, her smile stretching from ear to ear.

"Do you have a pretty dress on?" he asked.

"Yes." Donna actually purchased a new outfit for the occasion. Her evening gown was strapless and form-fitting. It hugged her waist and hips like an insatiable lover. It had a low neckline that revealed a great deal of chocolaty cleavage.

"Come outside then," Marcel said and hung up.

Donna looked out of the window and nearly screamed when she saw a stretch limo parked outside her home. She felt like a princess as she stepped daintily down her sidewalk, towards the magnificent carriage. Rather than Marcel, the driver got out and held the back door open for her. Marcel sat inside wearing a black suit with a white shirt and no tie. He had a few buttons open on his shirt. Donna thought he was GQ smooth.

She fell into his arms the moment the door closed behind her, and they neglected the champagne that was chilling in a bucket of ice. Instead they feasted on each other. Marcel buried his face in her cleavage and had her lying flat on the bench seat by the time they arrived at the downtown Hilton. He told the driver to, "Drive around some more," so he could make out with her a while longer.

They ate in a beautiful dining hall while a nearby pianist tickled the ivory for their listening pleasure. Donna didn't think she'd ever been treated so royally. Marcel told her he reserved a suite for them upstairs. Donna was eager to see it.

During dinner she told him, "You've made me a very happy woman, Mr. Webber. When we get upstairs, I'm going to make you a very happy man."

Marcel grinned at her. "Is that right?"

She nodded and nibbled on her bottom lip.

"I like the sound of that," he said. "But there's one more thing."

He waved a hand in the air, and their waiter appeared, this time carrying an elegant silver plate with a dazzlingly shiny lid on it. He approached Marcel and removed the lid. Marcel stood and took the one object off the plate. Donna didn't see what it was until Marcel dropped to one knee in front of her and presented the ring box. He cracked it open. Donna began to hyperventilate as she stared at a beautiful diamond ring.

"I'm not a perfect man," he said. "I've made some mistakes in my life. Done some real stupid things. The one thing that scared me the most is when I almost lost you. If you'll marry me, I promise to be a good husband and provider. I'll *always* protect you. I never want to see you cry again, unless they're happy tears. Please say you'll make me the happiest man on the planet..."

A cyclone of thoughts rushed through Donna's head. She was vaguely aware of how she walked out on him the last time Marcel dropped to his knees for her. That seemed like a long time ago. She knew it was something she would never do again.

"Yes," she said as her eyes filled with tears. "Yes, baby. *Yes!*"

She wasn't aware that nearly everyone in the dining hall was watching them until they erupted in cheers and the pianist embarked on a beautiful rendition of *Adore* by Prince.

Donna's hand was shaking so badly, Marcel had a little trouble sliding the ring over her finger. Unfortunately it didn't fit.

"Aww, baby. It's too big," he said. "I told that damned jeweler. He said it's better to get it big than too small. I'll take it back and–"

"No!" Donna's fist squeezed closed, preventing him from taking the ring back.

"But baby, I can–"

"I'll get it sized," she said.

"But the guy–"

"Leave it alone," Donna said sternly.

Marcel looked up and chuckled when he saw the seriousness in her eyes.

"Okay, baby. Damn. Can I at least get my finger back?"

She released her grip long enough for him to remove his finger. Marcel shook his hand playfully as he returned to his seat.

"You, um, you got quite a grip there."

Donna blushed and giggled.

"I hope you don't lose it," Marcel said.

"I won't," she said. "I'll lose my car before I lose this ring."

"Okay," Marcel said. He leaned back and smiled at her while she admired her new ring. "You wanna go for another ride in the limo?" he asked. "I got it till ten. We can go downtown, see some sights..."

Donna looked him in the eyes. "I wanna go for a ride on my future husband."

Marcel grinned. "Why don't we do both?"

Donna giggled. "Really?"

"Sure. Once the driver rolls up that partition, it's all good."

Donna narrowed her eyes, still smiling. She didn't know Marcel had a voyeuristic side. She decided that she liked it very much.

●●●●●●●

They were wed five months later. It was a warm July afternoon. Donna's gown was beautiful. Marcel's tuxedo fit him perfectly. The church was packed with family and well-wishers. Many of Marcel's colleagues from the police force came, including Lieutenant Freddie, who looked regal in his full uniform. Colton was the most dapper groomsman. Tricia and Kendra were the prettiest bridesmaids.

Donna and Marcel exited the chapel amidst a flurry of cheers and confetti. They were all smiles as they entered a pristine white limousine that whisked them away to the Dallas/Overbrook Meadows Airport. Their destination: Long Beach, California.

Six hours later they walked hand in hand on a secluded beach that was only thirty yards away from a waterfront condo that was all theirs for the next six days. The sun was starting to fade in a magnificent blue sky that was not quite as beautiful as the pristine waters.

Marcel wore black trunks that sat low on his hips, revealing sexy lines on his stomach that framed his sexy abs. His belly had always been flat, but his muscles responded a lot better to his exercise regimen when he put down the bottle. Donna was proud to say that her husband had a bonafide six-pack. She had taken a liking to running her tongue down every crease, both horizontal and vertical.

Donna wore a blue and white beach dress. She held it up as she stepped, with recently pedicured bare feet. She loved the way the soft sand squished between her toes with each step, before the incoming tide washed them clean again. She loved the sound of the water, the slight ocean spray she felt with each soft breeze. The temperature was a wonderful 75 degrees, a far cry from the 102 degrees they left behind in Texas.

She felt an unexpected breeze between her thighs. She looked back and saw that Marcel had the back of her dress in his hands. He lifted it waist high and grinned at the sight of her bare butt cheeks straddling her thong panties.

"When are you gonna put on your swimsuit," he asked her.

"I thought I'd get in the water tomorrow," she said.

"Or you can just take this dress off," Marcel commented, still admiring her derriere.

Donna tried to push her dress down. "Stop, boy."

"I don't wanna."

She laughed and ran away from him. She managed to get a few paces ahead, but Marcel caught up with hardly any effort. He scooped her into his arms so effortlessly and unexpectedly, Donna couldn't stop a startled scream from escaping her.

"*Whoa*! What are you doing?"

He held her with one arm under her bent knees and the other behind her back.

"You have to change now," he said as he marched her towards the ocean. "Your dress is all wet."

Donna looked down and saw that he was knee deep in the water. "You'd better not." She held on to his arms and shoulders. Marcel smiled at her. He thought she was absolutely radiant.

"Or what?" he said, still walking.

Donna felt the cool water on her ass when he got waist deep.

"Stop it, Marcel! I'm getting wet."

"That's what I'm talking about," he said. "I like it when you're wet."

His smile was mischievous. Donna rolled her eyes playfully.

"You ready?" he asked.

Her eyes widened. "Marcel, if you drop me in the water, you're gonna have a very *boring* wedding night."

"You wouldn't."

"You wanna try me?"

Marcel knew she was kidding, but he wasn't taking any chances. He turned and headed back towards the beach. He sat her down on the sand and took a seat beside her. They were close enough to the water for the surf to lap at their feet with each incoming tide. Marcel watched her for a while without words. Donna smiled, loving the way he made her feel beautiful, with only his eyes.

He said, "Have you ever thought about adopting?"

Donna was taken aback. That was totally unexpected. "Yes," she said. "I used to."

During her first marriage, she gave up her dream of having a large family because it wasn't on her husband's agenda. The conversation had been dead for so long, she never thought it was a possibility.

"I want a little girl," Marcel professed.

Donna's eyes grew large. Her heart tried to leap from her chest. "Me too."

"Really?"

She nodded quickly. "Yes. I've always wanted a little girl."

"You're not just saying that?"

"No. I'm serious. I stopped thinking about it years ago, but if that's what you want..."

"I do," Marcel said. "Not a baby, though. I can't do the diapers and crying at all hours of the night. But a four or five year old would be cool."

Donna's eyes filled with tears. She knew that Marcel was her soul mate, but it continued to amaze her how often they were on the same wavelength.

"Do you think it would be hard to find a four year old girl?" he asked.

She shook her head. She brought a hand to her mouth and tried to blink the tears away.

"Baby, are you alright?" he asked.

She nodded.

Marcel reached and moved her hand so that he could kiss her. Donna closed her eyes and savored the feel of his lips, the taste of his tongue. The warm California breeze. Her heart was completely full of love and happiness. She looked forward to opening her heart up even more to provide more love for their future daughter.

Marcel's hot kisses trailed down the side of her face and down her neck as he carefully lowered her, until her back was flat on the sand. Donna didn't care that her dress got messed or about her hair or anything else but the man holding her and the future that lay ahead of them.

Marcel crawled on top of her and nestled his hips between her thighs as she spread them for him. His kisses were like tiny bonfires on her skin that gradually raised her body temperature. Donna looked over his shoulder at the clear, blue sky. She closed her eyes and a joyful tear rolled down the side of her face.

"You got me wet anyway," she whispered.

Marcel's hand snaked between her legs and under her panties in one smooth motion. Donna gasped and her eyes popped open.

"Yeah, I did," Marcel noticed.

"That's not what I meant," she said with a chuckle.

"Do you think anyone can see us?" he asked as his fingers slipped between her moist labia and began to titillate her clitoris.

"*Ooh.* Probably not," Donna managed. She saw a few people on the beach an hour earlier, but they were at least a mile away. She didn't care if they were still there.

Marcel didn't care either. He pulled the drawstring on his trunks and stood on his knees, so he could remove her panties.

Donna was acutely aware that she was about to make love for the first time as *Mrs.* Marcel Webber. As far as first times go, this was the kind of love that dreams are made of.

THE END

BY KEITH THOMAS WALKER

ABOUT THE AUTHOR

Keith Thomas Walker, known as the Master of Romantic Suspense and Urban Fiction, is the author of more than a dozen novels, including *Fixin' Tyrone*, *Dripping Chocolate* and *The Realest Ever*. Keith enjoys reading, poetry and music of all genres. Originally from Fort Worth, he is a graduate of Texas Wesleyan University. Keith was nominated for an Emma Award in 2010 for Debut Author of the Year. In 2012 Keith was the recipient of a BRAB Book Club Award for Male Author of the Year (for Harlot) as well as a SORMAG Award for Fiction Author of the Year. In 2013 Keith was the recipient of a BRAB Book Club Award for Male Author of the Year (for Dripping Chocolate). Visit him at www.keithwalkerbooks.com.

CPSIA information can be obtained at www.ICGtesting.com
Printed in the USA
LVOW11s0709050614

388733LV00001B/72/P